Stepsister

STACY MCWILLIAMS

Editing by Karen Sanders
Cover- Shower of Schmit Designs
Proofreading- Judy
Formatting- Irish Ink

Dedication

This book is dedicated to my sisters, my girls, my ride or die team. Love you so much and I can't imagine my life without you in it.

Stacy

Chapter One

Cooper

My heart hammered in my ears as Bailey begged me to stay. I wanted to more than anything, but my dad had threatened her. He'd told me her dad had cashed in her trust fund and that Bailey was only able to buy into the gallery she part owned with his help.

I couldn't ruin her future. I'd already ruined her past. I was ruining everything with her and I hated myself for it.

The night of my bachelor party, I'd slipped and allowed myself to have just one more taste, but when she ran from me, I realized what a massive screwup it'd been. I was supposed to make her hate me more, not let myself fall in love with her all over again.

My voice broke, but not as much as my soul did when I answered her plea.

"I need to do this. I'm so sorry, Bailey. But I have to do this, for you and for me. Together we're fucked up, and we bring out the worst in each other. You deserve the world and some guy who's…" I had to suck in a breath. This shit hurt so much that my palms were sweating as we stood outside her car. "Some guy is gonna give you the world and treat you like a queen. I'm only sorry it's not me. Your arms are the only place I've ever felt at home, but I can't be the guy who gives you everything."

I wished I could be the one. The one to give her everything she deserved, but I wasn't. I never could be, and it was killing me. I pulled her into my arms one last time, breathing harshly as I pressed my lips to her forehead.

My heart broke as I whispered, "Goodbye, Bails."

As I turned to walk away from her, every step caused me physical pain, and I had to force myself to keep my eyes forward. If I looked back, I'd never leave, and my dad would screw her over.

I turned back once to see her scrubbing at her face, and my legs wobbled, but I grabbed onto the cart that held my luggage and managed to keep standing.

I heard a car start, and when I glanced back once more, she was gone. I'd lost Bailey Walker, probably forever. My legs shook and my palms were soaked in sweat as I pushed my luggage towards the check-in desk.

The girl there was cheery and chatted to me as she checked me in, putting my tags on my luggage, then waving me off.

I needed a drink.

Making my way to the airport bar, I spotted Jan's sister and her cousin and swerved to avoid them.

I couldn't deal with them. They were so excited, and I barely tolerated Jan. My temper was short, and my body shuddered in revulsion when she touched me. When Bailey touched me, I came alive, but with Jan it was as though something inside me died each time.

My eyes scanned the room, and I saw the first-class lounge up ahead, but Kirsty and Kayla were standing outside a shop directly across from it. Where their husbands were, I didn't know. I walked slowly towards them, hoping and praying they'd stay engrossed in whatever they were looking at.

I was so busy watching them that I didn't see Gregory or Martin until I walked right into them.

"Sorry," I said and turned away with a curse under my breath.

"Cooper, my man." Greg put his hand on my arm, stopping me. "How's it going? You all set for Saturday?"

I wanted to shake him off and run, but my dad's threat played over and over in my mind. He'd destroy Bailey if I did. He'd ruin her, and I'd never be able to forgive myself if I let that happen, so I smiled and shrugged, shaking his arm off.

The next second, Kirsty flew over with a shriek and started talking a million miles a minute. I tuned her out until she mentioned Bailey's name.

"Well, she just told Henri there was no way Bailey was coming and that was that. I mean, your stepmother trying to get her daughter to your wedding when she'd almost screwed you both up the first time. How absurd..."

I forced a smile, and she went on and on about how Bailey was such an inconvenience and how Zane had to stay away because he was a thief.

My fists tightened and I stepped around them. "Excuse me for a minute."

I stalked off without waiting on a reply and shot into the men's room. I stood by the sink and tried to breathe around the pain. But I was getting married, and my brother wasn't going to be there. Plus, I was marrying the wrong girl.

I heard the door open and saw Martin step into the bathroom, looking around until he spotted me leaning against the sink. His mouth was in a tight line, his forehead wrinkled above his eyes. His discomfort seemed to increase when he saw me watching him because his nostrils flared, and he squared his shoulders as he came towards me.

"Cooper, your dad asked me to give you a message." He stepped towards me and passed over a sealed letter. "He also said you'd likely want to leave, but I was to remind you that your futures are at stake, so to tread carefully."

I nodded once and he left the bathroom, letting the door hit him as he walked out. The stalls were empty and I went into one, closing the door behind me and leaning on it to open the letter.

COOPER,

I know you're probably thinking about running, but if you run from your responsibilities today, then you'll both suffer. Bailey is finally leaving the past behind, and if you care anything about her, you'll let her go and let her get some therapy. She still talks about her fictional dead brother and her mom is worried about her. I need you to let her go. Embrace your future with Jan and enjoy your promotion at work.

Dad

MY FINGERS CURLED INTO FISTS. TEARS STUNG MY EYES AS I read his words about Bailey again, and I'd never hated him more. I composed myself and went out to the bathroom, splashing water on my face and trying to hide the fact that my hands were shaking hard.

I walked out of the bathroom, seeing Martin and Greg standing across from me, but they had their backs to me, and I slipped into the first-class lounge unnoticed.

"What can I get you?" the barman asked as I approached.

I ordered a Scotch on the rocks. He was back within seconds and I downed it quickly, relishing the burn as it flowed into my stomach.

"Another?" he asked, and I bobbed my head as he poured me another drink.

I sank that one too, and he poured me a final drink before going to serve a few others.

I took my glass over to the window and sat sipping on it, watching the world go by. I desperately wanted to leave, but my dad's letter was burning a hole in my pocket.

Another drink appeared, and my dad's brother, Jake, sat down across from me. I barely saw him. He'd appear at family functions, but he was an outcast. My dad only put up with him for his mom, and as soon as she passed, he limited our interactions with Uncle Jake. I was never sure why. Perhaps it was because he was gay, or perhaps it was because my dad couldn't control him, and he hated not being in control.

"Hey, kid. You're supposed to look happier. We're flying out to your wedding."

Jake glanced at me, and he must have seen the bags under my eyes and the pain evident on my face.

"You wanna tell me why you look like it's your funeral we're flying to?" I shook my head and took another sip of my drink, glancing back out of the window. The first snow of the year was beginning to fall, and it fluttered down slowly as Jake and I sat in silence. "Cooper, I'm here for you. If you wanna talk, or if you need a getaway driver, then I'm your guy."

I smiled over at him and gave a brief nod, but our flight was being called. As it was announced, my cell pinged, and it was a message from my dad.

. . .

REMEMBER OUR DEAL, COOPER. DON'T MESS UP BAILEY'S life because you are selfish.

I SWORE AND CLOSED MY EYES, TOSSING BACK THE REST OF my drink and following my uncle Jake to our gate. He was seated at the back of first class and I was at the front. There were several people I knew on the flight, but no one I wanted to speak to, so I leaned back in my seat and tried to relax as the four drinks warmed me up inside.

My thoughts strayed to Bailey and how devastated she'd looked when I'd said no to staying. I knew I had to text her. I had to send a message to say it was okay to move on. I'd keep a part of her with me always. I took out the small half a heart that I'd cut from the bear I'd given her and rubbed my hand along it. It calmed me while I sat thinking of what I wanted to say to her.

After a few seconds, I composed a message and clicked send, just as the plane began to taxi down the runway. I poured my heart into the message and just hoped she'd understand how much I loved her. I'd do anything, even destroy my own future, if it meant she was happy.

I DIDN'T KNOW GOODBYES COULD BE SO HARD, BUT I FEEL like my heart has been ripped out. I've always loved you and I need you to do one thing before I delete this number. I need you to promise me one thing. Find someone who deserves you, who makes you smile and wants everything with you, because you deserve it, Bailey Walker. I've loved you forever, but I need to let you go and let you fly free because I want you to be happy, and all I do is make you miserable. Take care, my beautiful Bails.

Love always,
Coop

"SIR, CLIP YOUR SEAT BELT AND SET YOUR CHAIR UPRIGHT, please," the stewardess said as I sat numbly staring at my cell.

My head swam as I read back over the message I'd just sent. I turned my cell off with shaking hands as I realized I'd done it. I'd actually walked away from Bailey, even though my instincts screamed at me that I was making a huge mistake.

My numb fingers shoved my cell into my carry-on and then found my belt and clipped the two pieces together. What had I just done?

My heart began to race. I knew I needed to get off, to go back, but it was too late.

I'd officially left her to get married.

Tears ran down my cheeks as I thought of Bailey's face when I'd walked through the doors. Not only was I cinders and ash, but I'd ruined her. I closed my eyes as pain lashed at my insides.

The short flight did nothing to allay my nerves, and disembarking had me shaking like a leaf in a strong wind.

I can't do this. I can't do this.

My mantra repeated over and over as I climbed from the airplane. At the baggage area, there was a line, and I saw my dad staring through the crowds

A wave of nausea overtook me, and I ducked into the bathroom. I didn't want to do this. I wanted to go home to her, but my dad would never forgive me.

Do I really care? Does it matter if he never forgives me if I have Bailey? Is she worth it?

As my questions rolled over and over in my mind, I stared

at myself in the mirror and stiffened my back. I could do it. I could marry Jan, but what would that make me? I'd be using her, and it wasn't fair on her.

No. I wasn't going to do this.

I was going back, and I wouldn't let my dad control or manipulate me into making a huge mistake. I straightened my shoulders and walked out of the doors towards him. He had my bag in his hand and was looking around nervously. His face lightened with relief as I made my way towards him. He didn't speak until I was standing in front of him.

"Let's do this," he said before clapping my shoulder and leading me to the exit. We walked side by side until I froze.

"No…" I whispered. "Dad, I'm going back. I'm not doing this."

He grabbed my shoulder almost painfully. "Yes, you are." He moved me towards the door and I shrugged him off.

"No," I spat. "I will not. You will not do this to me." I was breathing heavily as I turned to face him.

"I'll ruin her. I told you. I'll ruin her future and yours if you do this."

My hands clenched and unclenched at my side. "I don't care. Do what you like, but remember, if you do it, we'll never forgive you. You'll grow into a lonely, spiteful old man."

His eyes widened and I turned away from him.

"I love her, Dad, and I don't care anymore. Do your worst."

As I walked away from him, I was lighter, almost floating above the ground. He followed me as I walked to the desk.

"I need a flight to Minnesota, please?" I asked the attendant behind the desk.

"Sure, sir. Let me check."

My dad was standing a little way away, frozen in horror as I stood at the desk, tapping my hand impatiently.

"The day after tomorrow is the first free flight," the girl said, and I nodded. Fine. That was fine. I could wait. Bailey wasn't leaving for a while yet, so I had time to get back to her and prove to her she was it for me.

"That's great," I told the girl as I handed over my card and she swiped it. I turned to face my puce-faced dad as he swung for me. His fist connected with my cheek and I fell backwards.

"We're done here," I replied as I pushed up and walked away from him.

He started ranting at me, but I walked calmly towards the row of cabs outside. I had to do this properly. I had to tell Jan it was over and make her understand that I couldn't be bullied or bought.

I climbed into one and gave the name of the hotel where the wedding was being held, seeing my dad speaking furiously on his cell outside the airport as I passed.

My eyes closed as I thought about Bailey and how much I couldn't wait to see her again. I had to tell her how I really felt. I'd pushed her away constantly, and each time she went was like a knife twisting in my gut. The cab was stiflingly hot, and the cabby spoke to me in broken English, but I was only half paying attention to him because my mind was caught up in how I was going to make Bailey understand.

Chapter Two

I LEANED BACK AND CLOSED MY EYES, THINKING OVER THE past few months and how hard it had been to stay away from Bailey when all I wanted was her.

My mind drifted back over the two months that had passed. Nausea rose in me as her face as I left her standing there appeared behind my eyelids. She looked broken, numb, and it was all my fault. I'd had to drag my legs forward because saying goodbye to her was never in my plan, but I had to do it. I had to leave her so she could be free of me, even though I'd never be free of her.

I tried to shake it off, desperately wanting to reach the hotel so I could get another drink, but like a glutton for punishment, my mind wandered back to my bachelor party.

I thought back to seeing Bailey again, and the days that passed in a blur as I fought against my attraction to my stepsister.

I bought my tux for the wedding, but standing in it, staring in the mirror, all I could see was the sadness that threatened to overwhelm me and the pain that came with every breath.

At my bachelor party, I'd made it my mission to be drunker than everyone. When Bailey walked in, my drunkenness seemed foolish. She'd seen right through me. She always did.

I was so drunk, and I only had vague memories that continuously assaulted me. I also had vague memories of Bailey taking me back to an apartment. I sobered up more in the shower, and when I went back out to the smell of coffee, I was much more sober than I'd been all night, but not enough, apparently.

As soon as my lips met hers, I'd known what was going to happen. It was inevitable, and incredible. She turned me on like nothing else and her creamy taste sent my mind into a tailspin. Seeing her had dredged up all of my old feelings, and I knew without a doubt I'd never really gotten over her.

The moment I moved towards her, I lost control. For the first time in years, I let my body take over and have what it craved. My heart hammered as we made love, because with Bails, it had never just been sex. It had always, always been love.

As soon as we came down, I tried to gather my thoughts to tell her how much I loved her, but before I'd gotten the words out, the look on her face stopped me and I knew she didn't feel the same. I was numb as she pulled away from me.

She made me feel everything, and as I brought her to orgasm, I was harder than I'd ever been in my life. My brain had disconnected, and it wasn't until afterwards that I realized what I'd done.

Bailey's horror-stricken face and the tears that left her eyes when I told her I was still marrying Jan destroyed me. I'd made her the other woman, when in reality, she'd been the only woman I'd wanted forever.

My dad's threats about Bailey bounced around in my head, and although we were adults now, he was still connected and I could risk her life, or her future. I wasn't worth it. I wasn't worthy of her, and my dad made sure I knew it. So, I left.

As I climbed into bed, my heart throbbed and I'd taken out my cell to call Bailey, but what could I say? *I'm sorry? I love you? I'm sorry we had sex?* But that wasn't true. I'd never be sorry for being with Bailey.

I left her behind and tried to put her behind me, but I stopped sleeping with Jan. Even the thought of having sex with her made me feel sick. I could usually compartmentalize, but Bailey had broken that part of me, and when I tried to move on with Jan, all I could see was Bailey's face as I made her come, and then an image of Bailey's eyes shining with tears would overwhelm me and I just couldn't do it.

I'd told Jan we shouldn't be together like that until after the wedding, because I couldn't make myself want her. I was broken, completely and utterly shattered because I'd realized that I still loved Bailey and I still wanted her.

A car horn sounded, and I opened my eyes, glancing around as I came back to the present.

"We have arrived."

The driver's voice interrupted my thoughts, and I quickly paid him before climbing out of the car. Henri was standing there, and she marched towards me with her face like thunder. As I climbed from the cab, she spoke in a deadly voice.

"Cooper, your dad was worried about you."

My eyes widened and I laughed. I couldn't help it. She looked utterly ridiculous with her body squeezed into a dress that was years too young for her and her overlarge glasses and floppy hat. I shrugged, stepping away from her towards the doors of the hotel.

"No need to worry, Henri. I'm here to do the right thing."

Her eyes narrowed, and I laughed again as her fists clenched at her sides. "The right thing for who? You? Bailey? Or Jan?"

My laugh stopped abruptly, and I spun back towards her. "The right thing for everyone."

My hissed words caused the bellhop to stop and glance in my direction.

"Cooper, don't be ridiculous. The right thing for Bailey would be for you to leave her alone and marry Jan…"

I could feel my face heat and I moved towards her.

"No. The right thing for Bailey would have been for you not to make out she was lying about Louis, for you to parent her and love her, and love the fact that she fell in love with someone…"

I broke off, breathing hard, and struggled to control my temper with her. I'd never wanted to get away from her as quickly as I did right then.

"She deserves so much more than you can give her!"

I closed my eyes and pinched the bridge of my nose. "No. She gets to choose. Not you, or my dad, or anyone else. Bailey gets to choose who she wants, and if it's me, then I will be the happiest guy in the world, and if it's not, then I'll be crushed, but at least it will be her fucking decision and not one that you made for her."

I spun around and stormed away from her into the hotel, passing Jan's family as they sat by the pool.

The maître d' was enthusiastic as I checked in, and I marched away to my room to shower and grab a few drinks from the minibar. Halfway to my room, I realized I needed to speak to Jan and end this quickly.

My eyes scanned the pool and the beach that was visible through a small gap, but I didn't see her anywhere.

My mind wandered back to Bailey. I knew I had to make the call to her to ask her to wait for me, but I had to end things with Jan first. I needed to be free of her, her family, and my dad before I went back to her.

I decided to go to my room and grab a shower before trying to track Jan down. I wanted to get this done so I could leave, and I knew that she'd try to tconvince me to go ahead with it. Every time she thought she was losing me, she hit out with some nonsense about being pregnant.

I always knew when she was lying, and I hated it when she tried to pretend she was pregnant to mess with my head. Three times she'd done it to me, and I'd learned from my mistakes. I wasn't about to let her bullshit me again.

I climbed the stairs to my room and found it blissfully empty. My luggage was sitting by the door, and I dragged it in. I wondered if my dad had made it back yet. He must have since Henri had accosted me, but I wasn't about to let them force me into making the wrong decision again. I was done dancing to their tune and it was time they knew it.

I ran the shower and cracked open a bottle of Jack from the minibar, downing it before taking another one with me to the bathroom.

I quickly scrubbed the grime of travelling off me. As I dried off, I considered calling Zane and checking in, but just as I decided to call him, there was a knock at my door. I quickly pulled my shorts on and shoved my arms into a t-shirt before answering the door. I set my cell down on the table by the door.

I knew it would be my dad, but I was surprised to see Jan's dad there too. He was the governor of Washington, and one of the most intimidating people I'd ever met.

"Cooper, can we come in?"

His gruff voice set warning bells off in my head, and I stood aside and let him and my father into my room. My dad walked towards the windows and glanced out, closing the window over as though he didn't want anyone to hear our conversation, as Finn sat on a chair by the bed.

Neither spoke until my dad had sat down on the edge of the bed. He stared at me with eyes that were hard as flint, and I squared my shoulders at them both.

Chapter Three

Cooper

"HOW CAN I HELP YOU, SIR?" I ASKED IN MY CONFIDENT lawyer voice, hoping to hide the fact that my palms were sweating.

"Your dad told me some worrying news today, and I wanted to come here and have a talk with you, man to man."

My eyes narrowed as I took both men in and my heart pounded even more.

"I hear you're planning on calling off the wedding, but before you do, I want you to think about who could be hurt by your actions."

My glare turned glacial as I stared between the two men. Finn met my glower and then stood and walked towards the minibar, getting out a few miniatures and passing them around. I held mine in my hand and watched as he slowly opened his and took a sip.

"So, where was I?" He paused, took another sip, and then sat back down, facing me. "I'm not sure if you know this, but your brother has just gotten a job with a company run by a dear friend of mine. He's been given a good salary, health benefits, and a steady contract, but if I were to call my friend and express my concerns, I'm afraid his job offer could disappear as quickly as it arrived."

"So, you want to bully me into marrying your daughter, is that it?"

He laughed. "No. Not at all. I'm merely pointing out that there are others who could suffer as a result of your actions."

"What you need to remember, Cooper," my dad interjected, "is that all actions have consequences, and you should think about that as you make decisions."

My heart pounded in my ears and I rubbed at my eyes as I took in the two snakes before me. They didn't care about my happiness, or Jan's. All that mattered to them was saving face.

"So, basically, what you're saying is if I don't marry Jan, then my brother, who has two small children, will lose a job he badly needs because of me?"

"Well, there's that, and a certain blonde girl is moving to Paris to open a gallery. The general manager of the gallery is someone who'll be keeping an eye on the situation for me, and if things don't go as planned, then he may have to get creative..."

He broke off as I stared between them.

"So, are you saying Bailey's life is in danger unless I follow through with this wedding?"

Both men nodded at each other, stood up, and finished their drinks.

My shoulders slumped in defeat. I couldn't risk her life because I was being selfish. I couldn't do that to her or Zane. I was stuck between a rock and a hard place, and they both knew it.

As they reached the door, Finn turned back and said with finality, "Glad to see you're finally getting it. Don't be late for the rehearsal dinner, and if you decide to leave, then don't be surprised when bad things happen around you."

With that, they left, and I paced around the room for a

while. I began to feel suffocated. If I left and didn't marry her, then they would punish those I cared about, and if I stayed and married her, then I would always feel trapped.

I needed to get out of the room. The walls were closing in on me, so I shoved my feet into my sneakers to go for a walk along the beach to try to clear my head.

I scooped up my cell and shoved it into my pocket, along with the key to my room.

As I left, I saw Henri and my dad standing by the pool with Jan's mom and grandma. My dad nodded at me, and I nodded in response before taking off down the path towards the beach.

I walked for ten minutes and then took my sneakers off and sat on the beach, letting my toes dip into the water.

I sat staring out at the ocean as I weighed up my options.

How could I leave when Zane would be punished for it? How could I let his babies suffer because of me? Was I being selfish for wanting to put myself first?

My head was swimming, and all I wanted was to run away from everything. Why was my life always so much of a clusterfuck? I'd never planned to fall for my stepmonster's daughter. She was always supposed to be a way to mess with Henri.

I knew who she was the first time I saw her at school. Her mom had shown me a picture of her a few weeks before, and I couldn't help my reaction.

Her bright blue eyes, blonde hair, and curves almost undid me. Fuck, I remember thinking she was exactly my type.

I couldn't believe it when we had to go to her school the following week and I saw her for the first time. It was as though someone had sucked all the air from the room. I watched her all through the debate and felt myself getting hard when her eyes met mine.

I held her gaze, but then I reminded myself who she was and tried to stop looking at her. My eyes were like magnets, drawn to her. I watched as she twirled her hair around her finger and bit her lip. I was so focused on the beauty across from me that I almost missed my question, but I got it just in time.

Pete laughed as he followed my gaze, but he knew me well enough to not comment on it. I glanced along my row and saw Abbi watching me. I smiled at her and she grinned at me as she pulled her top down slightly.

"Dude, get your head outta your dick…" Pete nudged me as I almost missed my question.

As the debate ended, our school won, and I slid my arm around Abbi, turned on by the girl, but not wanting to let it show. As we passed her, I made a point of barging into her, but the contact set my skin alight.

Pete and the guys laughed as she almost fell. My eyes followed her as she stood up, red-faced, and rushed away. Part of me felt victorious, but the other part of me wanted to go after her and make sure she was okay.

A HAND CLASPED MY SHOULDER, AND I STARTED. PETE WAS standing beside me.

"Hey, man. How's it going?"

I shrugged and kept my eyes forward. Pete didn't mind my reaction. He knew me well enough since he was one of my best friends and one of the few people who knew all about Bailey.

He sat down beside me and pulled out a few miniatures

from his pockets, passing me a Jack and keeping a Scotch for himself.

"So, you wanna tell me what's wrong?"

I shook my head, cracked the Jack open, and took a pull on the drink.

"Is it Bailey? Did something happen again with you two?"

I opened my mouth to tell him, but before I could get more than one word out, Jan and her friends arrived. She was smiling and laughing, and I leaned back, watching as they all screamed and giggled along the beachfront.

"I don't… I can't do this, man."

Pete looked at me in concern and leaned closer. "Do what? Get married?"

"Yeah. I don't want to marry her. I want a future with Bailey…" I broke off and swallowed as I remembered the threats to Zane and Bailey, and my chest began to ache because I knew I would protect them. I didn't care about myself, but I cared about Zane and his babies, and I loved Bailey. "But I can't have one."

Everything was so wrong, and I didn't know how to get out of the mess. Jan and her friends walked towards us, screaming and yelling, and all I wanted to do was run away. She smiled at me and my insides sloshed around.

"Coop, what are you going to do?" Pete's voice was low as the girls came closer. We stood up as they approached, and I spoke in a low voice, even though they were a bit away.

"I don't know. I guess I need to go through with this. If I don't, those I love are in danger and I can't live with that."

I stopped speaking as they reached us and I tried to plaster a grin on my face, but I wasn't sure I made it. I was usually a pro at masking my emotions. I'd had to be to hide how I felt about Bailey over the years, but I was so tired of pretending to be someone else.

"Hey, ladies," Pete said as they stood in front of us. Jan slithered her way towards me, wrapping her hands around my waist and pressing her lips to mine. I tried to feel something as I kissed her back, but all I felt were snakes writhing around in the pit of my stomach.

I hated her. I hated everything about her, from her brash overconfidence, to her voice, to the way she thought she was better than others because her daddy was a governor.

How had I gotten suckered into marrying this girl? How had my life become this?

The kiss ended and she stepped back from me, giggling. I wanted to shove her into the water away from me, but I couldn't. I had to pretend I was happy. I had to protect Bailey, Zane, Sam, and the kids.

"You girls having fun?" I asked, almost sighing with relief to hear my voice sounded almost normal. Only Pete who knew me so well could hear the panic, and he turned to look at me.

"Oh yeah," Marcy said, and I cringed.

We'd slept together Thanksgiving last year when Jan had been out of town. She was great in the sack and had no morals. I'd never been faithful to Jan.

"We've been drinking since breakfast," Carlie said.

She twirled her long blonde hair around her finger and grinned up at me. She'd given me a blow job in the sunroom on the night of her engagement party, and almost every time I saw her, we got into some compromising situation. She reminded me of Bailey, but there was no comparison, not really.

"Well, enjoy yourselves."

I met Jan's eyes and she grinned over at me, too drunk to

care that three of the girls present were openly flirting with me.

They all turned and left, heading back the way they'd come.

"Brunette and the two blondes?" He turned to me and I shrugged, knowing he'd got it. "You're such a dog, Coop."

I wanted to laugh, but I couldn't. I knew if I'd been with Bailey, there was no way I'd have been screwing around on her. If I was with her, I wouldn't even look at another girl because she was enough for me, but I didn't have that luxury.

"How many more?" Pete asked, and I shrugged, counting in my head.

"Seven, including the secretary at my last firm and her best friend."

I didn't include Bailey in the seven, because she'd never be a girl on the side. She was too special for that.

"Man, you really are a dog. Why would you fuck around though? Jan's hot."

Objectively, I could see what he meant. Jan *was* hot, with curves in the right places, a perfect body with tits that spilled over your palms, and long silky brown hair, but she wasn't who I wanted. Almost every girl I screwed around with had blonde hair, perfect tits, and a plump, round ass.

In short, they all reminded me of Bails.

"I dunno. I guess I just like sex."

He didn't speak again, and we started walking back towards the hotel.

"Are you gonna keep it up once you're married?"

I glanced at him and thought about the question. Was there any point in fucking people who weren't Bailey? They never measured up, and it hurt to think about, so I just shrugged and we walked the rest of the way back in silence.

As we reached the poolside, Pete went to find the other

guys, and I decided to go back to my room and have a nap. Maybe this was all a nightmare and I'd wake up from it as a teenager in the next room to the girl I was crushing on.

My head was starting to hurt, and all I wanted was an Advil and my bed. I stepped into my room, closing the door.

I crawled into bed and dropped my head back to the pillow, ignoring the nausea swimming in my gut and the spinning of the room as I pictured Bailey's face as I left. My chest throbbed, and I rolled onto my side, trying to escape the pain I carried everywhere with me, but it was futile.

I closed my eyes, and within a few seconds, I drifted off to sleep.

Chapter Four

Cooper

A SERIES OF LOUD BANGS WOKE ME, AND I SCRAMBLED around on the bed, searching for my cell.

Someone was hammering on my door.

I staggered over to it, still sleepy and confused. My hands shook as I made my way to the door, but just before I reached it, it burst open, and my dad ploughed into me, knocking me backwards onto my ass.

I slid along the floor and banged my wrist off the dresser, wincing as a throbbing pain shot through me.

"Where have you been?" my dad hissed as he stood over me, glaring down at my disheveled form on the floor. I was still so confused, and I grimaced as I tried to stand.

"I've been here. Where else would I be?"

"I thought you'd run back to her."

His eyes bore into me and I almost felt like a child again, about to face his wrath, but he didn't intimidate me anymore, and physical pain was nothing compared to the emotional pain he'd put me through over the years.

"Get up and get dressed. The rehearsal dinner starts in fifteen minutes. You will be there, and you will plaster a smile on your face, or I promise you, I'll make them suffer."

I wanted to roll over, but his eyes narrowed, so I dragged

my ass up from the floor and walked towards the bathroom, kicking off my sneakers as I went. Once in the bathroom, I took a leak and turned the shower on.

My stomach rolled at the thought of going out there and pretending to have a good time, when all the while I wanted to run. Somehow, I had to get myself out of this mess I'd made without hurting anyone I cared about. I wondered if Jan knew about the bribe.

Jan was who my dad had chosen for me, and like it or not, I was stuck with her. I banged my head on the tiles in the bathroom and the door flew open.

"If you're trying to drown yourself, I don't think a shower is going to work."

Jake's voice interrupted my thoughts and I jumped a foot into the air.

"You'd better get a move on. Your dad's going crazy because you're running late and Jan's already there."

"I'm coming now."

"God, I really hope you're not, 'cause that'd be hella inappropriate."

His laugh was deep and hearty, and I couldn't help joining in as I turned the shower off. Jake turned and left the bathroom, tossing a bath towel over his shoulder at me. I scooped up the towel and dried off, running my fingers through my hair.

I was supposed to get it cut last week, but I never made it to the barbers. In fact, I'd only left the house to go to work or the gym recently. I hadn't even gone to the store in weeks.

I pulled on my cream short-sleeved shirt and marveled at how tight it was around my biceps. As I pulled on my boxers, I thought about the wedding. My stomach rolled, making me retch, and I rushed over to the toilet bowl, throwing up nothing but bile and water. My throat burned and my eyes watered as I sat by the toilet, heaving and throwing up until there was nothing left.

Sometime around my third vomit, my dad had opened the door and glared at me. As soon as the vomiting had passed, he hissed at me.

"Get fucking dressed!"

The door slammed closed and I staggered over to the sink to wash my mouth out.

Fuck my actual life, I thought when I looked in the mirror.

My eyes were sunken and blacklined, and fury rolled over me. My fist made contact with the mirror before my head even realized what I was going to do. Glass fell in sharp shards and my knuckles were cut and bleeding.

I watched in fascination as my knuckles turned purple and blood ran down the fragmented mirror.

"Cooper, what the fuck?" Jake asked as he came back into the bathroom. He took my hand away from the mirror. "Well, you've broken at least three knuckles and your hand's a mess, but I can get these glass splinters out. Don't move."

He walked out of the bathroom in a flurry, returning a moment later with a pair of tweezers and a bottle of Scotch.

He poured the Scotch over the tweezers and set the bottle down on the vanity. He never said a word as he stood plucking pieces of glass from my hand, and five minutes later, when my dad returned, we still hadn't spoken.

"What the fuck happened to you?" My dad hissed the question at me, and Jake spun around to face him.

"The kid slipped. Now stop yelling at him and let him get dressed."

Jake shoved my dad out of the bathroom and turned back and winked at me as I stood numbly by the sink. "Wash your hand and I'll wrap it for you."

I nodded and turned the faucet on, wincing as the water

stung my hand. I pulled my pants on and walked out to see my dad pacing furiously, with Henri standing in a gold dress that was too tight and made her look my age.

"Finally. Calm down, dear. Cooper's ready, aren't you?"

She spoke to me like I was a child, and before I could answer her, Jake said, "No, he's not. I need to fix up his hand, otherwise it'll swell up like a balloon tomorrow. Why don't you guys go on ahead and let everyone know that Cooper will be along in the next half hour? Let them know he's had a minor accident and is really sorry about the delay."

I could see my dad turning this over, and when he nodded stiffly and walked towards Henri, I almost sighed in relief. As he met her at the door, he stopped and spun back towards me. His fist connected with my stomach and knocked the wind out of me.

"Shawn," Henri reprimanded, but it was Jake who surprised me as I dropped to the floor.

"GET OUT!" he hissed and stood in front of me. "Get the fuck outta here, brother, or Imma call the cops on your ass."

His fury scared me, and I could tell he was a good guy to have on my side. Suddenly, I didn't feel so alone anymore. Maybe I could tell him what was going on and finally have an ally, because I'd been alone with all of this since Zane had left home.

Everything was riding on me, and I was so tired of carrying the burden.

My dad turned and left, and Jake closed the door as I slowly crawled to my feet, unable to believe my dad had just done that. I was so tired that I wondered for a moment if I'd be better off just ending it all.

I shook the thought off as Jake sat across from me on the curved chair next to the window. I glanced around the room, and for the first time, noticed the décor. The room was decorated in muted tones, with palm trees blending into one another in shades of green, gold, and burnt orange.

The windows were open and there were mahogany shutters, and the bed was a mahogany four-poster with light net curtains tied to each post. There was a sofa and a coffee table, plus two curved chairs on the left-hand side of the room near the door, and on the right-hand side of the room was a full-length mirror and a wardrobe. Along the wall facing me was a desk with a mirror, the minibar, and a chest of drawers, upon which a TV sat.

I stared dead ahead until Jake cleared his throat, and I turned to meet my uncle's light brown eyes.

"Stay there while I run and get my bag and then you can tell me what's been going on."

He turned and left the room, returning a few moments later and sitting in the chair with his bag on the table beside him.

"Okay, kid, spill."

He looked at me with expectant eyes and I shrugged at him before he gave me a quizzical look, as I organized my thoughts in my head.

"I… I uh…"

I didn't know how to begin, and I broke off as I thought about all the people who could be hurt because of me, but I needed to tell someone and try to figure out how to get out of this mess.

"My dad wants me to marry Jan," I began slowly.

Jake's eyes shot to me and understanding dawned on his face. "And you don't want to marry her? Why?"

"I'm in love with someone else, but it's complicated. I have people relying on me and they'll get hurt if I don't follow through on this."

"Hurt how, Cooper?"

I swallowed and stood, pacing around. "My dad and Jan's dad threatened them. I have to keep them safe, but I'm so miserable."

As I spoke, I remembered my cut hand and glanced at the floor to see blood droplets where I was pacing.

"Sit down. I'll clean up your hand and then you can tell me all about it and why it's complicated."

I complied and he opened a bandage and began tying it around my hand.

"So, Cooper, what is it that's complicated?"

"She's my stepsister. Henri's daughter…" I broke off as a lump formed in my throat.

"So, you're in love with your stepsister? Isn't that a bit creepy?"

I snatched my hand away from Jake and shot up, towering over him.

"No! It's not fucking creepy! Do you think I like feeling this way? I have been battling this attraction to her since I was sixteen years old! I hate feeling like this, but I love her!" I paused and glanced at my uncle as he leaned back in his seat. My fury left me, and I slumped onto the chair beside him. "I love her. I love her so much that it kills me every day. She's my whole world, and I hate that because my dad and her mom met that we can't be together."

I put my head in my hands and Jake leaned forward, gently placing his hand on my arm.

"Cooper, why can't you be together?"

"Oh, where to start with this one? There's the fact that society thinks it's fucked up, and the fact that my dad forbids it, and the fact that I've caused Bails nothing but pain since I met her. I don't deserve her."

My voice was small, and I dropped my hands as a tear rolled from my eye. Jake said nothing, and I swallowed around the lump in my throat, speaking in a hoarse voice. "My dad has threatened her and Zane, and I've always done what he said. I've never stood up to him, and when I finally made a stand and said no to him, both he and Jan's dad threatened them. What am I supposed to do, Jake? Zane has two little kids depending on him, and Bailey's money for the gallery she's opening is coming from my dad. I… I don't know what to do."

Jake ran his fingers through his brown hair and sat back in the chair. "How do you know you love this girl?" he probed, and I thought back over the years.

"I think about her all the time, and I've always wanted her. She is the kindest, most forgiving person I've ever met and, believe me, I was a complete shit to her. I screwed around so much because I couldn't have her. I couldn't have the one I wanted and I was miserable, so I made it my mission to make her as miserable as I was, but in spite of that, she forgave me.

"She forgave me when I didn't go to her when the date she was on put her in danger. She forgave me when I hit her with a ball because I was pissed that someone else was into her and I was jealous. I'll never deserve her, but I want to be the person she sees when she looks at me. She makes me want to be better, to do better, and she doesn't care about my looks, or my job, or any of it. All she cares about is me. She sees the real me and not who I pretend to be."

"Does she know how you feel about her?"

I shook my head and dropped my eyes to my hands. "No. I pushed her away because I was worried about what my dad would do to her and I've regretted it every single day of my life since."

"Don't you think she deserves to know? Can't you call her?"

"I want to leave and go to her, but I can't, and it's killing me. I can't risk her future or Zane's because I love them too much to be selfish."

"Do you not think you're allowed to be selfish, Cooper?"

"No. I don't. I think if I give in and do what I want, then people will get hurt, and I can't stand the thought of them hurting because of me."

"Well, do you know what I think?" He paused and I looked at him, shaking my head. "I think you're scared. I think you're scared that if you go to her, she'll reject you and hold the past against you, but you won't know that unless you try. Don't you think it's unfair to Jan to marry her, even though you love someone else?"

"Yes. I do. I wanted to end it and leave. I have a flight booked for noon tomorrow."

"Cooper, do you think your dad knows how selfless you are and is using the fact that you love your brother and are in love with this girl against you?"

I pondered that for a moment and leaned back, staring up at the ceiling.

"Go to the rehearsal dinner and do the right thing. End this now, because you know if you go through with this, then you'll regret it forever."

"Yeah, that's what I'll do. I'll end it now. How can I do it without Bailey or Zane suffering as a consequence though?"

Jake drummed his fingers on his chair and then sat upright. "Use your cell. Record a private conversation with them and then inform them after you publicly end it that you will use the recording against them if anything happens to either Zane or Bailey!"

DINNER DECEPTIONS

Cooper

My heart began to race, and I realized what an excellent idea it was. Then they couldn't touch me. I could be free. Actually free! The thought of being free of my dad and being free to go to Bailey almost made me dizzy, but I nodded and stood up suddenly, pacing the room as I digested Jake's idea. I could do it. I could get the evidence I needed to break free and then there would be nothing stopping me from getting Bailey back.

I spun towards Jake, who was sitting quietly on the bed, watching me as I moved anxiously around the room. I met his gaze, breaking into a smile for the first time since I arrived. Excitement made my hands tingle, and I wanted to do it. I wanted to get it over with, so I could leave and break away from my dad's iron grip on me.

"Come on, Jake. I have breaking up to do."

We left the room and walked slowly across the hotel grounds to the beachfront restaurant where the rehearsal dinner was being held. I was almost bouncing, and just as we reached the hedges behind the restaurant, Jake put his hand on my arm.

"Cooper, put on your poker face. Don't give the game

away by smiling. Wait until the opportune moment before you do it."

I nodded slowly and relaxed my face. I had loads of practice over the years of acting one way when I felt another, so I knew I could do it. I sucked in a deep breath and turned to Jake with tears in my eyes.

"Thank you, Jake. Thank you for trying to help me."

He clasped my shoulder and gave me a gentle squeeze before we both turned to survey the festivities taking place. I spotted Jan floating around with her friends and I was desperate to go to her, but I had to sort things out with our fathers first. I had to get the recording, otherwise I'd never be free of them.

"Go get them, kiddo," he whispered as some people I didn't know moved towards us. After a beat where we waited on them to pass, my hands clenched into fists and my stomach rolled because I was so done with all this shit. They greeted me like a friend and I smiled at them and thanked them for coming, even though the words stung as they left my throat.

Once they were gone, Jake and I walked in and Jan sidled up beside me, hissing in my ear. "You're almost an hour late, Cooper!"

Her hand on my arm made my skin crawl, and I smiled blandly down at her. "Yeah, sorry. I fell asleep and then slipped when I got out of the shower."

"Oh my God. That's your ring hand. How are we supposed to get married when your hand is all wrapped up in a fucking bandage? And, oh my God, our photos."

She didn't care that I was hurt. All she cared about was what the photos would look like. I shook her hand off my arm and walked away in search of a stiff drink.

At the bar, I ordered a Scotch on the rocks and stood

slowly sipping it as I glanced around the room. All of the people there and I was completely alone. I didn't see my dad walk over and stand beside me, but I heard him as he ordered two drinks.

"Margarita with a twist, and a Scotch on the rocks."

I spun to look at him and he met my stare evenly.

"We need to talk!"

We both spoke at the same time, and I nodded towards a quiet corner.

I took my cell out and saw that it only had a small charge in it, so I hoped I had enough power to get the recordings I needed, and then I could escape from this sham.

I walked over and my dad joined me a few minutes later, but it was enough time to set my plan in motion. I'd set my cell up so it was hidden against a plant but could still see what was going on. After a few seconds, Finn walked over too.

They both stared at me as I sat sipping slowly on my drink, and I stared at them like a snake coiled and ready to pounce.

"I can't do this," I clarified, and they both shook their heads.

"Yes, you can!" my dad said, and I leaned back on my chair, watching as their faces turned puce.

"We've already discussed this. You will go through with this wedding," Finn began.

"Or you will be responsible for Bailey losing that gallery of hers and Zane losing a job he desperately needs," my dad cut in, and I rubbed at my face.

"Please, don't make me do this!" I begged, hoping they would say something more incriminating. I needed them both to incriminate themselves, so I could make sure that when I called this off, it would all be over and there would be no repercussions for me or anyone I cared about.

"You will do this, or, as your dad says, those you love will pay the price," Finn muttered, and then he leaned closer to me. "I will personally ensure that Bailey loses out and I will make it my mission to destroy you both, unless you do as you are told."

I snapped my teeth together because I was so sick of the threats, but it was awful for Jan too. She deserved to be with someone who loved her and wasn't being pushed into marrying her with threats and intimidation. I had to try to appeal to her dad for her.

"But don't you want Jan to marry someone who loves her?" I couldn't imagine forcing someone to marry someone they didn't love. It just wasn't right, and it was beyond belief that I had to try to convince them that this wasn't fair on Jan or acceptable at all.

"No. She's happy with you. She wants you and she has since you were kids. What my girl wants, she gets."

"So, my feelings on this don't matter? Can't you see how wrong that is? Forcing me to marry your daughter because I'm who she wants won't make either of us happy. In fact, I'm already miserable and, deep down, I think she is too."

"Enough," my dad cut in. "Cooper, you will go through with this, or I swear to you, you'll be sorry. I promise you that Bailey's life will be ruined, and Zane will never get a job again. Do you understand me?"

"Yes, sir. Loud and clear," I spat at him, and he met my glare with a vicious look in his eyes. I knew that, had I been younger, he'd have beaten me up so badly for daring to question him, and for trying to get out of this charade he was manipulating me into.

Just as I finished speaking, Jan's mom and Henri came over

and they all left. I reached into the plant pot and took out my cell, smiling as I rewound a little to make sure I'd caught it all, smiling wider when I saw I had. I quickly saved the video, emailed it to myself, and shared it via Facebook messenger with my office account before turning my cell off and putting it into my pocket.

Just as I pocketed my cell, Jake appeared. "Did you get it?"

I nodded slowly and he clapped me on the shoulder as excitement started to bubble up inside my gut. I was going to be free. Finally, totally and completely free, and it was a heady thought. I hadn't been free since that day he'd called me into his office, beat the shit out of me and told me he was financially responsible for Bailey. Seven years he'd held that over me and forced me to do what he wanted, but no more. Jake spoke and interrupted my trip down memory lane.

"Good. I got it too. I wanted to make sure you had a copy in case something went wrong."

"Thank you…" I began, but Jan interrupted us.

"Come on." She gripped my arm tightly and dragged me towards the top of the dance floor where the officiant for the next day was standing. I tried to shrug out of her grasp, but she spun around and gave me a sharp tug.

"Come on, Cooper. Everyone is waiting for us to get this done."

I shook my head and began to back away from her, but she followed me to the side before anyone noticed.

"What the fuck is going on with you?" she hissed as her friends cheered and giggled beside us.

"I don't…" I began, and then I closed my mouth as Pete and Toni appeared at our sides.

"Hey, we doing this or what?" Pete asked, and he met my eye. I knew he was checking if I was going to back out or not, but before I could say no, Jan tugged me to the center of the dance floor in front of the officiant.

The rehearsal passed quickly, and I stared around the room. We were told where to stand, and how to stand, and what each part of the ceremony would entail. I opened my mouth three times to end it, but I didn't know how to do it, and before I got the courage, the night was over.

Jake caught up to me at the end and shook his head, but we couldn't speak because there were too many people around us.

I made my way towards Jan and nausea rose in my stomach at the thought of being married to her.

"Jan, can I have a word?"

Her friends tittered and laughed as she walked towards me. I led her to a secluded spot and winced as she tried to kiss me. I unwrapped her arms from my neck and stepped away from her.

"Jan, I can't do this. We can't get married."

My heart was pounding, and she stood nonplussed for a second before she started laughing. "Oh, haha. Very funny, Cooper."

I wanted to shake her hard as she stood there in her pale cream dress, with her long brown hair floating in the slight breeze.

"I'm not kidding. I don't want to marry you. I love…"

She put her finger to my lips and hissed, "Do not say her name. I mean it, Cooper. I swear if you even utter her name here, I'll fucking ruin you!" She broke off, breathing hard, and shook her head. "No. It's fine. You just have cold feet, that's all. Go to bed, sleep on it, and I'll see you tomorrow." I could see her trying to convince herself that it was just cold feet; she was stubborn and refused to listen.

"Jan, I'm not going to change my mind," I told her as she just glared at me.

"No. I won't listen to this shit tonight. Don't fucking ruin this for me, Cooper. I mean it." She stepped towards me and gave me a soft kiss on my lips that made me step back in revulsion.

I watched in horror as she stalked quickly away without looking back at me. *Perhaps I should just leave.* Maybe if I left now, it'd be better than leaving her at the altar. Maybe it was kinder to just go. I mean, I had tried to tell her, and it wasn't my fault she wasn't willing to listen. But I couldn't do it. I had to do it right.

I had to end things publicly to protect Zane and Bailey, so she was right. She *would* see me the next day, but I wouldn't marry her. I'd tell her I wasn't going through with it.

I was leaving.

Chapter Six

Cooper

THE MORNING ARRIVED, AND I DRESSED IN MY CREAM trousers and white shirt with cream tie. I couldn't wait to have this all over and done with, but I was nervous.

I checked and re-checked the video, and I knew I had enough evidence to damn them, but I was still worried something would go wrong. Jake swung by my room with a bottle of Scotch and we had a few glasses each, along with croissants, muffins, and fruit.

I barely ate and was feeling pretty numb around the edges as Pete and the guys walked me to the wedding venue. The beach was glorious, and the sun was shining beautifully. If it had been Bailey about to walk towards me, this would have been the perfect location to get married.

My eyes scanned the beach and I could see the chairs on the sand. Two hundred guests were due to descend soon.

"Cooper, you look a little green. Here, have a sip." He handed me a bottle and I took a swig without looking at him. "Are you sure about this?" he pressed, and I nodded slowly.

"Yes, I'm sure."

I was sure I was going to end things. Sure I was leaving, and I couldn't wait to get it done so I could go and beg Bailey for forgiveness. The time passed quickly, and I watched everyone file into their seats in a detached sort of way.

All too soon, the ceremony began, and Jan walked down the aisle, beaming, but I couldn't wait to wipe the smile off her face. She'd been nothing but a bitch to Bailey, and I wanted to punish her for making me go through with this.

"We are gathered here today to celebrate the wedding of Jan Michaels and Cooper Christie," the officiant began, and I stared dumbfounded at Jan as she grinned at me.

"Cooper, smile, please? We're getting married."

Nope. No, we're not, I thought as she stood there and glared at me, and then I froze up because it was time for me to take what I wanted. After seven years of being told I couldn't have her, she was almost mine and I couldn't wait. My body went numb as the officiant continued speaking, I had to get out of this. I should never have let it get this far. My thoughts clamored around in my head as I tried to figure out what to say, how to get the man marrying us to stop speaking, and then my opportunity presented itself.

"If anyone knows of any reason why these two should not be joined together in marriage, speak now."

For a moment, the silence was deafening, and then four people spoke at once.

I found my voice and stepped back away from Jan. "Nope. Sorry, I can't do this."

Pete stepped around me and said, "Cooper, you can't marry her. You love someone else."

Jake also stepped forward. "He's not marrying you, sweetheart, and no amount of bullying or bribery will make him."

But it was the last person who rushed forward that surprised me the most.

"I object! This wedding isn't what you want, Cooper."

The noise from the guests was at fever pitch, and my dad stood up, trying to call them to order.

Zane moved slowly down the aisle towards me and I walked over, giving my brother a tight hug.

"Sorry, man, but I couldn't let you go through with this. You'll be fucking miserable."

My dad wrenched us apart and hissed at Zane, "I told you to leave us alone. I warned you what would happen if you didn't. I'm going to get those kids taken from you, and I'll ruin you…"

I spun around to face my dad, furious, my blood hammering in my ears. "You threatened his kids?" I spat.

My dad turned to me with hatred on his face and spoke to me through his teeth. "Of course I did. I will not let this worthless waste of space ruin any more lives."

I was about to lose my shit when Jan appeared in front of me.

"Cooper!" Her high-pitched, whiny voice made my skin crawl and fury erupted all over me.

Her dad appeared at my side, and I wanted to punch him as he stared meaningfully at me.

"Cooper. Remember our deal!"

Jan spun around and smirked at her dad, which was the final straw.

"Fuck you!" I yelled over at him, and then I faced my dad. "Fuck you too. I will not be bullied into marrying anyone!"

"Cooper!" Jan screeched, and I violently pulled my arm out of her grasp.

"No! You cannot force someone to marry you! I'm done with this shit. I'm done with you and your fucking games!" I turned around, pinning my dad and Finn with a glare as I pulled out my cell and played the video. "If either of you comes after anyone I love, then this goes to the media. I'm fucking done."

Turning, I clapped Pete on the shoulder, walking away with Zane at my side as my dad followed us. We just reached the edge of the aisle when he caught up to us.

"I'll end your career, you ungrateful little shit. I'll get your promotion taken from you and you'll end up a joke."

I turned to look at him and there was pity in my gaze, because I didn't understand how he could have gotten it so wrong. It was like he didn't know me at all. I didn't care about stature, or money, or being a partner. I cared about helping people, and I'd already applied for a new job with a bigger law firm. I was awaiting a call back, and if I got it, then I was out of the firm that my dad had recommended.

"I don't care! Don't you get it? I love Bailey and I'm going after her. Your threats are meaningless because I fucking love her. I've always been hers and I will love her 'til the day I die!"

My dad pulled back and punched me square on the jaw, sending me flying. Zane stood openmouthed as Dad approached me, saying, "You're done. I'm going to ruin you, you'll be nothing without me."

He hit me again, and I swiped his legs away from him.

"Enough!"

Henri stood watching, and her face was a picture of fury. "Cooper and Zane, leave, please. Shawn, you ever threaten my daughter again and I'll take you to the cleaners."

Zane helped me to stand, and we had to pass by Henri as my dad clambered to his feet. He opened his mouth to speak, but closed it when he caught Henri's eye. As we walked away, I heard her say, "How could you try to force your son to marry someone he didn't love? How could you lie to me about it?"

I didn't listen to his answer. I didn't care anymore. I was free. I was finally free of them and their games, and now I could go find Bailey and give her the love she deserved from me.

My breaths for the first time in a long time were easier, and I was optimistic about the future because I'd finally done it. I'd finally broken free.

WE MADE IT TO THE AIRPORT, AND I SWAYED WHERE I STOOD as the reality of going to Bailey threatened to overwhelm me. I was finally getting what I wanted. I was finally getting the girl I'd always dreamed of. At least, I would if she forgave me, but what if she couldn't? What if she wouldn't forgive me again?

My palms were sweating as I handed over my ticket, and I could barely hear the girl behind the desk as she asked for my ID.

Zane reached around me and handed it over because I was too numb to move.

"Zane, what if she won't forgive me?"

My anxiety began to soar and my breath started to come more quickly, but Zane smiled and led me to the bar. He shoved me into a chair and went to order some drinks, returning after a few minutes with a Scotch for me and a soft drink for himself.

"Here, drink this." He passed me my drink and I took a swallow, leaning back and enjoying the feel of the liquid as it warmed my throat. "You wanna tell me what's wrong, bro?"

I sat up and rubbed my trouser leg, removing a piece of lint. "What if she doesn't want me anymore?"

I spoke the thought out loud, and as much as I was scared of his answer, I had to know.

"She loves you. I haven't a clue why, but she's so in love with you that it almost killed her when you came back with Jan."

"Do you think she can forgive me? I mean, I've fucked things up so badly…"

I broke off and took another sip of my drink as Zane leaned forwards. "I think she'd be willing to hear you out. But, Cooper, you need to be honest with her." He paused and took a sip of his drink. "Why did you leave her? I could see that day in the park how unhappy you were with Jan. Why did you stay with her? Why didn't you tell Bailey how you felt?"

My dad's threats came back to me and I shrugged, wondering how to make him see that everything I'd ever done was to protect Bailey. I'd stayed with Jan to protect her, ran from her to stop her getting hurt, and now I was going to have to try to explain to Bailey what had happened over the years.

"I wanted to protect her. Dad threatened to pull the funding from her gallery, and I couldn't bear the thought of it. He also told me way back when we were kids that he wouldn't fund her even going to college if we were together, and he held the threat of hurting her over me for the last seven years That was why I didn't tell her, but I wanted to and I almost did on four separate occasions. I even asked her to stay with me, but when she asked me what I said, I lied because I'm a fucking coward when it comes to her."

His eyes widened and he leaned back. "Two things, Cooper. One, Dad hasn't funded anything for Bailey. Her dad paid her tuition for Princeton and she had a trust fund which kicked in when she was twenty-one. She owns part of the gallery on her own. And two, you are not a fucking coward. You gave up your chance at happiness to protect Bailey and me, and you are so fucking selfless. You always have been, and Dad used that against you, which is fucking shitty."

My stomach bottomed out as I realized that for all those years, I'd stayed away to let her go to school, to have her life, and it was all based on lies. All of it.

Bile rose in my stomach and I rushed for the bathroom, throwing up until there was nothing left. Everything I'd believed, everything I'd done was because of my dad and his fucked-up deceits. I'd hurt her, pushed her away, sickened myself, and it was all for nothing.

I leaned my head against my hands as fury rose in me. I wanted to go back to my dad and punch him in the face. All those years he'd kept me apart from her. Finding out he'd been lying had rocked me to my core.

I got up and cleaned my face with my good hand, walking out to see Zane speaking to a few people as I approached our table. Zane was frowning, and I wondered what was going on, but he shook his head gently at me just before I reached the table.

I ducked around the pillar near where we were sitting and stood listening to the people talking to him.

"Yes, we are looking for Mr. Christie in relation to an assault that took place earlier today. Could you ask him to come to the station, please?"

Zane nodded at them and I waited until they were out of sight before moving. Zane met me as I moved and nodded towards a different exit.

"What's going on?" I asked him in a low voice, but he didn't speak, just marched us through the airport until we reached our terminal.

"Jan's saying you assaulted her."

"What? When?" I asked, wide-eyed as horror over what that could do to my career hit me.

"The cops know you didn't do it, but they need to speak to you because they're worried she has a vendetta against you. They spoke to numerous wedding guests who stated that you just walked away from her."

"I'll call them now." I took out my cell and saw it was dead.

"No, don't call them now. If they want you to go in, you might miss Bailey."

"What do you mean?"

My hand clenched into a fist as I thought about what missing her would mean, and my heart hammered in my ears as nausea swept over me. I couldn't wait any longer. I'd waited long enough. I needed to get to her now, today, and beg her to love me. I knew she did, but I had to somehow convince her I would never hurt her again.

My eyes watered as the memory of her standing by the car washed over me again, and I knew that, even if she said no, there was no way I would ever love someone as much as I loved her.

"She's moved her moving date forward. She leaves on Monday, and if I can't get you back in time, then she'll leave without knowing you're coming for her."

Our flight was announced and we stood and began walking to the check-in desk. We didn't speak again and spent the flight separated, so I tried to sleep. When we landed, Zane quickly ushered me out of the airport.

Apparently, standing the governor of Washington's daughter up at the altar was newsworthy. It must have been a slow news week, but the vultures followed us out of the airport, shouting questions at us as we left.

We climbed into a cab and Zane gave Bailey's address.

"Zane, how did you get to Hawaii?"

I'd wondered on the flight and while we were waiting at the airport, but there wasn't a right time to ask him about it, or about how he'd paid for the flight for both of us when he was broke.

"I spoke to a lawyer and he freed up my trust fund. Dad had blocked it, but it was illegal, and although it will take a bit of time to come through, Mom's money will see Sam, the kids, and me through. Plus, Sam's got a job teaching elementary three days a week, and I've got a counseling job in a clinic four days a week. We'll be working around each other and one of us will be there when the other is at work."

"That's great, man. I'm so glad it's all taken care of."

"Yeah, well, we owe Sam's dad some money, so it'll be nice to pay him back, and we want to buy a swing set for the kids as a reward because they've been amazing. Oliver especially has settled in real well to Bailey's."

"Can I buy the kids a swing set?"

Zane turned to look at me, and I wondered if he'd let me. Since the day he'd gotten arrested, I'd felt guilty. I'd known my dad was lying, but I pushed my instincts down and ignored my better judgement. I'd punished him and hurt Bailey in the process, and I needed to start making amends to Zane, Sam, and Bailey.

"Sure you can," Zane answered, interrupting my thoughts.

"Can it be pretty big? 'Cause I got five Christmases and birthdays to make up for."

He laughed and glanced at his cell. I saw his demeanor change, and he swallowed before speaking again. "Yeah, that's fine."

He was distracted the rest of the way back to the farmhouse, but when we arrived, Sam flew out of the door and into his arms with tears streaming down her cheeks.

"God, I'm so glad you're home. I was so worried that your dad would mess things up for you or put you in jail or something that I couldn't sleep."

Zane glanced at me over her head and held her tightly as Oliver and Serena came out the door, followed by a man I hadn't met yet.

"Hi, I'm Kurt Kersley. I'm Sam's dad. It's nice to meet you."

He was tall with large arms and an intimidating stare, but he smiled as he came towards me, and I couldn't help relaxing as I shook hands with him.

"Zane, Cooper, you want some coffee?" he asked, and I nodded, thinking I'd add a little Jack to it to get some Dutch courage so I could speak to Bailey.

Chapter Seven

REPERCUSSIONS

I FOLLOWED THEM INSIDE AND WATCHED AS THEY ALL SAT down in the living room as I called my employers from the dining room and explained what had happened at my wedding. I also told them I'd be available to return to work, but Jack cut me off.

"We are aware of what happened," Jack Devon, one of the partners, stated in the conference call. "And quite frankly, we aren't sure what we want to do about the mess you've made yet. We work closely with your father's company, and with Finn Michaels too, so we need to evaluate and determine whether you are a good fit for our firm."

I tuned out for a moment as I wondered when Bails would be home. I was desperate to see her.

"Yes, quite an embarrassment for the firm, especially with you on the cusp of being made partner."

"I'm sorry," I muttered.

"Yes, well, sorry is all well and good, but I'm not sure what we can do about all the bad press." James Jackson spoke in his deep baritone.

"Bad press?" I asked, trying to keep up.

"Yes, Mr. Christie. There has been a ton of bad press because you dumped the governor's daughter at the altar. What did you expect would happen with such a public display of disrespect?"

"I'm sorry, but disrespect towards who?"

"Disrespect towards Governor Michaels, of course. If you didn't want to marry the girl, you should have handled things more privately." James spoke again.

"I move we vote for a suspension pending investigation," Jack said.

"Seconded," Chris Brown added.

"Carried," Alena Matthews said, and one by one, they clicked off until only Indie Parker and I were on the line. Indie was my line manager and my direct superior.

"Sorry, Cooper. I tried to get them to back off, but they're claiming you embarrassed the firm by not handling it more privately."

"So, I'm being punished for ending a relationship I was unhappy in."

"I think it was more the way you did it. I'm sorry. You're suspended for two weeks on full pay, but to be frank, I expect they'll want to fire you."

"Fire me? But I'm the best litigator in the firm."

She sighed and I could barely hear her as she spoke again. "Yes. I know that, but they love government contracts and they're worried that with you in the firm, these will dry up. Sorry, Cooper, but I've got to go. I have court in twenty minutes."

With that, she ended the call, and I was left sitting there wondering how my private relationship ending had resulted in me getting fired from my job. The sad thing was, I didn't even care. I enjoyed my job, but I was hoping to get the other job anyway, so it didn't matter. They'd need to give me a hell of a severance package since I'd been exemplary at my job since I'd started there.

I closed my eyes and rubbed at the spot between them as a headache was building, but I didn't care about the headache. I didn't care about the job, or the fact that everything I'd worked for was turning into a pile of rubbish before my eyes. All I cared about was seeing Bailey. I wanted to spend the night buried inside her and never leaving. The thought made me hard, and I squirmed as I wondered again where she was.

I needed to see her. I needed to hold her in my arms and beg her for forgiveness. I had a vague idea of what I wanted to do to her, but I needed her to be in front of me to do it.

I wandered from the dining room and into the living room, but Zane and Sam were sitting on the sofa with their babies between them, and I moved farther into the house.

I opened doors, looking for her room, and stopped outside a room that smelled so much like her it almost brought me to my knees. I knocked on the door, praying she was in there sleeping or something, but after a few moments, there was no answer, and I opened the door slightly to peek inside.

On a wooden desk near the window, beside a pile of boxes, was an envelope. My legs were leaden as they automatically carried me to the desk and I picked up the letter, seeing it addressed to Zane and Sam.

My heart pounded in my ears as I left her room and carried the envelope gingerly through to Zane. His eyes widened when he saw the envelope and I knew he was remembering our cousin who left an envelope addressed to his mom before he hanged himself.

My fingers trembled as I passed the envelope over to Zane, and he carefully opened it without disturbing Oliver and Serena. His eyes skimmed the letter and he sighed as he reached the bottom before passing the letter to Sam.

My heart hammered as I watched her read it and purse her lips before she and Zane did that couple thing where they communicated with each other with their eyes.

"I knew." Sam muttered in a small voice and Zane glared at her.

"You knew? Why didn't you say anything?" he asked her and I wondered what she knew, but then she nodded towards me and I understood that whatever was in the note, Sam already knew about it. I watched them and desperately wanted to snatch the letter out of Sam's hand, but before I could move, Zane nodded once at her and she passed the letter over.

I straightened it out. My heart was in my throat as I read.

DEAR SAM AND ZANE,

I'm so sorry to leave like this, but I can't bear to stay here any longer.

I've moved my flight up, and when you guys get this, I'll be gone.

I'll be back for Christmas and I'll miss you all terribly, but I can't stay because I need to move on. Cooper is getting married today and I honestly wish him all the happiness, but staying around to watch him begin married life with her would make me a total masochist, and he's caused me enough pain to last me a lifetime.

I'm so sorry for not saying goodbye, but I'll be in touch once I'm settled in Paris.

My love to you guys and the kids,
Bailey

I COULD FEEL THE TEARS WELLING UP AS I READ THE LETTER and realized she'd gone. I had to go after her. I had to make her see it was her I wanted. I didn't want Jan, and I didn't want to be the guy who let the love of his life walk away because it was complicated.

"Coop," Zane started, and I lifted my eyes from the letter to stare at him. "I'm sorry, man. I thought if I could get you back here in time, she'd change her mind."

"It's not your fault. It's mine. It's all my own fault."

I stood up, too restless to sit still, and began pacing around the room. I longed to hit something, but the babies were asleep, and I didn't want them to be afraid of me. I couldn't believe how much of a mess my life was.

All I wanted was Bailey and she'd gone. She'd left for Paris before I got a chance to tell her how I felt and how sorry I was for leaving her. I wanted to tell her I regretted it from the moment I left and I wished I could change what I'd done, but it was too late now. I walked through to the kitchen with the letter still clenched in my fist. What was I supposed to do now? Should I go to Paris and beg her for forgiveness, or should I stay and sort my life out so that, when I went after her, I had a job and a home to offer her?

I didn't know what to do. Without her, I was like a rudderless boat, spinning in a circle, not knowing which way to go.

I leaned over the sink and closed my eyes for a moment. I had to come up with a plan. I didn't even know if she'd accept me right away, and what if I went all the way over there and she rejected me?

Was it better for me to wait, or should I book a flight and just go to her?

My cell was still in the dining room charging, and I walked through to get it. Zane and Sam were speaking in the hallway, and I paused to give them privacy.

"She left because of him." Sam's tone was icy, and I could see Zane rubbing her arm from where I stood. "He should leave her alone. She deserves so much more than what he can give her."

"Sam, that's not fair. He really loves her and she loves him. Sometimes it's not about what we deserve, but what we want. You deserve so much better than me, a washed-up addict, but you love me regardless, and it's like that with them."

"I just don't think he's right for her. She was in a complete mess after she dropped him off. She begged him to stay. Did you know that?"

"Yeah, I knew, but he thought he was protecting her. You didn't see them when we were kids. They had this connection, and I hated it. It made me feel so alone, but now I can see that they needed each other because they were in love with each other. My dad hated it. He hates Bailey's dad because he put my grandpa in jail when Dad was younger for accounting fraud or something, and he's never forgiven him for it. That was why he was so against Bailey and Cooper. He wanted to punish her for her father's mistakes, but he didn't just punish her. He punished Cooper too because he wanted to make Coop his protégé."

I had no idea about my dad and Bailey's dad having history. No wonder he was so against us being together. But taking her dad's decisions out on us was unfair.

Was Sam right though? I wondered if I should just leave Bailey be and let her move on with her life. Would she be happier without me? I'd always wondered what would have happened if Bailey hadn't been Henri's daughter, or if my dad and Henri hadn't met, but now I see that, no matter what, my dad would have been against us because of her dad.

I stayed hidden as they passed and went to their room, closing the door softly, and continued into the living room where I sat with my head in my hands. I couldn't face going to bed as I pondered what to do. I wanted to go to her straight away, but I wasn't sure if she'd even speak to me.

I sat for the longest time and thought about my options.

One. Go to Paris on the next available flight and beg her to forgive me.

Two. Give her a few days to settle in and then go to Paris and beg her to forgive me.

Three. Call her and beg for forgiveness.

Four. Stay home and get my life in order, so I could go after her when the time was right and offer her everything she deserved.

I went around and around in my head and I couldn't decide what to do, but calling her seemed like the easiest option, so I swallowed my pride and called her cell. I didn't expect her to answer. I expected her to be on a flight still.

It rang once, then twice, and then her breathless voice answered.

"Hello." Her voice was hoarse, and I knew I'd just woken her up.

"Bails, it's Cooper."

Her intake of breath told me she wasn't expecting me to call, or to hear from me at all.

"Cooper, aren't you supposed to be with your wife?" Her voice was ice cold, and I flinched.

"I didn't get married. I couldn't, not when I love someone else."

"Cooper, I can't do this right now. You have to let me go."

I swallowed my pride and poured my heart out to her. "Bails, I know I've messed up. God, have I messed up, but I love you. I love you so much and I'll do anything to prove it to you. Please just give me a chance to prove it to you. I'll move to Paris if you want. I'll give up everything if you'll have me."

I paused to take a breath and heard her sigh down the line. "Coop, I've heard all this before and I'm always hurt. I love you too. I love you so much, but please, please, just let me go. I don't deserve to be your second choice. I want to be someone's everything. I can't keep being hurt and I can't see any way for us to be together right now. Give me some time and space and I'll call you when I'm ready to talk."

The line went dead, and I broke. I couldn't believe she thought she wasn't my first choice. She was my only choice, and all I wanted was to see her and hold her and be able to tell her that it was her. It had always been her, but I had to respect her wishes. Pushing her would only force her further away, and I knew she'd be home for Christmas.

I'd waited this long. I could wait another two months if it meant getting her back.

I lay back and tried to bury the pain of hearing her tell me I wasn't good enough for her. She did deserve better than me, but selfishly, I wanted her. I wanted to try and win her back, and I knew I'd do anything to make it happen.

I closed my eyes and pictured how to show her I was worthy, but I came up blank. I would figure it out. My whole world depended on it.

I wondered what I would do if she never forgave me, but it was too scary a thought, so I shook it off and turned over, drifting off to a dreamless sleep.

Cooper

THE NEXT FEW WEEKS WERE TOUGH AS I COLLECTED MY belongings from Washington and from our home in Minnesota. Jan had ruined all my suits and maxed out two of my credit cards.

The day I went to pick up my car and belongings, I found them all sitting out in the rain. My car was keyed and one of the tires was torn.

Jan stood watching me impassively as I gathered up my clothes, broken laptop, and the two mementos I wanted to take with me.

"I hate you, Cooper Christie. I really fucking hate you."

Her hiss made me straighten up and I turned to look at her in disgust. "Not half as much as I hate you. You are a manipulative, vile, conniving bitch and I'm only sorry I didn't end things sooner." She growled at me, but I continued. "I don't care what happens next, but at least I'm away from you and your poison."

My body tensed as she flew at me, scraping her nails down my face hard enough to draw blood. My arms were full of my belongings so I couldn't fight her off, but she shoved me back into my car and slapped me.

My instincts to defend myself warred with the fact I'd never hit a woman, but when her nail caught my lip and tore at me, bursting my lip open, enough was enough. I dropped what I was holding and pinned her hands to her side.

She started screaming, kicking, and cussing me out, but I didn't let go.

I couldn't. She stomped on my foot, caught my shin, and almost made my leg buckle, but I held on to her because I didn't want to hit her. No matter what, she did have a right to be angry.

After a few more minutes, a cop car pulled up and I glanced around, seeing Mrs. Kirkton standing by her door, watching. She glared at me as the cops got out of the car, then turned, walking back into her house and closing the door behind her.

"Can we help you?" a round, sandy-haired guy with a little neck asked, and I glanced over at him, surprised to see he wasn't looking at me, but at Jan.

"Yes. He won't let me go. Please help me."

She began to cry, and I shuddered in revulsion.

"Sir, can you drop your hands and step away from the lady now, please?"

The second officer came over, and as soon as I released Jan, he spun me around and pushed me against my car.

"You have the right to remain silent—" he began, but I cut him off.

"You're seriously arresting me? Are you blind?" I fumed, and he slammed me harder into the car.

"Yes. You assaulted that lady and held her against her will."

Fire shot through me as I considered what to say next. "I. Did. Not. Assault. Her. I. Was. Trying. To. Defend. Myself," I spoke through my teeth as he patted me down.

"Why did you have to defend yourself? Look at the size of her."

I rolled my eyes and faced the officer, spitting a little blood from my mouth. "Because she's furious with me for ending our sham of a relationship. She assaulted me and has fraudulently used my credit cards, destroyed my car and my belongings, and attacked me."

"It's true," a voice came from behind me. "I witnessed it all and recorded it."

Jan's face turned puce as I turned my head a little to see Pete standing there.

"You have evidence of her assaulting this man?" The first cop looked between Jan and me and began to laugh. "Okay, let me see it," he said while grinning at me, and I wanted to punch him.

Pete walked over and showed his cell to the officer, whose face turned stony. He turned to face Jan. "You assaulted this man without provocation?"

His tone was firm, and she shook her head. "No. He assaulted me first. He assaulted me before this video was recorded, look."

She lifted her top and showed a line of black and blue bruises.

"I didn't do that!" I told them, but the second officer had already decided I was guilty, and he shoved me into the back of the police cruiser, ignoring my protests.

I sat fuming as I pondered my next steps. I couldn't get a criminal record. I'd already lost my job, my home, and my dad. I couldn't afford to lose anything else.

My whole body shook as I waited on them to get into the car, and I saw Pete arguing with the officers. I couldn't make out what was said, but I could tell from the hand gestures that it was nothing good. After a few minutes, both officers returned to the car and officer one turned to look at me.

He had kind eyes and rough skin, a bald patch at the top of his head that was spreading, and a round stomach. "I don't think this kid is guilty," he muttered to his colleague, but Officer Dipshit, as I'd decided to call him, was taken in by Jan's angelic looks. "Look at the state of him, Tom."

Tom spun around to glare at me. "She got her own back on you, eh? She lose it 'cause you hit her one too many times?" His eyes narrowed on my face and he turned back around in disgust. "Beating her up and then wrecking your own stuff has to be the lowest, scummiest thing to do."

"I didn't beat her up. Today is the first time I've seen her in two weeks since I left her at the altar."

Officer Dipshit turned and brushed his blond hair out of his eyes as he eyed me up and down. "No way. You actually left her at the altar? Why would you do that? I don't believe it for a second. According to her, she dumped your ass at the altar because you were fucking your stepsister and that, to me, is all kinds of fucked up."

My face heated and fury rose in me, but I managed to keep a tenuous hold on my temper, spitting out, "Yeah, well, she's a lousy liar. It's all over the internet how I dumped Governor Michaels' daughter."

Franks, the first officer, showed Tom his cell, and Tom tutted.

"Oh, well. Looks like you're telling the truth. Still ruined your day though, didn't I?"

It was then that it dawned on me. Jan had a cousin in law enforcement, and she'd told me he'd be working in town once he qualified.

"Tom, are you by any chance related to Jan?"

His eyes darted to mine and he slammed on the breaks,

causing me to bounce forward into the Plexiglas that separated us.

"Oops, sorry!"

He didn't answer, and as we reached the station, Tom went inside without a backwards glance. Franks let me out, removing the cuffs that were cutting into my wrists.

"Come into the station, please, Mr. Christie. I'd like you to make a formal complaint against Tom. He's an arrogant, cocky little shit, and he purposefully chucked you into our squad car, even though all the evidence pointed to you being assaulted."

I nodded at the officer and we went inside where I made a complaint and pressed charges against Jan for fraud, assault, and destruction of property.

When I finally left two hours later, my face was aching, my lip throbbing, and I just wanted to go home and crawl into bed, but I didn't have a home.

My job interview was postponed, thankfully, but because my other firm had let me go with a hefty severance package, I had to find a new place to live, and my dad had frozen my trust fund.

I was still sleeping on Zane and Sam's couch. They'd offered to let me use Bailey's room, but I couldn't do that. I couldn't sleep in her bed when she wasn't there. I'd tried one night and the smell of her almost drove me to distraction.

Getting back to Zane's took another three hours by the time I'd collected my stuff from the townhouse and gotten my car towed to get fixed up. Jan's dad appeared as I collected my spare laptop, charging cords, and the remainder of my clothes. I put them all into my car and wished I could get away from all the stress and drama they'd caused me, but Governor Michaels was not about to let me off easily.

"What a mess you are, Cooper. No job, no family that

counts, little money. I bet you wish you'd done what you were told now."

His smug grin as I pushed past him made me want to hit him. My hands shook as I fought to maintain my composure, but I made it to my car and tossed in my belongings before turning back to face him.

"You know what? No, I don't wish I'd followed through. I wish I'd ended things sooner, and I honestly wish I hadn't let you and my dad try to force me to marry your psycho daughter. Now, if you'll excuse me, I'm getting the rest of my stuff and then I'm leaving. I will never come back here. Not ever."

His face was stony as I stormed past him and began shoving my shoes, work accessories, and files into a bag. When I was finally done, I left, leaving the door open, and passed him and Jan as they stood at the door.

Just as Pete arrived with my rental, which was in his name since Jan had messed up my credit, the cops rolled up and Jan was charged. Her face was purple, and she hissed at me as I passed her.

"I fucking hate you, Cooper."

I looked her up and down and continued to the rental, putting all my things from my car into the trunk as she was loaded into the back of a cop car.

I didn't pay attention to her dad or anyone else, but within a few moments of Jan being driven away, Finn approached me.

"You'll be sorry you did that to my daughter." His low voice made me chuckle, and I turned around to face him.

"I'm not sorry. I'm done with the threats and the games. Now, everyone is going to find out how corrupt you are and I'm here for it! Get out of my fucking way!" I shouted at him, unable to control my temper. Surprisingly, he stepped aside. I climbed into the driver's seat of the car, dropped Pete off at home and made my way back to Zane's.

What a day it had been. Zane was pacing the front porch as I drove up and he paused as I pulled into the driveway at the side of the house.

He moved towards the car and stared at me as I climbed out. I had my back to him as I tried to grab a couple of bags.

"Where's your Merc?"

I turned to answer him, and he gasped.

"Jesus, Coop. What the fuck happened to your face?"

My lip was stinging and split open. Every now and then I tasted blood. I lifted my shoulders and shrugged as Sam appeared on the porch, followed by Oliver and Serena.

"Cooper, we were getting worried." She looked at my face and her eyes widened. "Oh my God! You're a mess. What happened to you? Where's your car?"

I glanced between them and smiled at my nephew, who was staring at me. He began to cry, and Sam scooped him into her arms as Zane walked over and picked up Serena.

"It's a long story," I murmured and closed my eyes for a moment. My head was pounding, and I needed a drink. I'd not had one in days and my body was shaking from withdrawal.

I hadn't realized I had a problem, but Zane, who counseled troubled teens, noticed and pointed out to me that I was drinking way too much. I'd been drinking almost every day for the past few years as a way to numb myself to the pain of losing Bailey and having no choice over my life.

Zane led the way inside and I followed him, with Sam bringing up the rear.

"Your face is broken, Uncle Coop," Oliver whispered as

we entered the living room and sat on the couch. His little hands reached out and he pressed his finger to my cheek, causing a sting to burn through me. "Here, I kiss it better." He leaned up and pressed his lips to my cheek, and I gave him a hug, holding him for a second and taking comfort from this small boy who loved me. At that moment, I was okay.

Chapter Nine

THE NEXT SECOND, THE LANDLINE RANG, AND I STARED AT IT hopefully, but Sam smiled sadly as she answered the call. She turned her back to me and began speaking. I knew it was Bailey.

My heart started to race as I heard my name mentioned, and I wanted to both snatch the phone from Sam's hand, and run from the room and onto a plane.

Bailey had spoken to Sam and asked her to tell me not to come, but it was hard, and it went against every instinct I had to wait it out.

"He's fine." She paused and rolled her head from side to side. "Okay, sure thing."

Her fingers drummed on the table, and I prayed that Bails would ask to speak to me. Oliver wanted down and wandered off to play with Zane and Serena on the floor at the corner of the room. I watched for a beat, then turned back to Sam as she spoke again.

"Love ya."

My heart clattered against my chest because I knew she was going, and again, she didn't want to speak to me.

"Uh-huh, I will. Stay safe."

Sam turned and caught my eye as she spoke the one word that caused my heart to drop through my boots.

"Bye."

Her eyes were sad as she took me in, and she walked over to Zane and tapped him on the shoulder. They did that coupley thing again where they communicated without words, and I tuned them out, thinking about the week before when the landline rang and I'd answered it because Sam was at work and Zane was bathing Serena.

"Hello, Christie residence."

I answered with a professional lilt to my voice because I was waiting to hear back from the job I'd applied for before the wedding fiasco. My interview the previous day had gone very well, and I'd informally been offered the job, but I was waiting on their HR team to call me to give me the details.

"Is Sam or Zane there?" Bailey's voice cut into my thoughts about my job and my legs wobbled under me.

"No. I mean, yes, but no."

I couldn't get my thoughts together, and Bailey laughed. "Coop, you're confusing me. Are they there?"

Her tone was light, but there was an edge to it that I'd never heard before and I cleared my throat.

"Yes, Zane is, but he's bathing Serena. She got into the milk and poured a whole carton over herself."

I stopped because I was rambling and that wasn't what I wanted to say. I wanted to ask if I could go to her yet. I wanted to know if she was okay. Did she like Paris? Had she gotten her gallery? I had so many questions for her, but I knew she didn't want to talk to me.

Zane had told me the previous day that Bailey wanted a break from me and that my speaking to her would only serve to push her further away. If I wanted her back, then I had to give her time and space.

"Okay," she breathed, and I opened my mouth to say something to her when I heard a man call her name.

"Be right there!" she called out, and the lift in her tone was obvious. "I have to go. Tell Sam I'll call her later. Bye."

She hung up without letting me even say goodbye, and I stood numbly holding the telephone to my ear and listening to the dial tone.

My shoulders stooped and I punched out at the wall, cracking it a little, but cracking my knuckles too. Pain shot through me and I focused on that as I put the phone back on the hook.

I stood up from the sofa and decided to go get my running gear on. Going for a run was a great idea. It would help me clear my head and make me feel more alive. I was merely existing, and I needed something to focus on.

The new job at Lockhart, Brown, and Derbyshire had been postponed, so although I did have the job, my start date was after Christmas, and with nothing to distract me, I spent my days wallowing in pain.

I ran for five miles and got back to the house a shaking mess. I was generally fit, but not having any alcohol in my system for days was affecting me and I couldn't run any farther. When I got onto the porch, I leaned over and put my head between my legs as dizziness threatened to overwhelm me.

"Coop," Zane said from the porch, and I lifted my head slightly to see him sitting in a deck chair.

"A. Minute," I said as I struggled to get control over my breathing.

He waited patiently for me, and I went over and sat beside him. His face was serious, and his light brown hair was brushed back, with only his spiderweb tattoo visible between his hairline and his collar.

He turned his green eyes to me, and I balked at the seriousness of his expression. "Coop, we need to talk."

"Oh, God! You're not breaking up with me, are you?" I asked, trying to lighten the mood, and he grimaced.

His eyes went past me to the sky, and for a moment, we both sat looking out at the darkening sky. Raindrops started to fall and bounced off the ground, but we were protected by the overhanging porch.

"Coop, this is Bailey's house—" he began, and I knew what was coming. She didn't want me living in her house, even though it was only temporary. My trust fund was reactivated after a judge ruled that it couldn't legally be stopped by my dad since the money had come from my mom. I was looking for a place to live, but I hadn't found anywhere yet.

"And she wants me gone. I get it." I twisted the skin on my wrist around as I pondered where to go.

"She's hurt and angry with you, but I was hoping she'd come around."

"She hasn't though, has she?"

His eyes met mine, and I saw the sorrow in their depths. I had to leave. I couldn't stay and have them and Bailey on the outs. They needed this place.

"No. I'm sorry. I'm not... I don't..."

"Hey, it's okay. This was just temporary anyway. I'll go tonight."

I stood up and my legs shook again, but I forced myself to go into the house with Zane behind me.

Sam was holding her cell up when I walked in and then she dropped it, before nodding at Zane. He stepped around me and swept Sam into his arms, whispering in her ear.

"Cooper," she called as I passed them, and I turned to look at her.

"Stay the night. You can leave tomorrow."

I nodded once and left to take a shower.

How had my life gotten so far off track? How could I fix everything that was wrong when Bailey wouldn't see me or speak to me?

My face throbbed and my hand stung as I scrubbed at my skin with shaking hands. I needed to get a grip. I needed to get control over my life because this mess wasn't good enough. I had to sort myself out so that, if she did give me a second chance, I'd be worthy of her. No more drinking, no more screwing around. I had to sort myself out once and for all. And I would do it.

I climbed out of the shower and wiped the condensation from the mirror. I stared at my reflection and winced at the bruising appearing on my cheeks and below my eye, but I had to pull myself together. I wasn't a sniveling wreck, and I wouldn't let this define me. I was stronger than my demons, stronger than my father, and I knew that with Zane's help, I could overcome my demons.

I got dressed and sat on Bailey's bed as I found a listing for a townhouse downtown which was close to my office. I arranged a viewing and called a hotel to check in for a few nights, using the only credit card Jan hadn't maxed out.

For a few moments, I sat and breathed Bailey in, wishing she was there, but knowing that I had to give her time made me stand. I slowly walked to the living room to find Zane and Sam huddled together on the sofa.

"Hey," I murmured as I walked into the room, and they both looked at me. "I'm gonna go. I've booked a hotel for the night and I'm going to look at an apartment tomorrow."

Zane sat up straight and shook his head. "You were supposed to stay 'til tomorrow."

I cut him off because I knew it was upsetting him. "It's

fine. Bailey is your landlady and she doesn't want me here, so I'll go. I need to do this. I've wallowed enough for the past two weeks. I have to get myself together or I'll never deserve her."

"She cares about you, Cooper," Sam said, and I shrugged.

"I was speaking to her earlier and told her how worried we were about you. She doesn't want anything to happen to you and neither do we."

"I uh… that's good… I think."

I pondered what they meant about something happening to me and stared at Zane. He stood up and walked over to me, surprising me with a hug and whispering in my ear. "You've been so depressed that I was concerned about whether you would do something stupid."

I held on to him tightly, but we weren't usually huggers. We just survived Dad, and both of us had the scars to prove it.

"I'm fine. I wouldn't do that. I want to win her back and I can't do that if I'm dead."

He breathed a sigh of relief and stepped away from me as Sam walked over and hugged me tightly.

She spoke in a low voice, so only I could hear. "Go to Paris. Tell her how you feel and then give her the space she needs to make her decision. She misses you. I can hear it in her voice every time I speak to her."

She leaned back and pressed her lips to my cheek before stepping back into Zane's embrace. They were so lucky to have each other.

"Thank you." My eyes met Sam's and she nodded to show she knew why I was thanking her.

The drive to the hotel was short, and I checked in, flopping onto the bed and taking out my half a heart. I wondered where Bailey's was. I was going to look to see if the bear was there, but I couldn't bring myself to check. If it was there, then there was no hope for us, and if it wasn't, it could have been in the trash, or with her in Paris.

I didn't want to know either way. I just hoped she had it with her.

I closed my eyes and pondered what Sam had said. Did I dare go to Bailey? Could I really fly all the way over there and not get an answer?

My cell chimed, interrupting my thoughts, and my hand searched around the bed for it. I'd dropped it when I lay down and I scrambled around looking for it as another chime went off. Finally, I located it between the pillows and pulled it down towards me, keeping my head on the bed since it really was pounding.

I opened the messages.

One was from my dad, which I ignored. The other was from Bails.

COOP. I'M SORRY. I DON'T WANT YOU TO BE ALONE AND I called Sam back to say it was okay for you to stay when they told me you left. You can go back if you want. I was being mean and cruel, but I know you're hurting right now. Speak to Zane or Pete. Let them in and let them help you. Always, Bails xx

MY EYES WATERED AS I READ THE MESSAGE AND I PONDERED how to reply. I wanted to tell her how much I missed her, but I didn't want her to stop texting me, so I replied with a heart. I had so much more to say to her, but I wanted to give her the space she'd asked for and I decided to do just that.

I knew Sam wanted me to go to her, but if I went and she rejected me, then I'd have lost the only girl I'd ever really loved because I pushed her too hard. As hard as it was, I had to wait, so wait I did.

I bought a new townhouse and spent the next few weeks decorating it, buying furniture, and setting up my home office.

I'd gone with muted tones of gray, cream, and off-white in almost every room, and my furniture matched. My sofa was a dark gray, so dark it almost looked black, and my bed was gray with a TV that came out of the bottom. The furniture in my room was white, including an armchair I'd picked up from Pottery Barn.

Sam came to check in on me frequently, and so did Zane and Pete.

My dad tried to call me, but I didn't answer him. His messages were getting more and more frequent, but I knew he'd give up soon, or at least I hoped he would.

Every single day I checked out flights to Paris, and every day I convinced myself it wasn't the right time. I had to get my house ready. I'd signed all my paperwork for my new job, couriered all my files back to my old job, and bought a new car.

I bought a silver Toyota pickup truck because I'd had one when I was younger and I liked the memories it brought up.

On the twentieth of November, I ran out of excuses and sat staring at a flight to Paris for the next day. It was leaving in twelve hours, and I checked my cell for the one millionth time that day to see if Bailey had texted. She checked in with me every day or two, but I hadn't heard anything from her in three days.

My fingers drummed on my desk as I stared at the screen on my desktop.

Could I go? Yes!

Should I go? I didn't know.

Would I go? I wasn't sure.

I decided to go get dinner, and if she hadn't texted me back by the morning, I was booking the flight. I sent her a small message.

Hey, Bails. I saw Lish today. She was in the line at the grocery store with some guy. She's having a baby. I'm not sure if you guys are in touch still, but I figured that was something you might want to know if you're not. Speak soon, Coop xxx

I'd hidden from Lish because she hated me and I didn't want to face off against a pregnant lady in the middle of Walmart.

I threw some ingredients in the pan and made myself ignore my cell. If I could just get through dinner, then I could check again and then go to the gym before I went to bed. I could barely sleep because I had nothing to distract myself with, so I was hitting the gym two to three times a day.

My six-pack was now an eight-pack, and my abs were rock solid. I was eating loads because I was working out so much, but I knew I had to slow it down or I'd end up injured. *Not today though*, I thought as I fried chicken, veggies, eggs and rice in a pan on the stove.

I quickly served up my meal, desperate to get back to the gym and block out the world. As I scarfed my meal down, I sat thinking about what I would say to Bailey and if she'd even entertain me if I went to Paris when my cell chimed.

My heart dropped because if it was Bails, then I had no

excuse about going to Paris, but when I checked, it was Zane. I'd confided in him a few days ago about Bailey and me speaking, and he told me he already knew. It was him who encouraged Bailey to reach out because he was worried about me.

Hey, bro. You heard from Bails? It's been like three days and we've not heard from her at all!

My pulse began to race and I quickly texted back.

No, I haven't, but I looked and there's a flight to Paris tomorrow. Should I book us a few seats?

He didn't reply for a moment and then my cell rang.

"Hey," I answered quietly before taking a sip of water.

"Book the flight, Coop. I've got a few days off. Get a return for Friday or Saturday, so I can get back. Sam's working from home this week since Serena has chicken pox, so I'm good to go." I could hear the worry in his voice.

"Okay, I'll text you the flight details as soon as I've booked. She'll be fine, Zane. She has to be fine."

I was trying to reassure him, all the while panicking that something was wrong. I left my half-eaten dinner on the table and rushed back to my office, refreshing the page for the flights and booking Zane and me a roundtrip to Paris via Reykjavik.

I didn't care about the cost. All I cared about was finding

out if Bailey was okay. As the booking was confirmed, I texted Zane.

*P*ACK YOUR BAG. *W*E'RE GOING TO *P*ARIS AT NINE A.M. **tomorrow. We need to be at the Minneapolis airport by six, so I'll meet you at the door at five forty-five.**

FLIGHT OF FANCY

Cooper

I BARELY SLEPT ALL NIGHT. I TOSSED AND TURNED AND wondered what kind of response Zane and I would get. Was she going to be all right? Would she be happy to see us, or would she be mad?

I didn't care either way. As long as I knew she was okay, it didn't matter…

Okay, it mattered a lot. I wanted to win her back. I wanted her to be mine, so I had to be honest with myself. If she rejected me, I'd be crushed.

My eyes finally closed at four, and I drifted into a dreamless sleep, waking up fifty minutes later with my alarm tone sounding in my ear. I groaned and pulled my cover over my head, closing my eyes until an image of Bailey crossed my mind and I sat upright.

I grabbed a quick shower, shoving on a pair of jeans, a t-shirt, and a hoodie. I'd already packed my overnight bag and set my winter boots and my jacket beside it. My passport was in the front of the bag, along with my charging cord and my iPad.

I sat on the bottom step, pulling on my socks and boots. It took me longer than it should have because my fingers were shaking. I was so nervous that I had to stay seated for a moment as my cab arrived.

Climbing into the back of the cab, I stared out the window until we reached the airport. Zane was standing outside the terminal, waiting on me. We walked into the airport after nodding at each other.

Our flight to Reykjavik was economy, and we were squashed like sardines in a can. The hostess was pretty, and she smiled at me a little too often and sashayed by, wiggling her ass as she passed us. Zane laughed, but I ignored her obvious attempts at flirting and read on my iPad.

Really, I was only pretending to read, and after an hour, I leaned back, closing my eyes and drifting off to sleep. I was exhausted, and thankfully, slept most of the journey while Zane typed something on a small laptop.

Part of me was curious about what he was writing, but most of me was too tired to question him about it. When we made our descent into Iceland, Zane woke me up and I sat upright, bleary-eyed. We had a three-hour layover before our flight to Paris, and I was starving. I hoped the airport had food.

It was eight thirty in the morning local time when we landed, so most places were serving breakfast.

"You hungry?" I asked Zane as he checked his cell and texted Sam back.

"Yeah, I could eat." He was distracted, so I led us through the airport, finding a café that served all-day breakfast. We both had a specialty coffee and some pastries. We sat and ordered another coffee and then wandered to a bar where we had soft drinks.

I'd never needed a drink more, but I couldn't do it. It'd been a long few weeks since my last, but I was getting better at not reaching for the bottle whenever the mood struck me.

Zane sat drumming his fingers on the table, and I watched as his anxiety levels crept up. I didn't speak because I knew he was about to lose it, and I didn't know what to say to calm him because I was as anxious as he was.

We'd all tried to call Bailey's cell. I picked up my cell and tried again to call her. I needed to hear her voice. Needed her to reassure me that she was okay, that I was overreacting, but her cell went straight to voicemail and cut out before I could leave another message asking her to call me. I'd already called ahead and told her I was coming to Paris with Zane because we hadn't heard from her.

"Did she not answer?" Zane asked as I put my cell down on the table.

"No. It went to voicemail again."

Zane glanced around and leaned back on his chair, running his fingers through his shaggy hair. He checked his cell again and texted Sam back, ignoring me as he did.

"Sam's really worried because she hasn't heard a thing from Bailey in three days, and Bailey and Sam speak almost every day."

"Has anyone spoken to the people at her gallery?"

I was trying to think, but panic was threatening to overwhelm me. I had to stay calm though, so I focused on my breathing. If anything had happened to her… No. I cut myself off, refusing to finish the thought as Zane spoke again.

"Yeah. Sam spoke to Martine yesterday. That's Bailey's business partner, and she said that both her and Philip were getting worried because Bailey hadn't answered her emails or any messages in a few days." Zane paused and glanced around us before continuing. "They've given us the address of the gallery Bailey was interested in, so we can start there. They've also been trying to get ahold of the person Bailey was going to meet, but accidentally deleted his contact details, so it's proving to be a little impossible."

My heart pounded loudly in my ears as I sat staring at my brother and trying to control the panic I was feeling. I was trying to convince myself everything would be fine, but I had a ball of dread sitting in the pit of my stomach that I couldn't shift.

Our flight was called, and we walked in silence to the gate. I could barely function as we boarded and were shown to our business-class seats. I wanted to sleep again, but I was too wired.

I plucked my notebook out of my bag and decided to write Bailey a note I could give her when I saw her.

BAILS,

I haven't written you a note since we were kids. I want to write something profound and meaningful, but I'm so worried about you I can barely think straight. I'm on my way to Paris, currently on plane two from Iceland, and I miss you so much it hurts.

It hurts to breathe when you're not around. I know you asked for space, and I totally respect that, but I need to know you're safe. My heart feels torn in two right now.

I know you'll probably think I'm crazy or foolish or selfish for coming to you, but I couldn't help it. I need you, Bails. I need you in my life and as part of my family, whether that's as my stepsister or my lover. I don't care about titles.

It's up to you, but I need you to know that my dad threatened you. He threatened you over and over and held your future over me, which is why I always pushed you away. I never wanted to, and seeing your face on those days when you came home and found me in bed or in my room with someone else haunts me to this very day.

It was always you I loved. I never loved Jan. I never even really liked her, but I was coerced into a relationship with her as a way to keep you safe. I should have stood up to my dad. I should have prioritized you over me and fought harder for us, and for that I'm truly sorry. I just hope one day you can forgive me and know that I have loved you every day since forever and I will love you in all the days to come.

Always and forever,

Cooper.

I CLOSED MY JOURNAL AND LEANED BACK, LETTING MY EYES drift closed. I couldn't sleep, so I bought some earbuds and tuned into the in-flight movie. It was an Avengers movie, but I wasn't paying close attention to it, unless Black Widow was on the screen.

After what felt like an eternity, we landed in Charles De Gaulle Airport in Paris. Sam had booked our accommodation, so Zane checked his messages and led the way through customs, where there was a massive queue, and to the outside of the airport. We caught a cab and Zane showed the driver the address of the hotel.

He took us there and I paid. I'd changed a little money to euros in the airport back home because I didn't want us to be caught short. We went into the hotel and checked in. We both only had backpacks since we were flying out again three days later.

We dropped our bags off in the twin room on the third floor, used the facilities, and then left.

When we reached the hotel desk, we quickly asked for

directions to the Modus Art Gallery. The concierge called us a cab and told us to wait at the doors for it to arrive.

Within a few minutes, we were off across Paris, crossing the River Seine and passing the burned-out shell of Notre-Dame. After a few more terrifying moments when the driver sped along, taking corners at breakneck speed, we finally reached the gallery we were looking for.

My heart thundered in my chest as I paid for the cab ride. I couldn't control my shaking hands as I clambered from the car, closing the door quickly.

Zane had gone on ahead and came back after a few moments.

"It's closed," he said in a surprised voice, and we both turned as we saw a man on the sidewalk heading towards where we stood at the steps outside the gallery.

"Excuse me," Zane called out, and the man spun to face us.

His eyes narrowed in the late afternoon sun, and Zane rushed towards him. He was tall. Well over six foot with tanned skin and a head full of curls of dark hair. He had brown eyes and his teeth were bright white when he smiled at us.

"Bonjour. Puis-je vous aider?" the man asked, and his eyes lingered on me. He was smiling, but something about his expression was cold and set me on edge.

I shook my head at Zane, and he looked as perplexed as me.

''I'm sorry. I don't speak French.''

The man looked between us and then smiled widely at someone behind us. My whole body tensed as we heard footsteps on the paving stones behind us and the man spoke to whoever had just arrived.

"Ces messieurs ne parlent pas Français, chérie. Pouvez-vous traduire pour eux?"

My heart thundered as I slowly turned around to see Bailey there. Her face paled and she froze in surprise as she took in Zane and me. For a moment, she didn't move, and her eyes scanned my face, then she shook her head and walked around us, kissing the man on the cheek.

''Oui. Ce sont mes demi-frères, Zane et Cooper."

His eyes narrowed to a glare when she pointed at me, and he wrapped his hand possessively around her waist. She smiled, but her eyes lingered on me as she spoke.

Bailey shifted from foot to foot as we all stood there in the cold November air.

"Coffee," Zane almost shouted, breaking the tense silence.

"Zane, are you okay?" Bailey asked as she moved her eyes from me to look at him.

"Yes, sorry. I need a coffee. I'm freezing and I'm shattered."

"Okay," she answered. "I know a little café around the corner."

She turned to the man and spoke to him in a low voice, but it still carried across the small gap between us.

I didn't understand what she said, but when she reached up and pressed a gentle kiss to his lips, my hands clenched into fists. Zane looked at me and I rolled my shoulders, trying not to let the sight of her kissing someone else affect me, but it did. I wanted to rip his head off.

Bailey turned and stepped around me without looking at me at all. She didn't look at me the whole way to the café and spoke only to Zane when we were finally seated at a table.

She ordered the drinks, but kept her coat on, even though

it was a warm place. While we waited for the drinks to arrive, she and Zane chatted about Pierre and her gallery.

That was his name. The guy. Pierre. What a stupid fucking name, I thought, staring out of the window at the people bustling by. I couldn't bear to look at her, but I knew I had to at some point. When the waitress serving the coffee arrived after those few minutes that felt like weeks, I turned and saw Bails was watching me.

I picked up my cup and took a sip of the sweet nectar, and it warmed me from the inside. I didn't speak and let Zane and her chat as I sat there, wishing I could have gone back in time and stopped myself coming to Paris.

"So, you guys rushed all the way over here because you didn't hear from me for three days?" Her eyes darted between us and I nodded into the dregs of my coffee cup, wanting to drown myself in them. "But why would you do that?"

Zane reached over and covered her hand with his, making me green with envy. I wanted to do that. I wanted to be able to casually touch her without feeling as though my body was being set on fire, but I couldn't.

I wasn't sure whether to tell her about my feelings. She was making a life for herself in Paris, and she didn't need me or my baggage messing it up for her.

I sat back and decided to let her think I was being brotherly, though that title bothered me to no end. I wasn't her brother. I'd never been her brother, and I never would be.

I caught Bailey's eyes and she held my gaze, setting my insides alight and making me forget for a moment how devastated I was. Zane's cell rang, and he excused himself to go and speak to Sam, but neither Bailey nor I acknowledged his departure.

Chapter Eleven

"Coop," Bailey began.

"Bails," I muttered in a broken whisper, and she flinched. She hated my nickname for her, but I couldn't stop myself from using it.

"I'm sorry," we both said at the same time, and I nodded to her to go ahead. She reached out and slipped her fingers into mine, entwining our hands.

Warmth raced through me from the tips of my fingers to the bottom of my soul, and I gave her fingers a gentle squeeze.

"I'm sorry, but I can't do this with you. I need more time."

A tear rolled from her eye, and I reached over, wiping the moisture away with the pad of my thumb. I didn't speak because there was nothing to say. Her eyes said it all, and I knew in that moment I'd truly lost.

I bobbed my head at her, too overcome with emotion to speak.

"You came all this way for me, and I'll never forget it, but I'm finally happy. I'm finally moving on from you, from us, and I need to give this a chance."

She glanced around for a moment before she leaned over, pressing her soft lips to mine. It was a sweet kiss, a goodbye kiss, and I could feel the tears running down my cheeks, both from her and me. She pulled back and I rubbed my hands over my face, trying to get a grip of my emotions as she stood up.

"Cooper," she breathed, and I looked up to see her smiling sadly down at me. "I'll never regret a moment with you."

I nodded, unable to speak, and she brushed her hands down her skirt before she turned away from me.

"Goodbye, Cooper."

I watched as she walked out of the door of the café, and I sat there numbly, waiting on Zane to come back.

After twenty minutes, he returned, clapped me on my shoulder, and I started. I'd been staring at my coffee cup and wondering whether we could get an earlier flight home.

"Hey, man. You wanna go grab some dinner or just head back to the hotel?"

I thought about it for a moment and shook my head. "I'm not hungry. I just want today to be over with."

He nodded sadly at me as I rose from the chair and followed him outside to the bustling sidewalk. We followed the crowd along and I kept my eyes straight forward, but something ahead caught my eye.

Bailey was standing in her red coat with her dark jskirt, easily recognizable on the corner of the street, arguing with someone I couldn't see. I knew she was arguing because her back was poker straight and her hair whipped about her head as she gesticulated from side to side.

I didn't think. I just reacted on instinct and rushed towards her to see her and Pierre arguing.

"Problem?" I asked, and Pierre turned to me, punching me full in the face without warning and sending me staggering backwards, almost into the path of an oncoming car. If Zane hadn't reacted so quickly, I'd have been hit.

"Vous fils de pute!"

"You get that one for free, but you hit me again and it'll be the last thing you ever do," I hissed at him and went to move forward, but Bailey stepped between us and turned to face me.

"Cooper, leave, please. This is none of your business."

My heart broke and I spun around, walking blindly away from her. I paused, spitting blood onto the sidewalk before continuing. I knew Zane was beside me because he tried to stop me, but I shrugged him off and walked until we found a cab to take us back to the hotel.

Once there, I went straight to our room and checked my jaw. It was bruising, and my lip was swollen again. I had a scar on the left side of my lip where Jan had caught me, and now I had a split lip on my right side.

Zane came up to the room and tried to speak to me, but I brushed him off, too heartsick to speak to anyone. I locked myself in the bathroom for half an hour and took a long shower. I tried to wash off the feeling of her lips against mine, but I knew I'd never regret kissing her or wanting her.

Zane knocked on the door, so I went out into the room and climbed into the bed in my shorts and a t-shirt and pulled the covers over my head. I didn't want to think, didn't want to speak. I just wanted to block the world out and forget about her.

I heard Zane and Sam's conversation, even though I was trying hard to tune it out and he was in the bathroom with the door only slightly ajar.

"She's with someone else?" Sam asked. "Are you sure?"

"Yeah, we saw them together," Zane answered.

"Oh my God! Is Cooper okay?"

"No. He's devastated. I can't get him to talk to me. I'm worried about him."

"I know, babe, but all we can do is be there for him and help him to pick up the pieces."

"Yeah, I know. It's just so sad. They still love each other so much, but she doesn't trust him not to hurt her again. That was what she said to me outside when we spoke. She loves him, but she doesn't trust him with her heart anymore."

I couldn't listen to it anymore. I rolled over and pulled the pillow over my head, but it didn't block out the next words.

"What happened to her cell?" Sam asked, and Zane paused.

"She said Pierre accidentally knocked it into the sink when she was washing her hands, but he has a temper and I'm not sure if I believe that."

"You're worried about her?"

"Yeah. You should've seen their argument in the street. And he punched Coop for nothing."

Not nothing. That goodbye kiss. Somehow, I knew he'd seen or heard about the goodbye kiss and lost it.

I closed my eyes and pictured the kiss again. Her hair tickled my check and her breath warmed my skin as her lips met mine.

I drifted off to sleep, dreaming about that kiss, and woke up hours later to an empty room. Zane left a note propped up on the dressing table.

Dude, you were out of it, so I left you to it. Gone to meet B for brunch. Text when you're up and I'll let you know where we're at. Z

. . .

I grabbed my cell and saw a message from my dad, and one from Zane.

I ignored the one from my dad and opened the message from Zane eagerly.

She's quiet, man. I'm really worried. Can you come meet us? We're at a café called La Crème de la Culture. It's two blocks south.

The message had been sent twenty minutes prior, so I dres

sed at breakneck speed and rushed from the room with my cell and the room key in my hand. I didn't take my overcoat and it was pouring down with rain, but I ran the two blocks and found the café.

Zane was sitting facing me, and Bails had her back to me. As I opened the door, she turned and I saw a ghost of a smile cross her lips.

"Bonjour. Table pour un?" a young girl asked from the podium inside the door.

"No, I'm just joining those people."

She nodded at me with a look of boredom on her face and went back to texting on her cell while sucking a hard candy lollipop.

I moved past her as she took it out of her mouth with a pop that made me cringe. My eyes were fixed on Bailey and Zane, and I made my way towards them.

"Hey, how you feeling?" Bailey asked, and her eyes lingered on my chin. I hadn't looked in a mirror, so I had no idea how my chin looked.

"Wet," I muttered as raindrops ran down my fingers and

dripped onto the hardwood of the booth-like table they were sitting at.

"Scooch over," I commanded, and she slid across the bench.

I slid in beside her and sat across from Zane, pinching a slice of toasted bagel from his plate. I was trying to be nonchalant, but being this close to Bails was making me crazy. My left leg was pressed against her right.

She didn't move, but she didn't look too happy about something.

"Bails," I said in a low voice, and she turned to look at me with guarded eyes.

"What, Coop?"

"Are you okay?" I asked quietly, and she smiled sadly at me.

"You're seriously asking if I'm okay after my boyfriend assaulted you?" She paused for a moment as my eyes hardened, and I turned away to take a bite from the bagel. It was like cardboard. My mouth was dried out, and no matter how much I chewed, I couldn't swallow. "I'm fine."

Her answer did nothing to allay my fears, and I turned back to look at her, finally managing to swallow the piece of toasted bagel.

"Are you?" I asked, and I probed her with my eyes.

"Yes. I am, Cooper. I'm sorry about what happened yesterday, but I am happy with Pierre. He treats me better than anyone…" She broke off and glanced away.

Better than anyone ever has before. I nodded.

"I wish I could fix all that," I mumbled.

For a moment, there was silence, then she placed her hand gently on my knee, giving me a gentle squeeze. "Come and see me before you leave, okay?"

"Of course. I wouldn't leave without seeing you."

"Can you move though? Because I have a meeting at eleven and I can't be late."

I slid out of the bench and let her out, watching her as she walked out onto the street. Just before she left, she turned back and waved, then rushed off into the wet Parisian day.

"What do you think?" Zane asked as I sat back down. He picked up his coffee and I ordered one from a passing waitress.

"I'm not sure. I wish she'd tell me what's going on. Why did she have her coat on the whole time?"

"She never took it off. I didn't even notice."

I was worried she was hiding something from me, but I couldn't guess what it was. My worry was bruises or something.

We spent the day exploring Paris, and Zane told me he'd always wanted to bring Sam there because Sam was a big art lover. She devoured books, loved going to museums and looking at paintings, and she loved to paint. The basement was full of art supplies and canvases.

That night, we ate dinner in the hotel, and the next day, Bailey texted me.

CAN YOU COME AND MEET ME ON YOUR OWN, PLEASE?

ZANE WAS SLEEPING, SO I QUICKLY MESSAGED BACK AND SAID yes. I grabbed my windbreaker as I left the hotel room.

WHERE ARE WE MEETING?

. . .

I sent another message as I made my way down in the hotel elevator. As soon as I stepped into the lobby, I saw her. She was standing in a pale blue coat which brought out the color of her eyes, and her blonde hair was piled on top of her head in a messy topknot.

My feet moved without conscious thought towards her. When I reached her, I wanted nothing more than to pull her into my arms, but I clenched my fists by my sides to stop myself from reaching out to her.

"Shall we go for some coffee?" She shifted from foot to foot.

"Sure. I could drink some coffee."

She led the way to the café from the previous day, and we walked in, getting seated right away. I let her take care of the ordering as I drank her in with my eyes. She blushed when she caught me staring at her.

"Cooper, stop it."

"I'm sorry. I'm trying. I really am. But you're so damn beautiful. I can't help myself."

She smirked at me and I laughed at her expression.

"What is it, Bails? I know you and something is bothering you."

She sighed and leaned back on her seat, closing her eyes and resting her hands on the table. "I just wish things were different, Cooper. That's all. Part of me wishes that we really were just stepbrother and stepsister only, without our clusterfuck of a past behind us. Then another part of me wishes that we weren't related, because then I wouldn't feel so conflicted about how I feel about you." She paused and brushed her hair away from her eyes. "Stop watching me."

"Stop being so damn beautiful."

She chuckled. "I can't!"

"Then I can't stop watching you."

She seemed to relax as we sat there, and I saw the Bailey I loved shining through the hard shell of this Bailey.

"Want to play a game, Coop?"

I remembered playing twenty questions with her when we were young. When I was trying to figure out my feelings for her and her feelings for me.

"Twenty questions?" we both said at the same time, and then laughed.

"You go first. I went first the last time."

Her eyes widened and she reached part of the way across the table before she dropped her hand again and pulled it back. "You still remember that?"

Her whispered words made me sit up, and I stared at her. "I haven't forgotten a single moment with you. Not one single moment."

"Why did you come to Paris?"

I met her eyes with mine, and I could see her trying to work out my motives, but I didn't know if I could or should tell her I'd come because I couldn't not. I had to know she was safe.

"Next?" I would answer the question, but not right away. I had to check out how she was feeling, and if she truly was happy with Pierre.

"Oh, come on, Coop!"

I laughed and shook my head, and she rolled her eyes. I wondered if she remembered the first time we ever played twenty questions. The memory was one of my favorites.

We were driving home on a wild, wet day, and we'd both gotten soaked to the skin at school. I'd been at practice and she'd been on a field trip.

As we drove back from school, she took her jacket off and I saw that her blouse was soaked and see-through. I could see everything. I turned my attention back onto the road, forcing myself to concentrate on something other than the fact I could see her pert nipples through the linen of her blouse.

She'd gone to get changed, and I followed her with my eyes as she left me sitting in my car. My boner was rock solid and I was waiting for it to subside before I got out.

Her smell was everywhere, and every time I'd looked at her, I'd wanted nothing more than to reach out and pull her onto my lap before tasting her skin.

After a few minutes, I'd followed her into the house, rushing upstairs to get changed and passing her in the hallway. We didn't touch each other after my dad had threatened us, but I wanted nothing more than to take her into my room and go down on her. The thought made my mouth water, and I quickly ran into my bathroom, turning the shower to the coolest setting and stepping into the freezing cold spray as I tried to make my boner disappear.

When I'd come downstairs, I found Bailey sitting with snacks, watching the TV show about the vampires she loved. She was engrossed, and I stopped and just watched her for a moment. Her hair was up and I could see wisps of it touching her neck. Her eyes were fixed on the screen and she picked up a chip, putting it into her mouth almost delicately.

My heart thudded against my chest as she sucked the excess flavor from her finger and then picked up another chip. I began to harden again, and I knew it was a bad idea. I was supposed to be avoiding her, but instead I'd gone ahead into the living room and flopped down on the opposite side of the couch.

My mouth lifted in a smile when I saw that she'd gotten me a soda and a granola bar.

"Thanks, Bails," I murmured, and she turned to me, blushing as she met my gaze.

I needed something to distract me, so I decided to ask her a question, and thus the game of twenty questions began.

94

Chapter Twelve

TWENTY QUESTIONS INTERRUPTED

"Cooper," Bailey asked, and I glanced up at her, meeting her blue eyes with my green ones. "Where'd you go?"

"Sorry, I was distracted. I thought about the day we started to play twenty questions."

Her smile widened and she blushed before picking up her coffee cup and taking a sip.

"Bails, are you happy?"

Her bright smile and relaxed posture told me she was, but I couldn't help wondering if she could be happier with me.

"Yes. I really am. Cooper, are you okay?"

Her eyes lingered on my jaw and then she moved them slowly up my face to meet my burning gaze.

"I am right now."

"But what about when you're at home?"

"I'm getting there. I've got a new job starting in the New Year, and I have Zane, Sam, and the kids, so I'll be fine."

I didn't want to say I'd be happy because I knew that was a stretch, but I saw a little tension leave her. She reached over and took my hand, which was resting on the table, linking her fingers with mine and just sitting with me.

"Coop, why did you come to Paris?" she asked a second time, and my eyes darted guiltily away.

"I needed to know you were safe—" I broke off as she leaned closer to me.

"And?" she probed, and I knew that she'd spoken to Sam or Zane about how much I was struggling with giving her space.

"And I needed to know if you were happy."

She nodded once and gave my fingers a soft squeeze. "Is that all?"

I thought back again to our promise not to ever lie to each other during this game, and I hated it. Stupid rule. Stupid game. How could I tell her that I'd come here hoping to convince her to give me a chance when she'd finally moved on and was happy?

"No," I began, and she leaned closer still. We were almost nose to nose as we sat in our bubble, ignoring the outside world. "Bails, are you sure you want to hear this?" I asked her, both wanting her to say yes and no.

Before she could answer, a hand covered her arm and she started, looking up to see Pierre standing there. She dropped my hand quickly and sat back away from me. I instantly closed up and leaned back, watching as she relaxed into Pierre's embrace.

I'd almost forgotten about him, and I hated that he'd interrupted us just as I was about to tell her everything. Another wasted opportunity passed, and I knew I wouldn't get many more.

They conversed quickly in French and he stood, walking to the door and pointedly waiting on her.

"Coop, I'm sorry. I have to go."

Her eyes shone with disappointment, but I had one question for her. One that I had to ask her before she left.

"Bails, can I see you again before I leave?"

She stood up and bit her lip. She wanted to, but

something was holding her back. "I'll see what I can do. I'll text you, okay?"

"Please, Bails? I can't leave without seeing you again."

"I'll try. I promise." She opened her mouth, but she didn't get a chance to say whatever it was because Pierre took her hand, pulling her away.

I watched her leave until she was out of sight, saw her turn back and then shake her head before she walked out of the door as he marched her away from me. I wanted to punch him. I owed him for the pain in my jaw, but I couldn't do that to her. I just prayed she'd let me see her before we left in the morning.

I spent the rest of the day in a state of nervous anticipation as I waited to hear from Bails. I wanted to go to her, but I knew I couldn't. I had to let her come to me.

When I hadn't heard from her by seven p.m., I assumed she wasn't coming and stared dejectedly at my food, moving it around my plate.

Zane was talking about his plans for his job, and I was half listening, nodding along appropriately.

Zane stopped speaking and stared at me hard until I met his eyes.

"Call her!" he ordered, and I smirked at him. He knew me so well. I'd told him about how our game had been interrupted so he knew that was where my head was at.

"I can't. I want to, but I can't!"

His nod of acceptance crushed my hopes. He spoke to her more than me and I knew if he didn't think she was coming, then she probably wasn't.

We made our way back to our room and Zane disappeared into the shower before collapsing into bed and falling asleep. He told me the day before that he tired more easily since his overdose. I hated thinking about that time. I'd been so worried about him, but Bailey's reaction to seeing him made me angry. It was as though she couldn't see past it, and when I found out that she'd seen her brother have a seizure in front of her, I felt so guilty.

I sat staring at my iPad, wondering if I should go to sleep. Should I call her? My thoughts went around in circles. I didn't know what to do for the best. If I called her and he answered, then I'd know she wasn't coming, but if I called her and she answered, then I could talk to her.

It would be easier to say what I wanted over a call rather than face to face.

My cell chimed, interrupting my internal debate, and I quickly looked down. My heart leaped in my chest when I saw a message from Bails. It had been sent a few hours ago, but had only just arrived.

I'M SO SORRY, COOP. I CAN'T GET AWAY. I'LL TEXT YOU IN A few days and check you got home okay. Take care of yourself. Love, B. xx

I LEANED BACK ON MY BED, DROPPING MY CELL AND CLOSING my eyes as I looked to the ceiling. I wanted to text her back and beg her. I wasn't too proud to beg her to see me, but I didn't want to ruin her happiness, so I forced myself to relax. I had just about fallen asleep when my cell chimed again.

I opened one bleary eye and glanced down, seeing a message from Bailey on the screen.

WHAT'S YOUR ROOM NUMBER?

. . .

MY HEART RACED AND MY FINGERS SHOOK AS I QUICKLY typed three eleven into the message and sent it.

A few moments later, she texted again.

OPEN THE DOOR.

I BOLTED TO THE DOOR AND OPENED IT TO SEE HER STANDING there in a pair of sweats and an oversized hoodie. She was the most beautiful thing I'd ever seen, and my breath caught in my throat as she marched past me into the room.

I quickly shut the door and followed her, watching as she took in Zane's sleeping form in his bed. She turned to me and quietly kicked off her shoes before crawling into my bed. I stood frozen, watching her as she settled back against my pillows.

She didn't speak, just patted the bed beside her, and I unstuck my feet from the floor, crawling up the bed until I was half over her.

"Coop, I can't!" she uttered breathlessly. Her eyes roamed my body and all my blood rushed to my cock, making me so hard for this beautiful, complicated woman in front of me. "I didn't come here to sleep with you."

Her quiet whisper made the hairs on my neck rise and gooseflesh appear on my arms.

"No?" I asked her, watching as she licked her lips and color rose in her cheeks.

"No. I came to talk to you."

I sat back on my heels, trying to figure out what she wanted. Her body was telling me she wanted me, but she was saying no.

Her eyes widened as she took in my erection, but after

staring at it for a moment, she shook her head and relaxed against my pillows once more.

"Coop, can you just hold me?"

Hold her? I would happily spend my life holding on to her and never letting her go, so I scooted up beside her and pulled her into my arms.

For a beat, we were silent, and then she whispered against my chest. "Earlier, you asked me if I was ready to hear what you had to say. I wasn't then, but I am now."

I closed my eyes and just breathed her in, feeling my heartbeat rise as she ran her fingers across my abs. Her touch had always had the power to set me alight, and this time was no exception.

"Bails," I mumbled hoarsely as I tightened my arms around her. "Are you sure?"

She pressed her lips against my chest and muttered softly, "Coop, why did you come to Paris?"

I took a deep breath and considered where to begin. "For you. I came to Paris for you."

Her back stiffened, but I held her until she relaxed again.

"Bails, with you I've made so many mistakes. I've let myself be coerced and manipulated to stay away from you, but I always knew I loved you. I didn't ever stop. You had my heart, Bailey Walker, and you've never given it back.

"I only wish I'd known then what I know now because I'd have fought harder for us, for you. I'd never have gone to Hawaii and never have left the apartment that night if I'd known you'd be safe."

Her breathing sped up and she peeked up at me. "Coop, I know you want more from me, but for now, is friendship okay?"

"I'll happily take whatever you're willing to give me. I've loved you for the longest time and I'll wait until you're ready to be with me, if at all. Just say the words and I'm yours. I'm all yours. I always have been anyway."

Her arms tightened around my waist, and somehow, I knew the moment was ending. I knew she was getting ready to leave me. I just hoped that someday she'd find her way back to me.

"Coop, I have to go."

"I know, but give me a few more minutes. Please?"

I leaned down and pressed my lips softly to her hair. For a minute, neither of us spoke, and then she pressed her lips softly to my chest, right above my heart before she pulled herself out of my arms.

She moved down the bed and put her sneakers back on. Once she had them on, she glanced up at me, smiling. "Walk me out, Coop."

I nodded and grabbed my sweats, pulling them on, along with a t-shirt that was beside me. I grabbed my room key and we left in silence. We didn't speak until we reached the lobby.

"Goodbye, Coop," she said and went to walk away from me, but I reached out, tugging on her arm gently until she came back into my arms for a moment. She hesitated and then wrapped her arms around me.

"This is harder than I thought it was going to be." She sniffed against my chest, and I tightened my hold. "I wish I could stay in this moment forever."

I wanted to say something profound in response, but my brain was muddled, so I whispered, "Me too. I don't know how to let you go, Bails."

My voice broke and she hugged me tightly for a moment before she stepped away. My hand held on to her arm as she looked sadly up at me.

"Yes. You do, Coop. You've done it loads of times before."

I dropped my arm as the pain of her words overwhelmed me, and I watched as she rushed away from me and out of the doors into the dark night.

Tears clouded my vision as I stumbled back to the bank of elevators. I pressed the key to call the elevator and closed my eyes against the onslaught of pain that lashed at me, jumping in surprise when a hand closed over mine.

I knew instantly it was Bailey, and I turned back to face her. Her face was red and blotchy, and tears ran from her eyes, but the instant I turned, she kissed me hard and with a passion that took my breath away.

"I love you, Coop," she whispered before she turned tail and ran. I heard the ding of the elevator and I walked into it with my heart beating fast. The elevator rose quickly and I returned to my room, climbing into bed for a quick nap before our wake-up call for our flight home.

I'd never wanted to go anywhere less, but she didn't want to be with me and she'd said she was happy in Paris, so I had to accept it and go home. I prayed she'd come back to me, but I knew it would take a miracle before she'd give in and let me back into her heart and her life.

I'd be her friend, but I wouldn't push. I had to give her space and time to realize how much we belonged together. I knew I could do it. I could be strong enough to wait a bit longer. I'd wait forever and a day if it meant getting her back.

I closed my eyes and drifted off to sleep with the taste of her desperate kiss still on my lips, and for the first time in months, I slept soundly.

Chapter Thirteen

Cooper

Zane woke me after a few hours of sleep, and I was groggy and confused. My heart hammered as we left the hotel, and I prayed the whole time that Bailey would come back home with us. I knew she wouldn't though, and that the previous night was a kind of goodbye for her, but I couldn't stop hope blossoming inside me.

Our ride to the airport was silent as I battled with the crushing disappointment of leaving her in a strange city, but I had to do what she asked. I had to honor her request for time, no matter the cost to me. I'd caused her enough damage over the years, and this was one of the only things she'd ever asked of me.

I just wished I'd stayed when she'd asked me to. We could have been embarking on our life together if I'd stayed. I'd known I'd regret that decision as soon as I'd made it, but I'd had no idea how much it would haunt me.

We reached Charles De Gaulle Airport, and Zane paid the driver while I checked my cell again. I'd texted Bailey and was waiting on a reply. There was nothing, and my heart sank a little further as I climbed from the cab and took my backpack from Zane's outstretched fingers.

"You okay?" he asked me as we walked towards the

entrance of the airport.

"Yeah," I muttered around a sigh. "Yeah. I'm fine."

We checked in and went to the bar, and I sat staring dejectedly into my ice-cold glass of Coke. I rubbed at the condensation as I waited for Zane to come back from the bathroom. Our flight wasn't for another hour, but all I wanted to do was get home.

Eventually, Zane returned, and I stood up, running my fingers through my hair. We walked through the airport, but I was dragging my feet, praying for her to show up, and the closer we got to our flight time, the more despondent and dejected I became.

By the time we were seated, I was completely closed off, and nothing Zane said could break me from my mood. Our layover was six hours in Keflavik airport, and while the weather in Iceland was clear and dry, I had no desire to go anywhere.

Zane sat in the chair with his eyes closed, and I sat staring into space. My cell chimed with a text, but I didn't bother checking it. It was probably from someone else, so I ignored it and looked out of the window at the gate we'd be leaving from.

Zane got us sandwiches and chips, and we ate in silence, though I was sure it was about to break because I could see Zane gearing up to speak to me.

After a few more minutes, he moved closer to me and sat down beside me. "Cooper," he began in a soft voice. "You wanna tell me why you look as devastated as the day you came home and found out she was gone?"

I just stared at him and chewed on the sandwich he'd gotten me. I finally swallowed and tried to find my voice. Just as I opened my mouth to speak to him, he spoke again.

"Did you really think going there would be enough to

make her change her mind?"

Had I thought that? Partly, yes. If I was being honest with myself. I had hoped she'd come back home when we found her. I knew it was an empty hope and that she couldn't leave, but I couldn't help wishing that she'd come back with me. I'd never expected to find her in a relationship with some guy, or to feel as though I was missing a vital piece of the puzzle.

"You did, didn't you?" Zane probed in a cool voice.

"Yeah. I think part of me hoped she'd come back home, but I don't blame her for not wanting to. I don't blame her for not wanting me. If I were her, I wouldn't want to be with me either."

My voice cracked. I was being honest, and it killed me, but when I thought back over the years to how I'd treated her, I didn't blame her in the slightest for staying away from me.

"You think she deserves better than you?" Zane asked, and I leaned back, taking a sip of the soda he'd picked up for me.

"Yeah, don't you? I mean, it's not like I was ever nice to her or treated her well. I was a dick to her because I was scared. I was scared of the way I felt about her, scared of what people would think about me hooking up with our stepsister, and scared of Dad." I paused and took another sip of my soda. "I know now that none of that matters. That I am so in love with her I can't think straight, but does she deserve better than me?" I glanced at him and saw he was watching me with wide eyes. "Yes. She deserves everything. She is perfect and she'll always be the girl I've always, always wanted. She's my first love and I want to be her last love, but I'm scared that because of how much of an idiot I've been, that I've lost her forever."

"You haven't."

"How do you know? How can you possibly know that?"

My voice was pleading, and I struggled to control the emotion bubbling in my chest.

"Because, dumbass, she came to our room last night. She is still in love with you and she always has been. It's always been you who's fought against your feelings, not her. She'll come back to you because she sees past the asshole on the outside to the guy inside. The guy who loves her regardless of the past and in spite of the hatred from our father. You're her other half and she's yours. You complete each other. It's always been that way, and whether it takes her one year or five years, eventually she'll realize that she can't be happy with anyone else because you are her soul mate."

He stopped speaking, clapped me on the shoulder, and stood, walking away from me, leaving me reeling. Was I really Bailey's soul mate? Did I even deserve to be called that with all the shit I'd pulled on her?

Our flight was called, and it stopped me going round and round with Zane's words, but just as we sat down, I thought about what he'd said.

"How did you know Bailey came by our room?"

He laughed as he clipped his belt into place. "I heard the door and saw you two sitting together."

"Why didn't you tell us you'd woken up?"

"Because you needed the time to be together alone."

He turned away from me and leaned back against the seat, closing his eyes as the airplane began to taxi down the runway.

"Thanks, Zane." I turned to stare out of the window. I eventually leaned back and drifted off, waking as we made our descent.

We got off the plane and he ran into Sam's waiting arms. I smiled at them and left them to their reunion, sighing gratefully as I climbed into the back of a cab.

The ride home was short, and I was glad when I reached my house that I could just go in, grab a quick shower, and head to bed.

I closed my eyes in bed and then remembered the message I'd gotten. My hands searched around the bed for my cell, but I'd left it downstairs in my carry-on. I decided to wait until the morning and was glad I did, because if I'd read that message before I left, I probably wouldn't have gone.

COOPER

I'm sorry I'm not with you. I need to stay here a while to get this gallery up and running. I didn't expect it to hurt this much, but saying goodbye to you last night was one of the hardest things I had to do because this time it was my choice. All the other times we parted was your choice, and although they hurt, it never hurt me as much as me making the choice. I will always, always love you. I still sleep with my bear in my bed and I've never been apart from it. It goes everywhere with me because I'll always have a part of you with me. I hope you're coping okay, and good luck with your new job when it starts. I know you'll be amazing. I'm gonna stay away for a while, and I know I said friends, but I need a little time before I can fully be your friend. I hope you understand.

Love you always, Cooper.

Your Bailey xxx

I LEANED BACK AND PONDERED HER MESSAGE. I COULDN'T believe she still had the bear I'd given her. I'd never told her, but stitched into the bear was a ring I'd been planning to give her for prom. The ring was my mom's, and I'd gotten it cleaned and sized, and it was all ready to go to her, but then everything happened with Jan and me and she didn't want to speak to me.

I thought back to that night and wished for the millionth time I hadn't listened to her mom. I wished I'd just asked her to prom and taken her as my date, but I couldn't change it. I wondered for a moment whether to text her and let her know about the ring, or whether to leave it and tell her when I saw her next.

I decided to leave it and sent her a small reply.

TAKE ALL THE TIME YOU NEED. I'LL BE HERE WAITING. Always and forever. Xxx

I SPENT THE DAY MOPING, AND THEN THE NEXT DAY, I BEGAN getting ready for my new job. I had six weeks before I was due to start, so I contacted some friends and began making trips to see all my lawyer friends.

One of my friends called me after I emailed him. I hadn't heard from Luke Jones in over a year. He hadn't been able to come to my wedding because he was working on a big case.

"Hey, Luke. How's it going, man?" I tried to inject some enthusiasm into my voice and leaned back in my leather office chair to chat to him.

"All right, man. I won the case I was working on, so workwise, things are good."

Something in his tone was off. I knew Luke well. He was one of my best friends from school and we still met up every now and again to shoot the shit. I didn't much like his fiancée, Elena. She was very much like Jan; stuck up and selfish. I'd never told him that, but I'd always felt it.

"Congrats, man. I know how much work it takes to close a case. Are you okay, though?"

It was nice to focus on someone else. I'd been so selfish recently that I'd forgotten other people could be struggling with things too.

"Yes and no. Elena and I are over," he told me in a sad voice. "I'm glad we're done, but I need to finalize the divorce."

Divorce? Wait, what?

"Wow, you actually married her?"

"Yeah, I made a huge mistake and it cost me so much."

I knew the feeling, and I knew the mistakes I'd made with Bailey had cost me her trust and her love.

"Coop, you still there, man?" Luke's voice broke into my thoughts and I shook my head at how easily my thoughts strayed to Bails.

"Yeah, I'm still here. Are you busy this weekend?" I asked on a whim, checking out flights to New York and wondering if I could just go there for a few days.

"Nah, man, I'm not busy. You wanna come up for a few days?"

His voice sounded lighter, and I thought about it for a moment. I had nothing waiting for me here, so a trip to see my friend was just what I needed.

"Yeah, if that's okay?"

I checked flights and found one leaving the next morning at five a.m. It was a two-and-a-half-hour flight, with a return coming back Monday afternoon.

"Sure it is, man. I can't wait to see you. It's been too long and you can fill me in with what happened at your wedding. Logan said it was crazy."

I knew he'd want to know about that, but I was tired of talking about it. I would tell him, but only because he was one of the few people I'd ever told about Bailey. He didn't know that she was my stepsister. He only knew she was the forbidden fruit I wanted, but could never have.

"Okay, I gotta go, man. Text me your flight deets and I'll see ya tomorrow."

I heard voices calling to him and I quickly said goodbye and ended the call. I booked the flight, putting it on my credit card and then wincing when I checked the balance. It was near its limit. I'd need to start treading carefully, otherwise I'd struggle to pay my bills.

My trust fund was available to me, but I didn't really want to touch it. I didn't want any of my dad's dirty money, but I wasn't sure I had a choice. I'd always wondered if he was the one with money or if it was my mom. He always made out that he was the richer one, and my mom didn't correct him. Something she told me stuck with me over the years.

"Cooper," she told me when I was eight or nine and she'd been diagnosed again with cancer. "Marry for money and you'll earn every penny, but marry for love, and you'll spend your days broke, but happy."

I'd forgotten about it until that moment. My mind skipped through her getting sicker and sicker and finding out her treatments had stopped working. I hated remembering it all because it hurt so much. She was an amazing mom. She was sweet, kind, and funny, and when she died, I was so lost.

My dad, who'd rarely been home, had to stay home to care for Zane and me and he hated us. He'd never paid us much attention, and he was so cruel.

My back ached from sitting in my office chair, so I decided to go for a run to clear my head. I quickly changed into my running clothes and left, running along a path perpendicular to my house. I tried to outrun the painful memories that had surfaced.

When I got home, I swore I wouldn't call Bailey or send her a message, but I couldn't stop myself.

BAILS, I KNOW YOU ASKED FOR SPACE AND I SWEAR I'M going to give it to you, but I just wanted to let you know Zane and I arrived home safe.

I PAUSED FOR A MOMENT AS I THOUGHT ABOUT WHAT TO write next. I wanted to write *I miss you*, but I didn't think that was fair, so I deleted and tried again.

I LOVE YOU.

NOPE, DELETED THAT TOO.

THINKING OF YOU. COOP.

PERFECT.

I then texted Zane and told him I was flying out to New York the next morning and that I'd be back after the weekend. He replied with "kay," and I wondered why his reply had been so short, but I didn't dwell on it. After a shower, a pretend beer, and an omelet, I went to bed, setting my alarm for two a.m. so I could pack some clothes and then go to the airport.

Chapter Fourteen

NEW YORK STATE OF MIND

I woke up before my alarm and rolled over, trying to shake the nightmare off. It was about my mom. It was always the same nightmare, but this time Bailey was there too, and she watched me as I watched my mom fly away from me. I ran after her, trying to catch up, but it was never fast enough and she always flew away from me.

My body was covered in sweat, and I tried to calm my heartbeat. I focused on my breathing as my therapist had taught me to do after my mom died, and focused on three things I could see, three things I could feel, and three things I could smell.

Just as my breathing began to slow, my alarm clock went off and I groaned as I sat up slowly, the panic from the dream trickling away from me. I quickly packed a few shirts, some jeans and boxer briefs, and threw in my toiletry bag. I grabbed a fleece hoodie and stuffed that into my carry-on, then pulled my warm Barbour jacket on.

At the bottom of the stairs, I stuffed my feet into my winter boots and picked my wallet up from the side table. My ID was underneath, and as I shoved that into my inside pocket, the cab I'd ordered the night before arrived.

The airport was busy, but I kept my head down and arrived just in time to make the flight. As I was seated, I checked my cell and saw Bailey had texted me a heart emoji back. That was all. Nothing else. I pondered replying, but before I could make up my mind, the stewardess came round and told me to turn my cell off.

The flight was quick and painless, but I wished I could have had a drink to take the edge off. I didn't though. Hard as it was, I'd made a promise to myself to stay sober and I intended to keep it.

I called Luke once I was outside his building and he directed me to his office.

"The office is on Varick Street. Number two twelve. Take a cab and have them wait and I'll leave my key with Mel at the desk. My office is on the fourth floor and the firm is Lendon, Carter, Crewes, and Jones."

"Okay, man. I'll see you later today."

"I'm in court 'til noon and then I have a meeting with a client, but it's near my place, so I should be done around three. Help yourself to any food and drinks."

He sounded distracted and hung up. Even though it was only seven forty, he was already busy. I missed the hustle and bustle of my day in the office. I couldn't wait to get back to it and I hoped my new job would keep me as busy as my old one because I desperately needed the distraction.

He texted me his address, and I sat back, only speaking to the cab driver to give directions. He waited for me as I went into the office and then he took off towards Manhattan where Luke's place was.

His apartment building was in a great location, close to the subway. The apartment was on the sixth floor and had featured bay windows that looked out over City Hall Park.

There were two beds and two baths, and the open-plan living room was joined to a kitchen with oak cabinets and marble countertops with integrated appliances. Luke had texted to say that there was a key card on the table by the door that would get me access to the sauna, steam room, gym, or pool if I wanted to use it.

His gray leather sofa sat facing an eighty-inch plasma, so I took a shower and sat watching baseball until he arrived home.

His blond hair was gelled back from his face, but I couldn't miss the hollowness of his cheeks or the dark circles under his eyes. His suit was black, Italian, and expensive looking. He quickly typed out a message as I stood to greet him, picking up my empty soda can and chips wrapper to put them into the trash can.

"Hey, man. How are you?" I asked him as he moved farther into his apartment.

"Good. Well, not good, but okay. You?"

I wondered again what had happened to my friend to have him looking so dejected. Was it his divorce, or something else?

"I'm good."

We both stood sizing each other up and then he nodded towards the sofa, gesturing for me to sit down.

"You want a coffee or a Scotch?"

"A coffee would be great," I answered as he moved towards the kitchen and put a cup under the coffee maker.

"I'm just going to get changed," he called over his shoulder. "Stick a cup on for me, will ya?"

He left the room and I walked into the kitchen, placing my trash in the can, and then stood waiting on the coffee to finish brewing.

He came back in a few minutes later as I sipped my coffee at the island and he took his out, adding cream and sugar. For a moment, we stood in silence and then he turned, walking to sit on the sofa.

I followed him over and sat beside him. For a while

neither of us spoke as we watched a basketball game. It was an old game, but it held our attention for a while.

Eventually, he turned to me and leaned back with a thoughtful expression as he surveyed me.

"So," he asked, "you wanna tell me what happened on your wedding day? Why didn't you go through with the wedding?"

Wow. Way to start small. I leaned forwards, resting my elbows on my knees and speaking to the ground.

"You remember me telling you about Bailey?" I began, wondering if I should tell him everything, but at the same time worrying about his reaction.

"Yeah, man. She was the girl you loved at home when we met, right? But what does she have to do with you calling off your wedding?"

"Everything," I whispered. "She has everything to do with me calling it off. Bailey was— is my um... she's my stepsister."

"Whoa, seriously, man? That's a little fucked up." His tone was cool. I turned to look at him and he burst out laughing. "You should see your face, Cooper. You look like you wanna swing at me."

I glared at him and was about to stand up when he put his hand on my shoulder. I shrugged his hand off and stood up, letting my anger and frustration out.

"You've no idea about what I've been through, or what she's been through!"

"Coop, calm down, man." Luke's voice was calm, and I tried to focus on my breathing so I didn't hit him. I needed to chill the fuck out, but hearing him say that Bailey and I were fucked up had set me off.

"Sorry, Luke," I said as I collapsed onto the sofa again. I

put my hands over my eyes and rubbed at the headache that was pressing into my skull.

Luke got up and left for a moment, and then I heard the clinking of the glasses. He poured Scotch into a glass and shoved it into my hand and then sat and sipped at his. My fingers shook and I fought against the urge to bring the glass to my lips.

I knew I'd regret it, but at that moment, I just didn't care. I lifted the glass and took a small sip, feeling my body finally relax, and I melted against the sofa.

"So, now that we have a drink, why don't you tell me how you managed to fall in love with your stepsister?"

I turned my head on the couch and looked at him, wondering if I'd see judgement, or hatred, or disgust, but all I could see was curiosity, so I told him everything and he let me talk without interrupting.

"My dad remarried when I was sixteen. The woman he married had a teenage daughter, and she'd shown me a picture of the girl. I'd been at her school a few days after seeing her picture for the first time. Then I realized after she moved in, I had real feelings for her, but I tried to hide it, pushed her away constantly and then would cave and hate myself for it. I loved her so fucking much, even as a kid, but my dad hated it and pushed me into a relationship with Jan."

"Wait, is that how you knew Jan?" Luke intoned and I scrubbed at my face as I nodded.

"Yeah. I'd been with her as a teenager, but she was a bitch then and I realized on our wedding day that I couldn't marry her because I still loved Bailey. I also cheated on Jan with Bailey just before our wedding and the feelings... man... I never had those kinds of feelings with Jan."

"So why aren't you with Bailey now?" he asked, and I met his gaze as a wave of heartache settled over me.

"I was too late. She's moved to Paris and has a new boyfriend and a new life, and I'm home, alone, waiting to start my new job and trying to get my shit together."

"And you came here because you miss her and can't stand being at home when she's not there."

I glanced at him and wondered how he knew how I was feeling. My confusion must have shown on my face because he poured us another drink and then relaxed against the sofa.

"Yeah. Exactly," I muttered, and took another sip of the Scotch, feeling a slight burn starting in my abdomen because it'd been a few weeks since I'd had a drink.

"So enough about me and my shit, what happened with you and Elena? I thought you really loved her?" I asked, but Luke shook his head and picked up his cell, ignoring me as he typed out a message. I wanted to ask him about what was going on with him, but before I could try again, he stood up.

"Come on. We're going out. You need a good night out, and I know I do. I need to get out of my head. Let's get dressed and go get fucked up."

I shrugged. What the hell? Perhaps it would help to just forget about everything for one damn night. Perhaps I could try to forget about how much my life had gone to shit and have fun.

"Fuck it. Let's do this," I said, and Luke walked down to his bedroom, shutting the door. I wandered into the guest room, changing into a pair of black slacks and a dress shirt. I only had my winter boots with me, so I had no choice but to wear them.

I walked out to the sitting room and Luke handed me another Scotch, which I downed gratefully before he tossed a dark gray sports coat at me.

"Dude, put this on. You can't go out in a sweater or with a winter coat on."

He smirked at me as I tried the coat on, but while I was a little broader in the shoulders than Luke, it still fit and went well with my outfit.

"You ready?" he asked with a grin, which got wider as I nodded. He led the way from the apartment and we grabbed a cab, heading into Soho.

Chapter Fifteen

BAD CHOICES

WE ENDED UP IN A RESTAURANT, EATING STEAKS AFTER A FEW hours in a bar, and by the time we left, I was feeling the effects of the alcohol. Luke chatted about work, about the holidays coming up, but refused to tell me about what had happened to him.

I wanted to probe him, but I knew him well enough to know he'd open up when he felt like it.

"To a club," Luke slurred as we walked along the sidewalk.

"Yeah. Let's do it."

We reached a club and Luke chatted to the doorman. He seemed to know him, and I stood silently by his side for a moment. The doorman nodded at us and in we went.

It was a massive club with four floors. Each floor had a different theme and was decorated slightly differently. The floor we ended up on was decorated with silver paneling and had a giant disco ball on the roof.

Eighties music blared out from the speakers, and the dance floor was packed. We picked our way through the crowd and ordered more drinks. As we stood there, a few girls came up and one of them shrieked when she spotted Luke, throwing herself into his arms.

He smiled at her, but it didn't quite reach his eyes.

"This is Geri," he shouted above the music, with his arm

wrapped around her small waist. She had a nice figure and was pretty enough, like a five or a six, with long brown hair and a pretty smile. Her friend caught my attention, though.

"This is Abbie," Geri called over the music as I stared at the girl beside her. Abbie lifted her eyes and smiled at me. She was similar to Bailey in build, and her hair color was the same, but her eyes were different.

"Let's go dance," Luke said, and we all moved to the center of the dance floor. After an awkward minute where I tried to introduce myself to Abbie, she stopped me by taking my hand and leading me deeper into the crowds.

He spun Geri around as I moved with Abbie. I closed my eyes and pulled her tight, enjoying the feel of her body against mine. I let myself enjoy the moment, pushing out any thoughts of Bailey whenever they tried to enter.

Abbie turned away from me, and with her hair swishing down her back, I could almost imagine it was Bailey I was feeling against me. Her short black dress rode up, and I ran my hand along her thigh. My other hand pulled on her stomach until she was dancing against me.

I let myself get lost in the music and enjoyed the touch of her body as she moved against me. My lips found her exposed neck and I kissed her there, gently running my lips up and down and moving my fingers along her abdomen.

She squirmed in my hands and spun around to face me. I leaned down to kiss her, capturing her lips and closing my eyes, because seeing her face reminded me she wasn't who I wanted to be kissing.

My heart hammered as I allowed my mind to drift and imagined it was Bailey in the club with me. It was so easy to let myself imagine it was her as I pulled Abbie against me. We broke apart breathlessly as Luke tapped me on the shoulder, nodding to the bar.

Abbie and I followed him and Geri to the bar, and we ordered a couple more drinks. I quickly knocked back mine and then Luke shouted over the music.

"You wanna get out of here? Take the girls back to my place?"

I nodded. We left and hailed a cab, heading back to Luke's apartment. The cab ride was quiet, but I sat with my arm around Abbie, running my fingers up and down the bare flesh of her arm and gently touching her breast.

She ran her fingers along my pant leg and my erection was getting harder. Once we reached Luke's building, we piled out of the car and into the elevator. Abbie was facing away from me, and I ran my tongue along her neck, sucking at the skin and feeling her flesh heat under my lips.

Luke stood with Geri, and her lips were on his neck. We reached Luke's floor and stumbled into his apartment. Luke went to get more drinks, and I slumped onto the sofa, pulling Abbie down beside me.

Luke led Geri from the room and Abbie turned on the sofa and crawled onto my lap.

She began kissing me in earnest, and I picked her up, carrying her into the bedroom. I stumbled against the door, but eventually managed to get her safely to the bed. I lowered her down without breaking our kiss and was tugging her dress up when I thought of Bailey.

I clamped down hard on the thought and continued undressing Abbie. Once she was out of her dress, I leaned back and stared at her before flipping her over on the bed. She was facing away from me, and from that angle, she looked so much like Bails that I almost came there and then.

I shrugged my shirt off and ran my fingers over her creamy skin. It was perfect, unmarked in the low light from the window.

My erection throbbed in my pants, and I shrugged out of them, grabbing a condom out of my pocket and pulling it on as she writhed on the bed. I shoved her panties to the side and quickly thrust my cock into her.

I tugged on her hair and pounded into her, hearing her moans, and my head transported me to the last time with Bailey. Seeing her face and hearing her moans in my mind's eye spurred me on, but when Abbie moaned, it was different, and it stopped me in my tracks.

"Huh, what's wrong, darlin'?" she asked in her New York twang, and I could feel my erection sinking as I realized I was using this girl to get off.

"Nothing," I whispered hoarsely, and I began sliding in and out of her again. She was breathing heavily, but it was wrong. It wasn't Bailey and I began to feel a little sick.

I ignored it and continued fucking her. She writhed on the bed beneath me as I hammered into her hard, trying to fuck the knowledge that she wasn't who I wanted from my system. I eventually lost myself in the rhythm and came hard, shooting my load into the condom.

I pulled quickly out of her and walked over to the trash can, taking the condom off and knotting it before tossing it. When I turned around, Abbie was lying on the bed with a Cheshire Cat grin on her face as she stared at me.

Her tits were spilling out of her bra, and her long hair was mussed up from where I'd been tugging on it, but I just wanted her gone. She was attractive enough, but she wasn't who I wanted to be with, and the knowledge that she was the first girl I'd been with since the last time with Bailey tore me apart.

Hot and cold flushes ran through me, and I shuddered as I walked towards the bed. Abbie moved over and tried to straddle my waist, but I moved her to sit on the bed beside me as nausea rolled through my stomach. I put my head in my hands and breathed in through my mouth and out through my nose. After a few seconds, the bed shifted.

She moved around and then dropped to her knees in front of me. I wanted to push her away, but then she began running her finger along my cock and I sat up, leaning back a little. Once I was back out of the way, she leaned down and ran her tongue along the underside of my cock.

With my eyes still firmly closed, nausea forgotten about for the moment, I enjoyed the feel of her mouth as it covered the tip, and then she worked her way down. With deliberate movements, she twisted her hand around and sucked my cock deeper into her mouth. My hands twisted in her hair and I began thrusting up and hitting the back of her throat.

I got lost in the fantasy, thinking of Bails, and came harder and faster than I was expecting, shooting my load down Abbie's throat. She swallowed it all and rocked back onto her heels, staring up at me through hooded eyes.

"You enjoy that, darlin'?" she asked as she wiped her lips.

My stomach rolled as I looked at her and I struggled to keep the nausea at bay. She moved closer to me, and smelling her sickly-sweet smell set me off. I retched, brushing past her as I raced to the bathroom, making it to the toilet just in time.

My body ached as I threw up everything from earlier. After a while of sitting on the cool tiles, I tried to stand and ended up throwing up again. This was not how I planned to spend my weekend at Luke's, naked and vomiting in his guest bath.

Another hour passed before I could finally stand up without retching. I dragged my ass in for a shower and washed out my mouth with hot water. After my shower, I ran the faucet and brushed my teeth, trying to rid myself of the taste of alcohol.

Once I'd composed myself, I walked out to the room to find my companion for the night gone. My clothes from earlier lay scattered about on the floor. I walked over to the bed on unsteady legs and moved around it. My overnight bag was there, and I quickly pulled out some boxers and put them on before climbing into bed.

I woke up a few hours later with a dry throat, throbbing head, and a horrid taste in my mouth. That was when I knew I was in for a rough day.

I hadn't had a hangover this bad since my freshman year at college, but I knew the best thing I could do would be to try and sleep it off. I went to the kitchen and searched through Luke's cabinets to unearth some Advil, which I swallowed gratefully.

My head throbbed painfully, and when I saw the time on the microwave, I realized I was going to suffer all day because it was only just after seven a.m. I dragged my ass back to bed, putting the water bottle on the bedside nightstand, and climbed in, pulling the covers over my head and praying that sleep would take me.

After what felt like an eternity of tossing and turning, I decided to get up and use the sauna. Luke had left the access card in the hallway, so I shoved on a pair of running shorts and a shirt that I found in the guest room, and managed to find a pair of Luke's sneakers.

Once downstairs, I went to the gym, running hard on the treadmill and then rowing for half an hour. Afterwards, I went to the weight room and Luke joined me there.

"You look like shit, Coop." He laughed as he spotted me on the weight bench. After doing my reps, we switched around and he concentrated on what he was doing.

"You fuck her?" he asked as he stood, and we walked towards the cable machine.

"Yeah, man. You fuck her friend?" I asked, and he shook his head.

"Nah. I meant to, but I wasn't drunk enough to get Hailey outta my head and it didn't feel right to fuck another girl if you get what I mean."

"Wait. Who the fuck is Hailey?"

"Hailey is the girl I told you about. I was with her when I was a teenager, but I dumped her senior year…"

"But how is she relevant now? I thought you were married to Elena? How does Hailey even come into that?" I probed because it didn't make any sense.

He began pulling on the cables and didn't speak for a second, then he turned and stared at me.

"I fucked up. Hayley's the one that got away and I've always loved her, but I married Elena because I was supposed to love her, and by the time I realized I didn't, it was already too late and I fucked everything up."

He moved over to the punching bag and began whaling on it. I wanted to go and stop him, but I knew he needed to let it out.

Wow, I thought as I squatted and pulled the weights over my shoulders. *At least I'm not the only person who's fucked up and lost the one they love.*

We didn't speak again for a while as we exercised, and in the steam room, it was too hot to speak. Once we were in the sauna, I asked Luke if he was okay.

"I'm coping," he answered without looking at me. He was examining his fingers and picking at a loose bit of skin. "I'm throwing myself into work because I can't deal with how much I fucked up and how much I miss her. It's shit."

"You wanna talk about it?"

He clenched his fists and then shook his hands out. "Nah, man. I'm not a chick. It's all good."

I shrugged at his brushoff and we sat in silence for a while before he stood and motioned to me to follow him. We rode the elevator in silence, not speaking until he opened the door.

"You wanna head out for something to eat?" he asked as we walked in.

"Sure. What time is it anyway?" I hadn't checked my cell and I couldn't remember where it was, but I was desperate to check it now. Bails might have called or texted, and a wave of guilt crashed into me because if she had called while I was fucking someone else, I wasn't sure I wanted to know about it.

"It's only just after ten. Grab a shower and we can head out for the day."

After my shower, I searched the room for my cell and then checked the living room, finding it on the floor, but I couldn't get it to turn on. I picked up my wallet from the coffee table and carried my cell into the bedroom, plugging it into the charger to power up.

After a few minutes, there was nothing, and I hoped it just needed a bit longer to power up. Leaving it connected, I left with Luke and we went to a local coffee place for breakfast. I ate gingerly but felt much better after my workout.

After breakfast, we went shopping, and I used my credit card to buy some t-shirts and a new sweater. I also got Bails a little half-heart keyring. After a few hours, Luke wanted to hit a bar, but my stomach was less than up for alcohol and I knew I'd made a mistake drinking the day before, so I'd asked if we could just chill with takeout and a few sodas instead.

We headed back to his apartment and got takeout Chinese food on the way. Stopping into the grocery store I grabbed a bottle of soda as Luke picked up some beers. I didn't want to make him drink alone, so I decided to pick up a few low-alcohol beers because then I could still feel like an adult without feeling like shit afterwards.

Back in his place, he plated up the food and we sat in front of his TV, watching a movie about underground fighting. It was gruesome, bloody, and enjoyable. He took a call just as the movie was ending and I left him to check on my cell, but it was still dead.

I had my iPad which I could text from, but it was at home, so I'd need to wait until the following day to text Zane or check to see if Bails had messaged me.

Luke knocked at the door and poked his head around to ask if I needed anything and I shook my head.

"Nah, man. I'm beat. I'm gonna turn in early, if that's okay?"

He grinned and laughed as I tried again to get my cell working, but it was no use. I'd need to order another one when I got home, but I could live without it for a few days.

"Okay, I'm just gonna head out for a bit. Got me a date," he told me, and I gave him a nod. I opened my mouth to wish him luck, but then closed it again because he didn't need luck. Luke had been a ladies' man all through college, but he never stayed with any girl for longer than two dates.

We all used to joke that he was a two-date dick, but I remembered him telling me he couldn't get over his high school girlfriend because he really loved her and no one he'd been out with ever measured up.

The sound of the door closing jarred me back to the present and I lay down on the bed and thought of Bailey. It was good to get a bit of distance and it didn't feel so much like my world was ending when I was distracted. Maybe that was the key to me feeling better. I just had to keep busy and keep my mind off her and our situation.

She'd made a choice, and while it blew, I knew she did love me, and that if she ever asked me to be there, I'd go to her in a heartbeat.

I managed to drift off to sleep and didn't see Luke before I had to leave the next day. He was still passed out, so I wrote a note on his fridge to let him know I'd had to leave or I'd miss my flight.

The flight home was quick, and I couldn't wait to get back home because I was exhausted. Flying to New York so soon after Paris wasn't smart, but fuck if I'd needed it. I went home feeling much more content and a little happier than I had been, but I wished I'd been stronger and stayed off the booze. I just hoped I wouldn't indulge again, but I was only human and I knew I was likely to fall off the wagon on occasion.

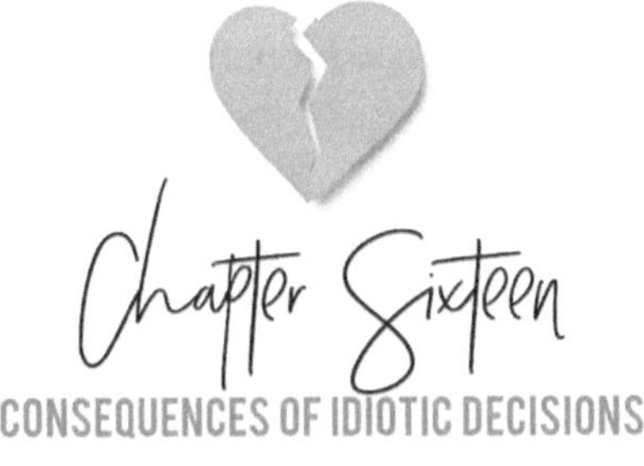

CONSEQUENCES OF IDIOTIC DECISIONS

Cooper

THE CAB RIDE BACK TO MY PLACE WAS BLISSFULLY QUIET, and I made it home in record time, partly because my cabby was a maniac on the roads, and partly because the roads were still pretty quiet.

Once home, I let myself in and scooped up my mail from the mat, setting it on the side table in the hallway. I climbed the stairs in a sleepy daze and stripped down to my boxers before throwing myself into bed and curling up under the covers.

Hours passed and I eventually woke up mid-afternoon with someone trying to break down my door. The banging sound went right through me. I shoved my legs into some joggers, pulling them up, then putting on a t-shirt as I rushed down the stairs.

Zane was standing in the doorway and his eyes narrowed furiously on me as I opened the door.

"Coop, where the fuck have you been? Why haven't you answered your cell? Or called me or Bailey?"

Bailey. My heart rate sped up as I stared at my brother and he shook his head. "She's here, but she's leaving in the morning. She said she left you a note."

I turned around and saw the note sticking out of the mail, and I rushed over and scooped it out.

Coop,

I know you're not home now. I called Zane. I need to talk to you, so can you call me when you get home, please? It's important.

Bailey

I turned to Zane and held the note up.

"Get dressed and come over to the farmhouse. She doesn't know I'm here. I told her and Sam I had a crisis at work to deal with, but I need you to get your ass over there."

I nodded at him and rushed up the stairs to get dressed. My heart was hammering in my ears. She was here. Bailey was here. I could barely think straight, and I jumped as Zane put his hand on my arm.

"Coop, what the fuck happened to you? And why are your hands shaking?"

I glanced down at my hands and tried to shake the shakes off, but Zane glared at me. I wanted to lie, but there were enough lies between us.

"I had a few drinks in New York, but I felt like shit—"

"Cooper, you can't. You need to be serious about this."

He cut me off, and even though I knew his words came from a place of love and that he cared about me, I was angry with myself for indulging, and with Zane for calling me out. I didn't need a lecture from him of all people.

"I know, and I am. I won't be drinking again."

He stared at me and shook his head. "Maybe you need a

program. AA might be good for you," he said thoughtfully as I pulled socks on and shoved my feet into my sneakers.

"I don't need a program. I'm fine."

My words were spoken with a bite of impatience, and he stood in front of me, staring at me through eyes that were narrowed in distrust or disgust.

"Cooper, I want to believe you, but I'm not sure if I can. You used alcohol as a crutch to get you through the shit you were in, but it's a hard habit to break."

"Look, Zane," I spat furiously, "I will consider it, but right now, all I want is to get to Bails. If you don't get out of my way, then Imma lose my shit."

He stared thoughtfully at me for a minute and then nodded once. "Fine, but, Coop, we need to seriously talk about this later."

I nodded once, pulled on my hoodie, and followed him back down the stairs.

"I'll go home and then you follow me. Come in about half an hour. And whatever you do, don't tell Sam and Bailey I came to get you."

I bounced on the balls of my feet as Zane climbed into his dark green sedan. I wanted to leave right then and go after him, but I couldn't do that. I didn't know what to do, so I stepped back, closed the door, and wandered into the kitchen.

I put my coffee machine on and waited impatiently for it to heat. Just as I placed my cup underneath and chose my coffee, there was a bang at the door again.

Bailey! I couldn't help hoping it would be her, but when I got to the door and saw Jan standing there in a dark brown coat with her hair blowing wildly behind her, my hope burst like a balloon.

"Cooper, may I come in, please?"

Her formal tone and demeanor did nothing to alleviate the

ball of anxiety that had taken root in my stomach as soon as I saw her. I stepped aside and let her in, showing her into the living room. My coffee went ignored and I didn't bother to offer her one because I wanted her gone.

Her eyes appraised the room and she nodded in approval. For a moment, neither of us spoke, and then finally she turned to look at me.

"Cooper," she began, and my insides shriveled at the look on her face. "You're looking well."

I just stared at her without speaking. She surely hadn't come to say I was looking well. When I didn't respond, she took a breath and then smirked at me.

"This is weird, isn't it?"

It was so much worse than weird. It was fucked up and I wanted her gone. Her presence was keeping me from Bailey, and I needed to get her out of my house without causing too much of a scene. She was being pleasant, and I knew how difficult she could get. Perhaps if I played along and was nice to her, she'd leave quicker and I could get to Bailey.

"Yeah, it is," I answered, and her smile grew wider.

"This is nice." She waved her hand around the room and then her face darkened. "I suppose this is all for her."

I didn't want to speak about Bailey, not with her.

"What do you want, Jan?" I tried to keep my tone friendly, but I couldn't help the annoyance that shone through in my tone.

"You know what I want, Cooper. I want what's mine. She ruined everything, and I'm gonna make her pay, but if you come back to me, I swear I'll leave her alone and she can live her happy little life in Paris with Pierre."

My whole body froze, and Jan stalked towards me, putting her hands on my chest. Her touch made my skin crawl, but her words reverberated around in my head and I couldn't help the sliver of fear rising that she would somehow hurt Bailey.

"No!" I hissed, stepping back and shoving her hands off me. "We're not doing this. I can't play these fucking games anymore."

I wanted to shout at her, but I was so exhausted with it all that I couldn't muster up the energy.

"Okay. I gave you a chance, but whatever happens next is on you." Her evil smile stayed with me long after she left the room, and it took me a while before I could get myself together enough to go drink my coffee. I knew I had to follow Zane, but I waited a little longer. I had to make sure Jan was really gone before I went to the farmhouse.

After an hour, I got into my truck and drove towards Zane's. I didn't stop, but I continuously checked my mirrors. No one was there, and I made it there a little after six. Zane and Sam were in the kitchen when I arrived, and I sat for a moment in my truck, taking in the beauty of the sun setting behind the farmhouse.

Bailey was out in the garden, playing with Serena and Ollie, and she spun Serena around, laughing at her as Serena giggled. My chest was heavy as I imagined what she'd be like as a mother. I knew she'd make a wonderful mom one day, and I just hoped it would be to my kids.

The thought of her being with someone else and having kids with them sent a pang of longing through me. I watched a little longer as I tried to get a grip on my emotions, and then she looked over and caught my eye.

My heart hammered in my chest and I didn't think. I climbed down from the cab of my truck and made my way towards my niece, nephew, and the love of my life. Guilt for my weekend washed over me, but I shook it off and scooped

Ollie up, spinning him around before setting him down beside Serena.

For a moment, Bailey and I just stood there, taking each other in, and then I stepped forward, pulling her into my arms and holding her.

Serena and Oliver continued playing as I stood, just breathing her in. I didn't want to let her go, but I knew I had to. Just as I was releasing her, Serena screamed, and Bailey and I turned towards her in time to see her screaming and holding her hand to her chest.

Fuck! I ran towards her, hearing the telltale rattle. I scooped her up into my arms as Bailey ran towards the house with Ollie. I held her hand still, squeezing some blood out as I rushed backwards, keeping my eye on the curled-up snake.

Once clear, I ran towards the house, hearing Zane on a call to 911. I kept her hand down and saw it swelling, but I didn't let her go until we were safely in the kitchen. Sam scooped her out of my arms and ran her hand under the faucet, squeezing out more blood.

Within a few minutes, the paramedics arrived and Sam left with them. Zane stood watching his wife and baby for a moment as they were bundled into the ambulance and then he spun to face me.

"What the fuck happened?"

I knew it was the fear talking, but it was my fault. I was the one who'd distracted Bailey.

"It's my fault. I was giving Bailey a hug and Serena wandered about the garden. I'm so sorry—"

I didn't get to finish what I was saying because Zane lashed out and punched me square on the jaw. I moved back a step with the force of it, but I didn't even try to defend myself as he swung at me again.

His next punch connected with my nose, and the crunch

of bone almost brought me to my knees. My eyes watered, but the pain overwhelmed me and I stumbled backwards, feeling the drip of blood.

"Daddy," Ollie spoke from the doorway, and Zane turned towards him, scooping him up and carrying him from the room. I moved to the sink on shaking legs and found a cloth. I was wetting the cloth when Bailey came in.

She moved towards me and took the cloth from my hand. "It wasn't just your fault, Cooper," she said as she led me to the kitchen table and pushed me into a chair.

"Yes, it was. It always is. Bad shit always happens around me."

I didn't say anything else, because I couldn't. She put the cool cloth to my nose and was putting pressure on it. It was burning like a motherfucker, and I was struggling to control the nausea when Zane came back into the kitchen.

"I need to call pest control," he told Bailey, ignoring me completely.

"Where's Ollie?" Bailey asked, and he looked at her sadly.

"He's in his room watching Mickey Mouse. I think I scared him."

Zane's eyes darted to me and then away, but he didn't say anything, and Bailey sat down across from me.

"It was my fault too. I just didn't think there would be a rattler in the yard at this time of year."

I met her blue eyes and saw fear there. "Hey, it's okay. She'll be okay."

Just as I spoke, her cell rang, and I saw Sam's name flash up. She took a breath before answering it.

"Yeah, okay. That's good, right? Uh-huh. I will. Okay. See you later."

She ended the call and then turned to Zane.

"Sam tried to call you. Serena is okay. She's responding well, but they are keeping her in overnight to make sure. Sam said you should call her."

Zane nodded at Bailey and then rushed from the room. For a moment, Bailey and I sat facing each other without speaking. There was so much I wanted to say, so much I wanted to do, but I was frozen in fear.

She stood up, and I knew she was going to leave, but I couldn't just let her go. I had to try and stop her. Zane came in and sat down on the sofa again, typing furiously on his cell as Bailey moved towards the door.

"Bails, wait!" I begged, and she turned back to look at me.

"You're gonna have to let me go sometime, Cooper," she told me firmly before she turned and left the room.

Let her go. Her words reverberated around my head and I couldn't concentrate on anything else.

How the fuck am I supposed to let her go? I wanted her back and it wasn't because I was possessive or a douche. It was because she was meant for me, but I didn't know how to make her see that when she wouldn't speak to me.

After ten minutes, she didn't come back, and I wasn't sure whether to go looking for her. I stood up and was about to try and find her when Zane came back into the room. He stared at me sheepishly.

"Sorry, bro. I shouldn't have hit you, but she's my little girl."

"It's fine. I get it. Is she okay?"

I was praying she was with everything I had. I'd never forgive myself if something happened to my niece because I was too preoccupied with Bailey.

"She's fine. It was only a baby rattler and it didn't put much venom into her, so she's going to be okay. They've given her a dose of anti-venom and she's in for observation, but her vitals look good, according to the doctor."

I smiled over at him and he crossed the room, pulling me into his arms for a rough hug.

"I was so scared, and I took it out on you. I'm sorry."

His voice was muffled against my shirt. I was about to answer when Bailey came back into the room. Her eyes were glassy as she watched us, and then she shook her head and walked to the refrigerator.

My eyes followed her as she twisted her hands nervously around her wrists. After a beat, Zane stepped back, scrubbed at his face and then turned and left the kitchen, closing the door softly behind him.

Chapter Seventeen

FOR A MOMENT, I STOOD AND STARED AT BAILEY, TRYING TO ignore the longing I felt. She wouldn't look at me.

"Bails, you okay?" I asked as I moved towards her. She was standing still, looking out of the window, her back ramrod straight and her shoulders tense. She sighed before she turned her head slowly to look at me, and I almost took a step back at the pain in her eyes.

"It was our fault. We're always so wrapped up in each other that we miss everything that's going on around us."

Her face looked miserable, and her tone was low and full of pain. I wondered for a moment if I could somehow stop making her feel that way.

"That's not true—" I began, but she cut me off.

"Yes, it is, Coop. You know it and I know it. We don't... We can't... ugh."

Her voice began to break, and I didn't think, I just reacted and pulled her into my arms. My soul relaxed as I breathed her in, and I knew in these brief moments that this was what home felt like. Home was in her arms. It always had been, and I had never had it with anyone else because this was always where I belonged.

"You are my home, Bails," I insisted.

"No!" She stepped back, shaking her head. "No." There

was a coldness in her voice as she swiped at her eyes. "I'm not! I can't be."

Her panicked words and the way her eyes darted around caused my heart rate to speed up. It took me a moment to process and I sucked in a breath as what she said bounced around in my head.

"Are you saying no, not ever?" I asked in a horrified croak around the lump that had appeared in my throat. My eyes were burning with unshed tears, and I watched in horror as she nodded. Her eyes spilled over and she spoke in an anguished voice.

"I can't, Cooper. Every time we're together, something bad happens, and I can't take that chance. Not anymore. It's killing me, but I have to end us. Once and for all. We're over for good. Forever."

She turned to leave and I could hardly breathe around the pain in my chest. My whole body was frozen as I heard her words over and over again. She stepped slowly away from me, which sent a wave of complete agony over me.

"Bails," I begged in an agonized whisper. "Please." I dropped to my knees and reached out to her. "Please."

She turned back and I saw the same agony I was feeling written all over her face, but she simply shook her head and turned around, running from the room as I collapsed in a heap on the floor.

The next few minutes were like days as I struggled to breathe. She'd really done it. She'd really ended all hope I had of us being together. I couldn't take it in. Every part of me hurt, and I stood up on shaking legs and stumbled, tripping and falling as I made my way to my truck.

I climbed in and sat there, letting my cries out where no one could hear me. After a while, I knew I needed to leave, but I couldn't make my numb hands turn the ignition on.

Zane came out and climbed in beside me without a word. He handed me a hot drink and I sat holding it, staring dead ahead without a word.

"Cooper, she's scared," he began. When I didn't say anything, he continued. "Her flight leaves at nine a.m. tomorrow. Meet us at the airport and you can talk to her before she goes."

I couldn't speak, so I nodded, and he clapped me on my shoulder. "She doesn't mean it. She can't. She loves you as much as you love her."

We sat for ten minutes without speaking and I held on to the drink, feeling the mug go cooler and cooler in my hands. I didn't take a sip because my stomach was rolling at hearing Bailey say *not ever*. She really said it and she meant it too, but it sucked. And it hurt so fucking much.

Zane glanced over at me, and after a beat where I stared numbly back at him, he took the untouched cup from my hands. He turned and opened the door, letting the chilly November air into the cab.

"Go home, Coop, and sleep on it. She'll be better tomorrow."

I didn't remember the drive home. I didn't remember if I slept or showered, but I did remember going to the airport. I used my iPad, and Zane messaged me to meet them in the morning at the coffee shop in the airport. I changed into different clothes. I put a shirt on, and it took me ages to do the buttons. Even then I was sure that the buttons were all wrong.

I pulled a sweater on, and a pair of slacks, slipped my feet into my loafers and drove to the airport. I was there an hour before I was due to meet them, but I just sat in my car in the airport parking lot for a while. When it was just after seven, I left the car and made my way inside.

It was busy for a cold, wet, windy November morning, but I was barely paying attention. Once I was inside the airport, I followed the signs to the coffee shop, then found a table and sat down. I hadn't even planned out what I was going to say. Every time I thought of what to say, how to reassure her, I came up blank. I just had to hope that she was just afraid of how she was feeling and that she'd give me a chance to prove how much I loved her.

Zane saw me first and he led her over to my table. I'd gotten them a coffee each, and Zane took his gratefully when he reached me. Bailey hadn't even noticed me, but her eyes widened when she finally looked up and saw me sitting at the table.

She took one look at me and then turned, fleeing the coffee shop. Zane turned to go after her, but I blew by him. I caught up to her just a little way along the corridor.

"Bails, please," I begged as I caught her arm, and she turned towards me.

"Go home, Cooper! I don't want you here!" she hissed, enunciating each word. My heart dropped.

"But you said in the note…"

"Yeah, that was before everything happened. It's not important now."

"Please, Bails. Just hear me out?" I begged her with tears in my swollen eyes.

My face was a mess. I had a bruise on my cheek and across the bridge of my nose where Zane had hit me, and both my eyes were swollen and puffed up with a lovely shade of black underneath.

"No. I can't. Don't you get it, Cooper? It's too hard. This! Us! It's too hard!"

She burst into tears and I stepped closer to her, pulling her into my arms. "I am so sorry," I whispered into her hair, breathing her scent in and trying to hold my broken heart together long enough to speak to her. "I don't want to hurt you anymore. I just want to tell you, before you leave me forever." The word caused agony to burn in my chest. "I love you. I love you so much." I held her tightly as she vibrated against me. "I was never whole until the first time you hugged me, and I need you to know that I will never love anyone like I've loved you, Bails. I wish I could make you stay, beg you to be with me, but I know I can't. I will always, always be here for you and I will always love you. You're my lobster, Bails."

She sobbed against me and held on to my sweater, tears soaking through into my skin, but I didn't care. Her body shook and I held her as tightly as I could because I knew this would be the last time I would ever get to do this. She looked up into my eyes and I reacted on impulse.

My lips found hers, and for a moment, we just breathed against each other's lips, letting our tears mingle on our cheeks. Our eyes locked and we stayed like that for a beat until she blinked.

"I'm so sorry, Cooper." She shrugged out of my arms and then turned and rushed away from me. She didn't say goodbye or turn back, and I watched her until she was out of sight.

Once she turned the corner, my legs buckled and I sank to the ground, letting my tears fall harder as the realization that I'd lost her hit me. Zane appeared a few moments later and helped me up. He walked me to my truck, and I climbed in, closing the door without speaking to him.

I drove home in a daze and climbed into bed, sleeping the whole day away. When I woke up, I wasn't numb or hurt anymore. I was furious. I was furious with her for coming back just to break my heart. I was furious with Zane for convincing me to go to the airport, and I was furious with myself for ever believing I was enough for her when I clearly wasn't.

I spent the next few weeks holding on to my fury and not speaking to anyone. I threw myself into reading for work, having convinced my boss to give me a few cases to look over and went into my new office on a number of occasions before the Christmas holidays arrived.

I'd ordered gifts for Zane, Sam, and the kids, but I hadn't spoken to any of them since that day at the airport. Four days before Christmas, Zane came over and refused to leave. I had to let him in since it was snowing, but I didn't want to. I wanted to be left alone, but my brother was tenacious, and stubborn, and refused to listen to me.

"So, you are alive, then?" he muttered when I finally stepped aside and let him in.

I led him through to the kitchen and poured him a coffee before sitting down at the breakfast bar. I didn't say a word to him. I didn't look up from the paper I was pretending to study.

Eventually, he sighed, and my eyes flicked over to him, seeing concern all over his face.

"Are you okay?" he asked me in a low voice.

I thought about it for a moment as I contemplated my answer. Should I tell him how I wasn't sleeping? How I had to force myself to eat, and how I'd sat at the bridge wondering if it would hurt if I drove over? It was always only a fleeting thought, but I knew no one would really miss me too much if I was gone.

My dad had said words to that effect in my voicemail a few days before. I'd tried to ignore it, but I eventually listened to the message.

"I'm fine," I whispered when Zane cleared his throat.

"Are you though?" he asked, and I turned to look at him.

"You want the truth? No. I'm not okay. I'm a million different emotions every day, but mostly I'm angry. I'm angry with everyone and I hate myself—" I broke off, breathing rapidly and trying to control my anger. My hands shook and Zane's eyes widened as I finally verbalized the words I was keeping inside. He seemed to relax a little against the chair and took a sip of his coffee.

He coughed and spluttered when he tasted it as I'd known he would because there was about half a bottle of Scotch in it. What did being sober matter when there was no one to be sober for?

"Coop?" Zane asked quietly, and I glared at him.

"What, Zane?" I hissed, and he reached out to me. When he didn't answer, I got angry again and stood up, pacing around. "Spit it out, big brother. I know you want to lecture me. I can see it written all over your face."

I was goading him into a response and he just stared at me sadly as the fight left me and I slumped back down at the island.

"You think this is helping?" he asked seriously, as I lifted my cup to my lips and sipped my Irish- or Scottish-style coffee.

"No. I don't think it's helping. Nothing fucking helps."

He nodded at me and then stood, emptying the coffee pot down the sink and pouring our coffees out. He then turned back to face me and I shrank back at the look of determination on his face.

"Go pack a bag. You're coming back to stay with us."

I shook my head and stood up, backing away from him in horror. What if Bailey was there? I couldn't be around her. I couldn't face it. I didn't want to. My thoughts all began to jumble together and my breathing sped as I snapped at him.

"No. I'm not. I can't."

Zane stepped towards me, putting his hands on my shoulders to stop me spiraling out of control. "It's okay. She's not there. She's not coming, okay?"

His words were delivered clearly and concisely, and I began to relax a little.

"She's really not coming?" I asked quietly. Part of me was relieved, and the other part was disappointed. I didn't know what I wanted anymore. I was desperate to see her, but I also dreaded seeing her again. I couldn't make my mind up.

"No. She said she'd try, but she didn't think she'd be able to make it."

His words reassured me and hurt me all over again. I stepped back away from him, running my fingers through my hair as I contemplated what I was going to do.

"Zane, please, just leave me alone. I can't…"

"Cooper, I've spent the last six Christmases without my family, so I'm asking you to come for me. Not for Bailey, or because you're hurt or angry with her, but to celebrate Christmas with me, my wife, and my kids."

His words hurt, and I tried to brush off how selfish I was being. He was right. It'd only been a few months since we'd reconnected, and I was hiding away from him. It wasn't his fault I was hurting.

"Sure," I whispered. "Okay. I'll come."

He stepped further back and leaned against the breakfast bar, smiling. "When?" he asked, and I knew I didn't have a choice. I'd have to go with him then or face his wrath when I backed out again, which he knew I would.

"Now. I'll go pack a bag."

I left him in the kitchen and went upstairs, throwing some clothes into a bag. Then I went into my closet and gathered up all the gifts I'd ordered, including the ones for Bailey that I'd purchased before.

I didn't want to see her, but I didn't want to spend another Christmas without her. I missed her so much, but she hadn't texted me since she arrived back in Paris, and I couldn't bring myself to send her a message.

My eyes darted around my room, and I picked up my cell, charger, and MacBook from my bedside table. I quickly gathered up the takeout containers and shoved them into the bin. Then I gathered up the cups beside the bed, feeling my stomach roll at the smell of days' old coffee and whiskey.

Carrying them and my bags downstairs precariously, I dropped my bags at the door and walked to the kitchen. Zane was on his cell, and I saw his face darkening as he spoke. He didn't see me standing just outside the kitchen doorway.

"Well, I don't care, Sam. He's my brother and he's a mess. He's coming for Christmas with us." He paced around the room and sighed. "No. If she comes, we'll deal with it then. She doesn't have to know."

He paused and my cups began slipping. My palms were sweating, and I needed to go into the kitchen and put them down before I dropped them. I pushed open the door with my shoulder, ignoring Zane as he stood at the patio doors, and walked across the kitchen to the sink. I emptied the cups out and rinsed them before popping them into the dishwasher.

Zane turned and looked at me with furrowed brows, then relaxed his expression. "We're just about to leave. Set up the guest room."

I didn't hear Sam's answer, but Zane ended the call and then typed out a message I assumed was to her.

"Ready?" he asked cheerfully, and I nodded, feeling guilty about going.

"Zane," I began as he strode to the chair he'd been sitting

on and scooped up his winter coat. He ignored me for a minute and then turned to look at me when he saw I hadn't moved.

"Coop, what is it?" There was a bite of impatience in his tone, and I balked.

"Are you sure this is okay? I don't want to put you guys out."

He stared at me for a moment and then smiled widely. "Of course it's okay. Why wouldn't it be?"

He didn't speak again, but walked around me, leading me to his station wagon and tossing my bags into the back seat. Once I was sitting inside, he turned up the music and began singing along to the radio as he drove.

It relaxed me a little and reminded me of a simpler time, when were younger and Zane would drive me around places. That was before the drugs, before Bailey, and before my dad began staying home so much.

It was a happier time, and I relished the memories of my mom and how much she loved us. She made every day a joy, and I could still remember Christmas morning with her as she had us searching around for our gifts from her, Dad, and from Santa Claus.

Chapter Eighteen

Zane climbed out of his station wagon, and I sat nervously fidgeting with my zipper in the passenger seat. I didn't really want to move because I was scared. I was scared Bailey would show up, and I was also scared she wouldn't.

I'd managed to get through so many Christmases without her, but this one was different. This one, there was no hope of more with us, and I hated it. I was tired and grumpy when Zane came around and opened the door, letting flakes of snow drift in and hit me. It was freezing cold out, but I followed him slowly into the house.

Sam was in the kitchen as we entered. Her eyes widened as she took us in. I hadn't looked in a mirror in weeks, but I guessed from her reaction that I looked bad.

"Hey, Coop. How you doin'?" Her eyes roamed all over my face and narrowed on my collar.

I couldn't even remember what I'd pulled on earlier, so I hadn't a clue why she was glaring at my shirt.

"I'm okay." I answered her in a monotone and she just shook her head at me. She turned to Zane and he nodded at her.

"Come on, Coop. I've set you up in the guest room." Sam stepped around Zane, giving him a quick peck on the cheek. She led me downstairs into the basement. "Zane's been working on this for weeks and it's finally ready."

We walked down into a living room, complete with sofa, TV, and mini fridge. There was a large bed in the corner, and a dresser with a lamp on top.

"Cooper," Sam began, and I turned to face her. "He's worried about you. Are you coping okay?"

I didn't want to answer her because I wasn't coping okay. I was so far from okay that I couldn't even see any value in myself. But I'd been through worse when my mom died, so I knew I could get myself through this time.

"I'm not okay," I informed them softly, and Sam stepped forward, hugging me.

"I know how hard this is for you. I know how much you love her, but she's…"

Whatever she was, I didn't get to hear, because there was a commotion upstairs and Sam and I both turned to the stairs as we heard raised voices. She took off, and I dropped my bags onto the bed and sprinted after her.

I made it to the kitchen a few seconds after her. My mouth popped open at the sight of my dad and Zane standing face to face. Henri stood behind my dad.

"I didn't come here to see you," he hissed at Zane, and Zane flinched.

"Dad, why are you here?" I asked, hoping to break the tension, and my dad spun around, almost knocking Henri over.

"You! You ungrateful little shit! How could you? How could you stop the wedding like that?" He spat the words at me and I took a step back.

I had just opened my mouth to reply when Sam stepped between us.

"That is enough. This is my home and my children are in the next room. If you cannot be civil, then you need to leave right now!"

Her voice was low but deadly, and my dad took one last look at me and then stormed from the house, slamming the porch door.

Henri glanced once around the room and her eyes shone with disappointment, but she didn't say a word as she took off after my father. As usual, she let him shout and scream and still followed blindly after him.

"Zane?" I began, but the crunch of tires on the driveway stopped me speaking. My dad shot off too fast and without enough caution. He was going to kill them because he wasn't taking enough care on the roads, but it wasn't my problem. Not anymore.

"What, Cooper?" Zane asked in a quiet voice, and I moved beside him, picking up the drying cloth and drying off the plates.

"Is something wrong?" I picked up a dish and rubbed at it until it was dry and then placed it in the cabinet. Zane refused to look at me and didn't answer, so I asked him a different question. "Are you okay?"

He had a healing cut on his neck, and I couldn't help wondering what had caused it. He subconsciously rubbed at it as his eyes darted around.

"Yeah, I'm fine." He sounded exhausted, and when he turned to face me, I saw the tiredness in his eyes. For a moment, he didn't speak. He tugged his collar up a little and shrugged.

"It's fine," he told me when he saw where I was looking. "I had to get minor surgery. A fly bite got infected."

His words should have set me at ease, but I knew he was lying. Zane had a tell when he lied, and even though it'd been years, I knew he was lying to me still.

We didn't speak again as we finished the washing up, and

then he drove to the airport to pick up Sam's dad and his girlfriend.

Once they arrived, the house was busy and full of laughter and joy. They adored Ollie and Serena. Sam's dad, Kurt, was a great carpenter, and he'd made the kids a train set, a doll, and a car to play with, which amused the kids greatly.

The next few days passed in a flurry, and on Christmas Eve, I was sitting on the floor, playing with Ollie, while Sam was getting Serena bathed for bed. Kurt and Chrissie were sitting on the sofa, arguing over a crossword puzzle, and Zane was downstairs in the basement, building the kids' toys.

The door opened behind me, but I didn't bother looking round because I assumed it would be Zane.

"Hi," Kurt called to whoever had come in.

"Hi."

My whole body tensed. I lifted my eyes from the floor and turned to see Bailey standing in the doorway, laden with bags. Her cream wool coat clung to her, and I couldn't help noticing her figure had changed in the weeks since she'd left me. Her breasts looked fuller, and her face had filled out a little, but it suited her.

"I'm Kurt, Sam's dad. And you are?"

Kurt interrupted my perusal of Bailey's body. I turned away, unable to look at her any longer. Just seeing her standing there set my teeth on edge, but it was what happened a moment later that almost set me off.

"Mon amour, where shall I put the bags?" He spoke in broken English, and I clenched my hands into fists. Ollie crawled over to me and was making vroom vroom noises with his little car. I tried to ignore them, but I didn't miss his hiss when he walked into the living room and saw me sitting on the floor.

Bailey quickly ushered him out and turned to Kurt. "Hi,

I'm Bailey. It's so nice to finally meet you. I'm Zane's stepsister."

She didn't mention me, and for that, I was grateful, but just hearing her soft voice tore at the wounds I was so desperately trying to heal. I didn't know what to do, so I continued to ignore her and volunteered to put the kids to bed to allow Zane and Sam, Kurt and Chrissie, and Bailey and Pierre time alone to catch up.

I was sitting on the floor, reading *The Night Before Christmas* to Ollie with Serena on my lap when the door to the bedroom opened a little. Bailey stood in the doorway. The light behind her framed her figure, making her look like an angel.

She didn't speak, and I ignored her until I'd finished and tucked the sleeping form of Serena into her crib, and then turned, tucking Ollie into his bed. He said something and rolled over, and I walked quietly to the door, stepping out into the hallway.

Bailey was nowhere to be seen, but Pierre's voice sounded clearly from the kitchen. My legs were leaden as I made my way towards the kitchen. I paused just outside the door to take a breath, jumping a foot in the air when Bailey materialized behind me.

"Hey, can I get by, please?" she asked softly in my ear before she stepped around me and left me standing in the hallway. Her tone had been so formal that I was completely stunned. After a pause, I followed her into the kitchen, taking a bottle of water from the refrigerator and trying to avoid eye contact with everyone.

"Well, Cooper, don't you have a lady friend?" Kurt asked in a jovial tone, and Chrissie laughed as I stood stiffly behind Zane and Sam.

"No. I'm sworn off women. I've just had my heart broken."

He laughed and ran his fingers through his graying hair.

"Handsome guy like you," Chrissie began. "She must be out of her mind."

The atmosphere in the room became even more tense, and Zane stood up. He walked Kurt, Chrissie, and Sam into the living room. I didn't look at Pierre or Bailey as I decided to go outside and get some air.

I passed by them and walked out to the enclosed end of the porch, sitting down on the porch swing. My eyes burned at seeing her there. I'd known it would be hard if she came, but her coming with him was brutal, and I struggled to cope with the emotions that ravaged my insides.

I leaned back and covered my eyes with my hands as I listened to the howling wind. I didn't hear the footsteps, and even if I'd heard them, there was nowhere to run.

"May I?" Pierre asked, and I turned to look at him. He was pointing to the armchair across from me.

I shrugged and he sat down.

"It is nice here," he began, and I was already over the pleasantries. I just wanted to get tomorrow over with so I could start building my future, because seeing her there with him had told me everything I needed to know. While I'd spent weeks pining and hurting and angry with her, she'd already moved on.

"I know this must be hard for you," he continued, and I forced myself to look at him, "but she is happy with me and I with her. I don't want you to think I don't know how you feel about her."

He paused and looked at me again, but I didn't move. I just stared at him steadily until he continued again. His

English was better than I thought because he didn't skip words or mess up.

"You have to let her be free to move on. We are happy together and we are planning our future. I just need you to know that she is mine and will be from now on, so I need you to leave her alone because all you do is hurt her. She is being healed by my love, not torn apart by yours."

He stopped and began walking away without waiting on me to respond, but what could I say? I had nothing. I knew she was happy with him, but I still pursued her. I wanted her and I didn't care who got hurt in the process, but it was all for nothing because she didn't want me anymore.

I sat for a while longer, not feeling the chill, or at least attempting to ignore how cold I was. I didn't want to go back inside. I didn't want to face her at all. I just wanted to get away from her and from the situation I'd been forced in to.

Chapter Nineteen

CHRISTMAS SURPRISES

WHEN THE NEXT SET OF FOOTSTEPS SOUNDED, I DIDN'T NEED to turn around to know it was her. Her scent had carried on the wind and my stomach did a feeble wobble as she sat beside me on the swing.

"Hey, I brought you this." Her low voice startled me, but it was when she put the fleece on my lap and touched my arm that I jumped. "Jesus, Cooper. You're freezing."

Her high-pitched voice made me turn towards her, and I had to look away because she was so beautiful that it stole my breath and made my chest ache. Her face was glowing, and she looked happier than I had ever seen her, but the sight of her happiness just made the emptiness inside me more apparent.

"What is it, Bails?" I asked her tiredly, because I just couldn't anymore.

"I just wanted to see if you were okay." I could hear the pain in her voice, even though she was trying hard to mask it.

"I'm fine. Shouldn't you be inside with Pierre?" I asked in a harsh voice, and she sighed, standing up.

"Yeah, I should be, but I wanted to check on you."

She didn't say another word, and although I didn't want to, my eyes followed her until she went inside the house and I was left sitting outside alone.

I pulled the fleece on that she'd brought me and zipped it

up, trying to warm up, but it was impossible, so I conceded defeat and dragged my frozen ass back inside. Everyone was sitting in the living room, but I stood in the kitchen, making myself some coffee. My hands were shaking, and my whole body ached as I shivered.

I sipped on my coffee, relishing the burn on my tongue and contemplated going to bed, but Zane came in and caught me as I was just about to make my way downstairs.

"Hey, are you okay?" he asked me, and I didn't know what to say.

"Yeah, I'm fine. I mean, I'm never gonna be okay with her being with someone else, but at least he makes her happy, right?"

Zane met my eyes and opened his mouth to say something else when Sam interrupted.

"Listen, guys, I'm beat. I'm gonna head to bed. Wake me in the morning when the kids get up so I can see their faces when they see Santa has been."

I gave Zane a quick hug and Sam a peck on the cheek before I made my way downstairs. Once in the guest room, I pulled my jeans off and grabbed a pair of joggers from my bag. I pulled them on and put another pair of socks on, then I flopped into the bed and wrapped the covers tightly around me.

I didn't wake up until early the next morning, and I was up before the kids and everyone else. I didn't know where anyone else had slept, but I didn't care. My body was aching because I'd slept on the lumpy mattress and the springs spent the night attacking me. I couldn't find a spot where I wasn't poked or prodded, and I was exhausted because of it.

Upstairs in the kitchen, I put on the coffee pot and stood at the window, watching as more snow fell. A few feet of snow had fallen overnight, and it was clear and untouched. I went into the closet and pulled on my walking boots, taking my coffee outside and standing in the snow.

I'd always loved the snow, and when we were little, Zane and I would go out with my mom and make tracks in the fresh snow. It had always been our thing. It was still pretty dark out, but I didn't care. I walked around and around in circles and then made reindeer prints under the kids' window.

I met Zane and Sam in the kitchen as I went back inside, and within a few moments, heard Ollie running down the hall. He flew into his mama's arms and began chattering excitedly.

"Has Santa been? Has he? Dad? Did you see Santa? Did you, Uncle Coop?"

He was bouncing up and down and Serena was crying, so I left them and went into the kids' room, scooping up Serena and bringing her through to the kitchen. Sam was busying herself with the stove and Zane was pouring coffees when Pierre arrived.

"Your children are very noisy!" he told Zane, and Sam and I glared at him.

"Yeah, they are," Zane answered and met my eyes.

It was Christmas morning. I couldn't imagine any child not being noisy on Christmas morning.

"Santa's been!" Ollie told him, and Pierre turned to face Ollie.

"I'm sure he has, but children should not make so much noise."

Ollie's face fell, and I decided to teach him how to play drums on his plate. I gave him a spoon and we all sat bashing on our plates until Sam came over and confiscated our cutlery.

"Spoilsport," I observed, and she laughed.

"Who's been making all that noise?" Kurt said cheerily as

he entered the kitchen, followed closely by Chrissie and Bailey.

"We have, Grandpa. Uncle Coop taught us to play drums on our plates," Ollie told him excitedly as Kurt poured himself a cup of coffee. Bailey asked Sam if she needed any help and Sam shooed her away.

"Oh, did he now?" Kurt asked as he sat down at the table and began to tickle Ollie, who giggled and knocked his juice cup over.

Kurt scooped him up and I got a cloth and cleaned up the mess, while Pierre, Chrissie, and Bailey stood sipping on their coffees. Sam put down a plate of cinnamon buns, croissants, and scones, and everyone tucked in, eating, laughing, and chatting as they ate. I had another cup of coffee and managed to eat a few things.

Then Zane scooped up Ollie and Sam scooped up Serena, and we all headed through to the living room which looked a lot like Santa's workshop. The kids were excited and opened presents. At least, Ollie did. Serena was playing with the doll I'd gotten her and the baby stroller from Santa.

The adults exchanged gifts too, and I handed out my small gifts to Zane and Sam. I'd also gotten Kurt and Chrissie a gift certificate to a restaurant that everyone was raving about, but I didn't have anything for Bailey and Pierre. I had a gift for Bailey, but I wasn't giving it to her. I'd hidden it under the tree and shoved it right underneath where it wouldn't be found as we exchanged gifts.

Zane and Sam had gotten me a new briefcase, and Kurt and Chrissie had gotten me a new pen with my name engraved on it. Bailey and Pierre also gave me a gray silk tie, and I smiled and thanked them blandly.

"I'm sorry I didn't get you anything, but I didn't know you were coming."

Bailey smiled sadly at me and busied herself opening her gifts. Sam had gotten her some books, and Zane an organizer, and they'd given Pierre a bottle of Scotch, but it was the next gift that puzzled me. It looked like a pair of baby mittens.

Bailey smiled and said thanks and put them away quickly before I got a good look. They were probably adult gloves folded over. I sat on the floor for hours with Ollie. Kurt and I played trains with him until lunch was ready.

We all went into the dining room and sat down. I was sitting between the two kids at the center of the table, and Sam was next to Ollie on my left, and Zane next to Serena on my right. Kurt was at the head of the table and Chrissie was on his right, next to Pierre and then Bailey.

The food was delicious and we all enjoyed eating. I was feeding Serena bits of chocolate pudding when conversation broke out around the table.

"So, how far along are you?" Chrissie asked, and I looked up, thinking she was speaking to Sam, but I glanced at Sam and she was staring at Bailey.

Oh my God. No.

My eyes shot to Bailey's. She stared guiltily back at me and it was all the confirmation I needed.

"I'm eighteen weeks," she told Chrissie, and I leaned back in horror.

I stood up, pushing out from the table, and left the room without a word. I could barely see. She was eighteen weeks. Eighteen weeks. The phrase repeated over and over again in my head until nausea rose in me like a tidal wave. I rushed to the bathroom, making it just in time to empty the contents of my stomach.

Once I was sure I was done, I stood up and went into the kitchen. I blazed past Zane and Sam, grabbing my coat, and left the house, walking slowly along the road for a while.

I didn't know what to do. She was pregnant with my baby and she hadn't even told me. My heart hammered against my chest, and my head pounded. I just walked and walked, and too soon, I was at the graveyard where her brother was buried. I didn't know what possessed me to go there. I just walked, and when I saw the graveyard, I went inside because I didn't know what else to do. I couldn't believe I still remembered where it was after all these years.

I climbed slowly up the hill in the fading light and came to the headstone. It was just like I remembered, but I scooped the snow from the top of it and stood staring at her brother's gravestone. I didn't know what to say. I didn't even know if I wanted to say anything at all.

"She's pregnant," I hoarsely whispered. Then the pain I was trying hard not to feel overwhelmed me and I crumpled to my knees and sobbed. She didn't want me involved because I was a wreck. I didn't blame her, but the agony was killing me.

Eventually, I managed to compose myself, and I turned, walking back down the hill and out of the graveyard. I walked back towards the farmhouse, intending to ask Zane to give me a lift home. I couldn't stay there with her. Knowing that she didn't even want me to know about my baby hurt me in a way that nothing else she'd ever done had.

I was completely and utterly crushed. My legs ached from the walking, and I made it back to the farmhouse just after dark. Zane was pacing around the kitchen when I walked back inside, and he clenched his fists at the sight of me.

"Coop, how could you just leave like that?" he asked, and I could barely look at him. My eyes were burning, and I just wanted to run away.

"Can you—" I began, but the words were too much. I just needed a minute. Just one. My legs shook as I turned away from my brother and went to walk away from him, but I didn't get to even leave the kitchen before Bailey came inside.

Her face tightened, and I knew she was seeing the complete agony I was in because I couldn't hide it.

"Zane," she asked in a small voice. "Can you give us a minute, please?"

He stepped around me and left the room. I didn't look at her. I couldn't. It was killing me, knowing she was going to be bringing up our baby with another man.

"Cooper," she sniffed, and I could hear the pain in her voice, but it didn't matter. She'd chosen not to tell me. I tried to step around her because I didn't want to hear anything she had to say. She'd already gutted me completely and I couldn't take anymore.

"Wait, please. Let me explain!" Her begging in a broken voice made me stop, and I turned towards her.

"Explain what? That you don't think I'm good enough to even tell you're having my baby, or that I'm not enough to be a dad? Because I got that message, thanks."

I couldn't stop my tears from falling, and she sniffed as I struggled to compose myself.

"Please, just sit. It's not that."

Tears spilled from her eyes too, falling onto her cheeks and rolled down. She waited, and I half turned to the door, but she begged me again.

"Please, Cooper. Hear me out. You owe me that much."

Her words angered me, and I threw myself into the chair across from her. She breathed a sigh of relief and sat down across from me.

"First of all, I want to say I'm sorry." I snorted and she stared impassively at me. "No, I mean it, Cooper. I never meant for you to find out that way. I tried to tell you last night, but you were so defensive that I couldn't." She spoke quickly, as though she was scared I was going to lose it.

"How long have you known?" I asked in a croaky whisper, and her eyes widened. It was then I knew that she'd known for a while. "Since Paris?" I asked, and she shook her head. "Before Paris?" I asked again, and she nodded, a tear falling from her eye. "How long, Bailey?"

She stared up at me with fear in her expression. "When I dropped you off at the airport. I knew then."

Her confession rang in my ears and I stood up and began pacing around. Her eyes followed me, and after a moment, I collapsed back on to my chair.

"Three times I've seen you since then. Three fucking times, and I… You…" My voice was broken, devastated, and the tears rolled from my eyes and down my cheeks.

"Cooper, I'm so sorry. I wanted to tell you, but I was scared."

"You're scared of me?" I asked, and out of everything she'd said, it was this that completely destroyed me because she nodded. Pierre came into the kitchen and pulled her into his arms, glaring at me, and I wanted to punch him.

"I think this is enough. She's upset. You need to leave."

I sat for a moment, but when she didn't say anything else, I stood up and walked to the door.

"Bailey, I never expected you to hurt me like this. I've always loved you and I would go to hell and back for you, but not telling me I'm going to be a dad is the most devastating thing you could ever have done to me. I'm not like my dad. I know I've hurt you and pushed and pulled at you, but damn it, Bailey," I said in a broken whisper. "I'm nothing like him…" I sucked in a breath and continued, "And it's killing me that you would keep it from me."

I turned from the room and bumped into Zane in the hallway.

"Take me home. Please, Zane. I can't stay here anymore."

He nodded sadly at me. "Sure. I'll just go and let Sam know."

He clapped me on the shoulder and left me in the hallway. I went downstairs, throwing my things into my overnight bag. As soon as I had everything, I rushed upstairs and out the kitchen door. Once I was outside, I began to breathe a little easier, but I turned back as I crossed the driveway to Zane's car and saw Bailey watching me from the window.

The sight of her there stayed with me for weeks, and I couldn't get over what had happened. The last message I'd sent her was from the car on the way back to my house.

BAILEY, I KNOW I'VE HURT YOU, AND YOU FEEL LIKE I'VE used you, but I have always, always loved you. Today was one of the worst days of my life. Finding out that you're pregnant with my baby from someone else was probably the worst thing I've ever experienced. I get why you think I'd be awful. I mean, look at my dad, but I'm nothing like him and you of all people should know that. I'm only sorry that you couldn't see me for who I am. Cooper

SHE'D TEXTED ME, EMAILED ME, AND CALLED ME A FEW times, but I didn't answer. The pain was too great, and I was completely avoiding everything to do with her, her pregnancy, and our baby. Zane came over once a week and dragged me out to his house, but I could barely stand being there, because everything reminded me of Bailey.

Once I began working, I began socializing again, and I

screwed a different girl every night. I kept sober, but started using girls to fill the void. Once I'd been with a chick more than a few times, I moved on and didn't look back. I was always safe with them because I didn't invest too much and I didn't care about them.

CONFRONTATIONS AND COMPROMISES

THE MONTH OF JANUARY SPED AWAY FROM ME, AND ALL TOO soon, it was February. I was pulling twelve-hour days at the office, working out and going out with a different girl every night, which was fun, and a welcome distraction. I was also spending my weekends with Zane and Sam, but I refused to let them speak to me about Bailey.

Three times I'd begun trying to write an email to her, and every time, I'd ended up deleting it. Eventually, I would respond, but I couldn't do it yet. I'd gone over to Zane's on Valentine's Day to mind the kids because it was Sam's birthday, and I was bored of the girls I'd been seeing.

I was sitting on the sofa, watching TV after putting Ollie and Serena to bed, when I heard the door open. I got up and wandered through to the kitchen, then froze in my tracks because Bailey was standing there.

Her body was blooming in pregnancy, and it suited her.

"Zane's not here," I told her in a bored voice, as I tried to hide my surprise at seeing her. I didn't even know if it was safe for her to fly so much, but I didn't want to ask her. I couldn't because it was killing me seeing her. I just wanted her gone, so acting like I was bored seemed like a good way to go.

Her eyes narrowed into a glare as she took in my relaxed stance. For a moment, neither of us spoke.

"I didn't come here to see Zane. I'm here to see you." Her eyes were glacial.

"What? Why would you come here to see me?" I was stunned, but curious at the same time.

"Because," she hissed at me, and I stepped back away from her in shock at her tone. She was pissed at me? What a fucking crock of shit. What right did she have to be angry with me? Her next words were spoken through her teeth as she struggled to rein in her emotions, but like always, they were written all over her face. "I think we need to talk, don't you?"

She sat down at the kitchen table and I flopped down across from her. Her eyes roamed over my face and I could feel my heart thump hopefully in my chest.

"We need to work out how we're going to do this, Cooper."

"Do what?" I pressed, and she stared at me, clenching and unclenching her hands on the table in front of her.

"Have a baby!" She pointed to her stomach, and I chewed on my lip.

I stood and began to walk away from her because talking to her was killing me. My heart was already broken, and she was stomping all over the pieces.

"Cooper, will you just give me a fucking minute?" she yelled, and I spun back towards her.

"Give you a minute? Why, Bailey? So you can hurt me some more? Be a bit more of a bitch to me?" I asked in frustration. "Why wouldn't you just tell me?" My voice crackled as I begged her to answer me. "Did you not want me involved? I mean, you didn't tell me, did you? Would you ever… you know what, never mind."

Her sigh of exasperation and her narrowed eyes told me I was so far off the mark, but I didn't know what she wanted from me. Talking to her was like pulling my nails out one by one; useless, painful, and devastating. She took a deep breath and then moved to stand in front of me calmly.

"Cooper. I want you to be as involved as you like." She paused and I knew something was making her nervous. "As long as..." She paused, nervously fidgeting with her ring. "You can accept that Pierre and I are together, and he will be the baby's father too."

"No! He won't! He'll be the baby's stepfather. Nothing more! Nothing less!"

She glared at me and I glared right back at her. I wasn't letting some douchebag push me out of my child's life.

"Fine. It doesn't matter either way. I have an ultrasound tomorrow at Lincoln Memorial. I've decided to keep my antenatal care here and we'll be moving back here once the gallery is off the ground. The appointment is at ten a.m. Can you be there?"

Her tone was very matter-of-fact, and I sat back, thinking. It was Thursday, and I had court on most Friday mornings, but I was sure that the court case for the next day had pleaded out.

"Two seconds and I'll check."

I left the room and grabbed my iPad, logging into my work emails and accessing my calendar as I walked into the kitchen. She was on her cell, typing furiously, but stopped when I sat down.

"I'm free until lunch tomorrow." My words were clipped and formal, but it was easier to treat her like I treated my clients.

"Good. That's good. I'm back in Paris from Monday, but I'll be back in a few weeks for another appointment. Should I email you to set it up?"

She seemed to be treating me like a client too, and it made

me feel much better about things, because if we could take our emotions out of the equation, then we could maybe learn to co-parent.

"Yeah, that would be best."

She leaned back and nodded before picking up her cell and typing out another message. Moments later, my email pinged, and I checked to see a complete schedule of appointments for the baby.

"Cooper, I'm twenty-six weeks, and I'll be staying in Minnesota soon."

She ran her tongue along her lip, and I wanted to… Shaking my head to clear it, I stared across the room as I tried to tell myself I didn't want her, even though I knew I was lying to myself. I knew that, somehow, we needed to work together to become parents, and if the only way we could do that was to stay apart, then I'd do it. I wasn't about to let her walk out of my life with our baby because I couldn't control how much I loved Bailey and how much I wanted her. I had to get a grip, and I just hoped our baby didn't feel how hard it was between their mommy and me.

"Coop," Bailey whimpered, and I turned back to look at her.

"I am sorry I didn't tell you, and I swear I don't think you're anything like your dad. I just need you to know that." She leaned forward, speaking to me in earnest, and her eyes glassed over as she spoke again.

I gave her a small smile. I wished I could pull her in for a hug, but it was impossible. I knew if I hugged her, I'd never want to stop. I swallowed the longing down and gave her an apology I still wasn't sure she deserved.

"Okay. Thanks for saying that. I'm sorry I didn't listen when you tried to explain." My heart hurt as a tear rolled from her eye and she scrubbed it away, looking down and then meeting my eyes.

"You were hurt, and you had every right to be. With you, I can't switch off my emotions and that scares me, but we need to, Coop. We need to put our feelings aside because we need to do what is best for our baby."

I could hear the pain in her voice, so I reached out and slipped my fingers into hers, feeling my body relax as her fingers tightened around mine. My heartbeat sped, and for one moment, we sat without speaking and let ourselves feel everything.

She broke the moment, leaning back and breathing hard. She swallowed, and I watched as her throat moved with renewed longing. Her next words made me look away, because I wasn't sure I'd ever be able to separate how much I wanted her from how she felt about me.

"We can do this. Together, okay? We can do it as long as we support each other. We need each other, Cooper. You're our baby's dad, and I need you in my life, so please, just keep in touch with me and let me know you're okay."

She squeezed my hand and I looked up into her eyes, getting lost in their blueness. "I will. You don't need to worry about me. I'm okay."

I heard the lie in my tone. I'd never been further from okay. The pain of losing her love roared inside me, and I scrubbed at my eyes and took my hand from hers.

Her lips pursed, and I wrapped my hands around my waist as we sat in awkward silence again. She knew I'd lied to her and I couldn't think of anything to say to make my lie okay, so I said nothing.

"Cooper," she whispered, leaning forward, but the door opening made her jerk back, and I lifted my eyes to see Pierre glaring at us.

"I thought you said you'd only be a short time?"

His words and tone made my hands curl into fists, but it was his next action that really infuriated me. He stepped forward and grabbed Bailey's hand from the table, tugging her up and hissing at her. "We have to go. Come on."

Bailey smiled sadly at me as she allowed herself to be pulled from the seat, and I stood up with my blood ringing in my ears.

"Cooper," Bailey warned as my eyes narrowed, and I knew my fury was visible on my face. "Cooper, please."

I stared hard at her. She smiled at me while he shoved her coat into her hands, and I stood, clenching my teeth. My body instinctively leaned towards her, and I froze in horror as she reached up and kissed Pierre.

I couldn't watch, and Serena chose that moment to give me the perfect excuse to turn away from her and him. His smirk and bright smile as I turned away set my teeth on edge, and I left the room.

Serena was crying and squirming, and I quickly settled her back to sleep, trying to ignore the pangs of longing and loneliness.

Once she was sleeping, I walked back into the living room and sat on the sofa with my head in my hands. My life was such a mess, and I kept on screwing up. Every single thing I tried to get her out of my head didn't work, and I hated it. I hated that I was so weak and that I longed for her.

My hand still burned from our touch, and I wished I could somehow wake up and feel nothing for her, but life didn't work like that. And now we were having a baby. A baby I'd wished to have with her, if I was being completely honest, but not in this way.

Pierre was involved, and it was breaking my heart a little bit more every day that he'd get to be there for my baby, while I'd be brushed to the sidelines. He'd get to be with Bailey as she did feedings, and see her as a mom, and I'd get occasional weekends and holidays.

I couldn't stop the tears as my heart broke more, and I sat sobbing on the sofa at the loss of the life I'd always wanted but couldn't have.

I didn't hear the living room door open.

"Cooper," Bailey whispered, and I couldn't even look up at her, because I knew if I did, I'd never be able to hide the pain I was in.

"I'm okay," I half sobbed. "It's fine. You can go."

"No, I can't. I can't leave you like this." Her gentle words caused more anguish, and I wrapped my arms around my waist as I struggled to control how much this was hurting me.

"I'll be fine. I promise."

"Liar," she whispered, and I glanced to the side as she sat down beside me. "I hate that I'm hurting you." She reached out to touch me. I scooted away from her and she leaned back, watching me with wide eyes.

"No. Please, Bails. I can't… You can't." I didn't want her to touch me because I knew if she did, I wouldn't ever want to let her go again. It was bad enough she was there to see me melt down, but having her in my arms again would destroy me entirely. She didn't listen and moved closer to me, pulling me into her arms. I protested for a beat and then relaxed into her embrace.

For a while, neither of us said a word, and then she pressed her lips to my head, muttering against my skin.

"Just so you know, this isn't easy for me either. I still care about you, Cooper, and I don't want to see you hurting because of me."

Her tears dripped onto my forehead, and I shifted a little so I could wrap my arms around her waist. We sat holding each other, each taking the comfort we needed desperately from the other. I broke the silence as I confessed what was hurting me the most.

"I don't know how to stop loving you, how to stop wanting you, and it's killing me that you're with him and not me."

Her body stiffened and she pulled out of my arms. I didn't want to look at her, and I tried to avoid her, but she gently put her fingers underneath my chin and lifted my head so I was looking into her eyes.

"Cooper, I need you to accept it because he's going nowhere. I love him. I'm in love with him, and I need you to be okay with it."

Her words caused an ache in my chest, and I swallowed, trying to breathe through it. "Bails, I'm never gonna be okay with it, but I will accept it, somehow. You don't need to feel bad about moving on. I don't want you in pain because of me. I never wanted that."

Her eyes spilled over and she sniffed, rubbing her hands over her face and brushing her hair away from her face. After a moment's silence, she glanced at me, and I stared steadily back at her.

"I will always love you, Cooper, but I can't be with you. Too much has happened, and Pierre makes me happy in a way you never could and never did."

Her brutal honesty was like a knife to the gut, and I closed my eyes as her words clawed at me.

"I don't want to hurt you, but you need to know the truth. We have no future together. I can't forgive you for everything. I want to, but I can't, and if you won't accept that Pierre is with me, then I don't know how we move forward."

"So, if I can't accept you and him, then I don't get to be a father to our child?"

She nodded weakly at me and I glared at her.

"You get how unfair that is? You don't get to keep me from our child because of your personal relationship. That's not how this is going to be, is it?"

She stared at me hard and I sat up straighter and met her gaze with a glare. "Yes, that's exactly how it's going to be. I won't have you treating my fiancé like shit because you're jealous!"

Fiancé? Her fiancé? She was engaged to him.

Her hands covered her mouth as mine popped open in horror, and I just stared at her.

"Cooper, I'm sorry. You weren't supposed to find out like this."

She moved closer to me and I scuttled away from her. Her eyes widened and she brushed away a tear from her cheek.

"We always mess up with each other. I can't even tell my stepbrother good news about my life because it hurts. It hurts so damn much and it destroys every moment of happiness I find in my life. The look in your eyes and the pain I can see on your face breaks me, and I just can't do it anymore." She stood up and moved towards the door, turning back as she opened it. "Cooper, I really am sorry. I hope you know that, but I need you to only come tomorrow if you can promise you'll try to accept Pierre and me."

She didn't wait for my answer and rushed from the room. As soon as she was gone, my strength left me and I crumpled in a heap on the floor. I didn't cry. I had no tears left, but all I had ever wanted was gone, and somehow, I had to accept it and be okay with her decision.

Chapter Twenty One

Zane and Sam came home a little after midnight, and I left as soon as I could. I was supposed to spend the night, but I could barely stand being in the house, and I didn't want company as I tried to sort through my feelings.

Every time I started to get control over the pain, something would happen and throw me right back again. I didn't know how to break the cycle, but I thought it was maybe time for me to get some help.

I barely slept, and when my alarm sounded at five a.m., I reset it for seven thirty and rolled over. I couldn't get back to sleep because my mind wouldn't switch off, so I dragged my exhausted ass out of bed and into a shower.

When I was more awake, I made myself some coffee to drink as I pressed my clothes and set up my travel mug to take into the office. As I dressed, I tried to think of work and my meeting that afternoon, which worked for a little bit. At least until I checked my cell and saw six missed calls from Zane and four messages. Two from Zane, and one from a girl I'd been seeing kinda regularly, but the last one was from Bailey. I read the ones from Zane and ignored the ones from Bailey and Kim.

Coop, Bailey filled me in. Are you okay?

. . .

His text checking in had arrived and then another because I didn't answer straight away. I didn't sit on my cell all the time and I checked the time. The most recent one was sent minutes before I checked my cell.

Can you answer me, please?

I replied to his messages because I didn't want to worry him.

I'm fine. Just going to work. Will call tonight.

I drove to the office and sipped on my coffee as I waited on the elevators to descend. I was thinking about the emails I had to respond to and the appointment I needed to reschedule the following week when I heard a voice that made me want to run away.

I refused to turn around, and when the elevator doors opened, I rushed inside, pressing the button for the fourth floor, praying he wouldn't get on, but luck wasn't on my side. Before the elevator doors could quite close, they opened again, and I was left standing face to face with my father.

He pressed for the sixth floor, and I stood staring at my feet. For a moment, there was complete silence, and then the abuse started.

"Look at the state of you, Cooper."

His words whipped across me and I glanced up to meet his eyes.

"She's moving on and what are you left with? I'll tell you, nothing. You ruined your life and she left you anyway."

I didn't open my mouth. I just wanted out of the elevator, so I continued to ignore him until we reached my floor.

"Dad," I ranted as I passed him. "It's you who has nothing. Your sons don't want to know you and you are missing out on all of your grandkids."

I didn't wait for his response, and I walked away with my head held high and carried on into my office.

The next few hours passed quickly, and I stopped when my reminder went off in my calendar.

Bailey Ultrasound Appointment. I sat back, wondering if I should go with how we'd left things. I took out my cell and saw Bailey had messaged me a further four times.

COOPER, ARE YOU COMING TO MY APPOINTMENT TODAY?
I need to know if you can make it today.
Are you coming or not?
Cooper?

THEN THERE WAS THE ONE SHE SENT THE PREVIOUS NIGHT.

HEY, I'M SORRY ABOUT EARLIER. I KNOW THIS ISN'T EASY for you. It's not easy for me either and I'm sorry for just blurting out about Pierre and me getting engaged. Please just come tomorrow. I really do want you there. xxx

.   .   .

I typed out a quick reply, saying I was coming for the appointment and that I was on my way as I picked up my suit jacket and pulled it on over my shirt and tie. My shirt was light gray and my tie was the dark gray one Bailey had gotten me for Christmas. I'd put it on by accident, but it looked good with my suit and I decided to go with it.

I rushed into the bathroom and quickly splashed some cold water on my face before I ran from the office and down in the elevator. I emailed my secretary, telling her I was taking an early lunch and would be back after my lunch meeting.

My heart hammered in my chest as I rushed across town toward the hospital on foot. I arrived at quarter to ten, sweating profusely and red-faced. I marched into the hospital shop and picked up a bottle of water and a granola bar.

Once I'd paid, I went back outside and waited for Bailey to arrive. Just as I took a mouthful of my granola bar, she walked through the doors. She didn't see me for a moment, but I saw her smile at her companion who came in the door after her.

My eyes almost popped out of my head when I realized it wasn't Pierre. It was Henri. She'd brought her mother with her, and it was Henri who saw me first. She tried to distract Bailey, but I wouldn't let her keep me from seeing my baby.

"Bails," I called, and she turned towards me, her face lighting in relief when she saw me. Her eyes roamed over me and she blushed a little when she saw I'd noticed her.

She walked towards me and Henri followed, scowling at me the whole time.

"Hey, Bails," I remarked with a smile, relieved Pierre wasn't with her.

"Hello, Cooper," Henri said formally, breaking the moment between Bailey and me.

Bailey laughed and rolled her eyes at her mom, then linked her hand with mine. It seemed like a subconscious action. She frowned at me as I dropped her hand and moved towards Henri.

My eyes followed her and I saw her fiddling with something on her keys. It was the half-heart keychain I'd gotten her. It was what I was going to give her for Christmas before everything went to shit. Zane or Sam must have found it and given it to her.

I wondered if she knew what it meant to me, but I wasn't sure she would know because I hadn't had a chance to tell her why I'd gotten it for her.

The sunlight streaming in through the window caught on her hair and I watched as it glittered and blew in the light breeze coming in through the small opening of the window. She really was so beautiful that I choked a little and coughed as she led us towards the bank of elevators.

We went into the nearest one and Henri asked the question I needed the answer to, but she asked it in a way that let me know that I was unwelcome. "Where is darling Pierre?"

I glanced at Bailey and she grimaced up at me, picking up on her mom's not-so-subtle attempt to remind us that she was with someone else. Bailey reached for my hand again and gave my fingers a gentle squeeze as she faced her mom. I couldn't think how to get out of her hold without hurting her, so I left my hand there, even though the contact was setting me alight.

"He's at the gallery meeting with a few artists for our gallery in Paris He's going to try and come meet me a little later at the gallery."

My fingers contracted in hers and she gave my hand a reassuring squeeze. The elevator doors opened and Bailey tugged me along with her, reaching her doctor's office and dragging me over as she let the receptionist know she had arrived.

"I'm sorry. I didn't think you were coming and I didn't want to come alone." She hissed the words at me and then smiled as the receptionist turned to face us.

"Have a seat, dear."

Bailey grinned appreciatively as we walked over and sat down beside Henri, who ignored us both and flicked through a magazine.

Bailey fidgeted with her yellow dress and tied and retied it. Her nervousness was getting to me, so I quickly entwined our fingers and leaned closer, whispering into her ear. "It's fine, but can you stop panicking, please? You're making me nervous."

She turned quickly to look at me, and I didn't get a chance to move, so our lips brushed. It was only a second's contact, but the burn that went through me lasted much longer.

She blushed harder and looked away as Henri huffed on her other side. I didn't look at her. I couldn't take my eyes from Bailey.

We sat for a few more minutes and then Bailey's name was called. I stood automatically with Bails, and so did Henri, but the OB-GYN shook her head.

"Sorry, only one of you is allowed into the scanning room."

I glanced at Bailey and Henri squared her shoulders. "Cooper, while it's nice that you came today to support Bailey, I really think I should be the one to go in since this is my grandbaby."

I glanced at Bails and her face paled.

"No. Sorry, Henri, but the father of the baby trumps Grandma."

Bailey's hand squeezed mine so tightly my fingers began to tingle as Henri stumbled back dramatically. "This baby is yours? Why didn't you tell me this before, Bailey? How can this baby be yours? You were engaged when… Oh my… I feel faint…"

Her eyes narrowed as she looked between Bailey and me in complete horror, and I smirked at her.

"Yep. Bailey is having my baby."

Bailey looked at me with tear-filled eyes and I looked guiltily away. "Now isn't the time for this," she whispered before she turned to her mom. "Mom, can you wait here, please? Cooper, stop acting like a child and come with me."

Her tone was waspish, and I followed her slowly into the room, not sure how I was supposed to feel.

Once we were in the room, Bailey underwent some measurements, her blood pressure was taken, and they took some blood from her.

The doctor chattered away and Bailey answered all the questions, but I sat there with my hands clenched together on my lap without saying a word.

"Have you been eating well?" the doctor asked her, making a note on her file when Bailey answered that she had.

"And movements, you are feeling them?" Her eyes glanced between Bailey and me, and I sat up a little straighter.

"Yes, I feel movements. Lots."

"Excellent. Now, your blood pressure is a little high. Is something causing you stress?"

Bailey's eyes shot to mine and I stared steadily back at her. "Yeah," she mumbled, still looking at me. "I've been a little stressed recently."

"Okay. I suggest you try to eliminate anything that's causing you stress because it isn't good for you and the baby."

Bailey nodded and glanced away from me, meeting the doctor's eye. The next few moments passed quickly and then Bailey was asked to go up onto the ultrasound table.

She opened her dress and I caught a glimpse of her pearly flesh and a simple cream lace bra before she covered it up. She caught my eye and blushed before glancing away. Her blush made her more attractive, and I couldn't quench the desire that began to race through me even though I knew it was wrong and it wasn't fair on her or her new relationship.

I moved towards her and sat down on the stool beside her, unable to resist taking her soft hand in mine and running my thumb over the back.

The sonographer squeezed some gel onto her abdomen, and for a moment, there was nothing, and then there was a thumping sound. My eyes were glued to the screen, and within a few minutes, there was an outline of my baby on the screen.

I watched in fascination as the sonographer checked measurements and I sat staring at the screen in complete awe.

"Cooper," Bailey whispered, and I glanced at her, seeing her eyes filled with tears.

"Sshh, it's okay. I love you, Bailey Walker. I love you and our baby so, so much."

She didn't speak, but her tears began to fall and I leaned over, putting my head against hers and holding her hand.

"I want it all with you," she began softly, and then she leaned up and captured my lips in a gentle kiss. It took me by surprise and then I kissed her back.

"Ahem," the doctor called, and we broke apart and turned towards her, breathing hard.

Bailey squirmed and I turned to see her blushing furiously. The color red stained her chest, neck, and cheeks.

"All is good with the baby. All measurements are good. Here is a copy of your photo."

The lady handed over our image and left the room, leaving Bailey and me together. She tugged her hand out of mine and sat up, fixing her dress without looking at me.

"Bails," I whispered as she scooted forward and slipped her feet into her sandals. She either didn't hear me or ignored me, but my heart hammered in my chest as she bent over to pull up the strap at the back of the sandal.

"Bailey," I tried again, and she turned back to face me.

"Cooper, I'm sorry. That was a mistake. I got caught up in the moment."

Her eyes were wide and I could see the fear in them, so I stood up and used my jacket to hide my erection as I strode towards her.

"Hey, it's okay. I get it."

I didn't get it. I didn't get it at all, but I needed to take the burden off her. I didn't want her hurting or stressing because of me. The doctor had said it was dangerous for the baby, so I had to do what was best for them both.

She gave me a fleeting grin and then stepped closer to me, holding the image in her hand. "You take this. I have others at home."

I met her eyes as I reached over and plucked the image from her hand. I tried to do it without touching her, but our skin met for the briefest second and I quickly retracted my hand as electricity and longing raced through me.

She shook her head and rushed over to scoop up her handbag and coat. I waited patiently for her to put her coat on, staring only at the image and trying hard to push down the incredible rush of love and longing I felt for this crazy, complicated, beautiful girl in front of me.

She opened the door and walked out ahead of me without looking back and I knew, once again, that the moment was gone. Lost amongst her fear and distrust of me. I walked out to the waiting room with my head down and only looked up when I accidentally ploughed into her back.

BAILEY STOOD, FROZEN, AS SHE STARED INTO THE WAITING room, and I followed her gaze, surprised to see Pierre standing there with a furious look on his face. He only held my attention for a fleeting moment because behind him stood Henri and my dad.

My dad's eyes narrowed in disgust at me, and I shook my head, already over the drama this was about to cause. The doctor's warning about Bailey and our baby came to mind, and I quickly stepped around Bailey, shielding her behind me.

Pierre glared at me for a moment and then began to move forward. I held both hands out in front of me and gave them my most intimidating stare.

"Bailey has been advised to reduce stress, and since I'm the father of this baby, I will not let any of you stress her out."

Bailey sighed behind me and I peeked back over my shoulder to see her shaking her head and rubbing at her temples.

"She's mine," Pierre started, and I stepped in to face him.

"She's not a possession, and she's carrying my child, so you will back the fuck off." My voice was deadly serious, and he stepped back away from me, glaring at Bailey as he did.

He sneered at me as Bailey stepped around me and moved between us. "Cooper, it's fine."

Pierre gripped her arm and marched her down the corridor. He punched the elevator call button furiously and she turned back to look at me longingly as he stepped inside, pulling her with him.

I wanted to go after them, but I didn't want to cause her anymore stress, so I stayed where I was, turning eventually to face my dad and Henri.

My dad's face was scarlet, and I knew he was about to blow a gasket, but I didn't care. I only cared that the girl I loved, the girl I wanted more than anything, was gone again.

"Cooper," my dad hissed as he came and stood in front of me. My eyes darted around and I could see a few families waiting to go into the doctor's office, so I nodded down the hallway. As I stepped around my father, I knew he wasn't going to let me go or let me dictate where we had the conversation we were about to have.

"You knocked up your stepsister?" he asked in a carrying whisper, and I spun around to stare at him as the gasps from the waiting room rang in my ears.

"This. Is. Not. The. Place. To. Discuss. This," I spat out, enunciating each word, and he stepped closer to me so we were almost nose to nose.

"You disgust me. I cannot believe you got Bailey pregnant."

My fists clenched at my sides as I fought to control my temper. "It is none of your fucking business."

Henri came over and stepped between us, pushing us apart. Her gaze was glacial and I couldn't believe she'd called him. "Shawn, calm down, dear. You're making a scene."

Her words did the opposite of calm my dad. He stormed past me, barging by people like a bull in a china shop, and I breathed a sigh of relief. My eyes darted around the waiting area, and I saw many eyes on me, but as soon as I looked their way, they turned away.

I was just about to follow my dad when he barged up to me and pinned me to the wall. "You spiteful, arrogant little prick. How could you do this to us? What will people think? You could have let her be free from you and let her move on and be happy. All you do is make her miserable. Why didn't you just leave well enough alone? We believed the baby was Pierre's, but you…" He spat the words viciously into my face and pushed hard against my neck as I struggled to get his hand off me.

"That would have been difficult since the baby wouldn't look a thing like him."

"Better his than a bastard child of their step-uncle."

My blood pounded in my ears and I managed to break free of my dad, shoving him off me just as security arrived. My dad was escorted from the building. I left after them with his vile words floating around in my head.

It didn't surprise me that he'd just called his grandchild a bastard. Nothing surprised me anymore with my dad. Henri walked beside me and didn't say a single word the whole way out. My dad was pacing furiously outside and I wanted to avoid another showdown, so I turned away at the doors and left via a separate exit, heading northwest for my meeting.

I arrived in the restaurant a little before midday and ordered a coffee as I waited for my client to arrive. It began to rain as I sat down, and it hammered on the sidewalk. I stared out of the window and turned when the maître d' approached my table, clearing his throat.

"Mr. Christie, your lunch companion has just called to say that he won't be able to make it today. Would you still like to stay for lunch?"

I shook my head and asked for the bill, staring out of the

window at the pouring rain. Bailey's gallery was just down the street, and I wanted to go in for some cakes to take back to the office with me, but I wasn't sure if it would even be okay.

I decided to risk it, because the chance of her being there was slim, so I grabbed my jacket and cell and quickly paid the bill before rushing out into the wild weather.

I rushed along the street, feeling the water running down my head and soaking me to my skin. By the time I reached the gallery, I was soaked through and shivering. My eyes darted around, and when I saw Bails wasn't there, I breathed a sigh of relief. My office was only a few blocks away and I had an emergency suit hanging up behind my door.

I walked to the counter and ordered a few cream cakes, some glazed donuts, and a tray of sandwiches to take back, along with a coffee for me and one for my secretary, Kathie. She was an elderly lady, and the best secretary I'd ever had.

I called the office and was put through to her desk, but she was on her lunch break and I left a message, asking if she could reschedule my lunch date with my client. She'd know I meant Roman Richards. He was a singer who wanted advice about a divorce, but I had to be discreet, so I only said my twelve o'clock.

As I was standing at the end of the counter, waiting on my order, I heard raised voices coming from the corridor. I tuned them out until I heard my name mentioned, and a set of footsteps barreled towards me.

I glanced up and saw Pierre rushing at me. His face was a picture of fury. When he reached me, he pulled back his fist to hit me and I stepped out of the way, so he hit the glass cabinet beside me. He howled in fury and Bailey ran over towards us.

"Pierre, calm down. Cooper. Go. Just go." Her voice was high-pitched and she was pale.

"What the fuck, Bails?" I asked her, stunned by her dismissal of me and confused about why she was telling me to leave. "Bailey, are you okay?"

She turned around to face me, color rising in her cheeks. "No, Cooper. I am not all right. Everything is going to shit and it's all your fault."

I stepped back, wincing at her words. It would have hurt less if she'd slapped me. Pierre stepped between us and hissed at me, "I believe she asked you to leave, so why don't you go?"

"Ah, sir. Your order is ready. I've double bagged it as per your request."

The girl behind the counter watched everything with fascination, and I turned around, scooping up my purchases. The coffee was on a tray inside the bag, and I was careful to keep it upright as I stepped away from the counter.

I tried to look around Pierre but he moved so I couldn't see Bailey at all. I left, heading back out into the downpour and towards my office. I didn't understand what exactly I was at fault for.

I made it to my office in less than ten minutes and sloshed my way into the elevator, hitting the key forcefully for my floor. I was completely soaked through, and I left wet footprints as I walked along our dark paneled oak floors. I put the coffees out on the table and placed the rest of the items on the coffee table next to the window.

I went into the bathroom in my office with my other suit. I was so glad it was there, but it was my fancier court suit, and I had only had it dry-cleaned the day before. I had to strip completely and dried off on the company towels. Once I was stripped, I put on my lighter gray suit with a white shirt and mint green tie.

I didn't have a choice. My socks and shoes were soaked, so I placed them on the radiator and walked back out to my office, picking up my coffee cup and taking a sip. I sat down at my desk and began replying to emails.

A few hours passed and I was just typing out the legal precedent for a case I was working on when there was a commotion outside my door.

I spun around as the door flew open and rattled against the wall, knocking one of the only framed photographs to the floor.

"You arrogant son of a bitch," Jan hissed at me, and I leaned back as she advanced on me.

"Jan, what in the name of God are you doing in my office?"

"You got her pregnant. You cheated on me and got that little slut pregnant!"

Her voice was so high that it hurt my ears to listen to, and I stood up, walking towards her calmly and closing the door on my startled colleagues' faces.

"Sit down," I began, and she turned to me, slapping me hard across the face twice. She tried a third time, but I caught her hand and she screamed and yelled, so I stepped back away from her, dropping her hand as security stepped inside.

"Miss," Frank, our senior security guard, spoke gently to her. "We're going to have to ask you to leave."

She laughed at him and tried again to get to me, when Joey stepped in front of her. He was tall, with muscles that usually made women putty, and dark hair that curled at the edges.

"Miss, calm down," Joey said in his Australian twang, and she lost it again.

"Calm down? He knocked up his stepsister while we were engaged! You tell me how calm you'd be after finding that out!"

Both security guards turned to me and I glared at them. It didn't matter what I'd done or hadn't done. What mattered was that she'd burst into my office and attacked me.

"Seriously, you knocked up your stepsister?" Frank asked me with a surprised look on his face, and Jan stopped squirming.

"It's not important what I did or did not do. She has no right to be in my office, and I want you to remove her right now."

I used my most professional tone, and both guys shared a quick look before they turned back to Jan.

"Sorry, miss. He's right. You need to leave."

Joey spoke, and his tone told me everything I needed to know. He thought I deserved it. I waited until they were gone and closed the door. My body sagged against it, and for a moment, I just stood there, waiting on my racing pulse to calm down.

Just as I was about to move, there was a knock at the door, and the head partner in the firm pushed the door open.

"May I come in?" Walt asked, and he walked into my office with Terry, the HR person. They took in my disheveled suit and lack of socks and shoes.

"Sit down, Cooper," Walt instructed, and I sat at my desk while they took the armchairs. For a moment, no one spoke, and then Walt cleared his throat and pushed his glasses up his nose.

"I know you didn't ask for that performance, but I have to tell you that was entirely unprofessional." He turned to Terry, and Terry glanced at my feet. "If you continue to act in an unprofessional manner, I'm afraid that we'll have no choice but to let you go. Sitting in your office in your bare feet and having an ex or whatever she was screaming profanities at you while in the office is not appropriate."

Part of me wanted to answer sarcastically, but I knew it wouldn't do me any favors to tell them that I'd try to schedule my next assault out of office hours.

"I'm sorry. I don't know what came over her. I have a restraining order against her, but she just lost it today. And my socks and shoes are on the radiator because I got soaked while out for a meeting today and I don't have spare socks and shoes in the office."

Both men looked at me and Walt's eyes softened. "It's okay. Just try to make sure stuff like that never happens again. You've been formally warned."

They both stood and left my office, and I let my head bang against the desk. The door was closed for a few seconds and then Kathie came into the office.

"Mr. Christie," she said, and I turned to look at her. She shifted from foot to foot.

"Yes, Kathie?" I asked. I was bone tired and all I wanted to do was go home and sink into my bed.

"I'm sorry, but I can't work for you anymore."

I sat up straighter in my chair and stared at her hard. "What do you mean? Why not?" My voice was ice cold and I glared at the old lady.

"Because I'm a good, God-fearing woman, and what you did with your stepsister is wrong and immoral. I believe you'll go to Hell for it." She said the words in a rush, and I sat back with my mouth open in shock.

"I see. So, something that has nothing to do with our professional relationship, which is just hearsay, means that you won't work for me any longer. Is that correct?" She nodded and I rolled my shoulders, trying not to lose my temper. "Fine. Just go. I refuse to bring my personal life into my work, so you are free to leave, because I will not justify the rumors with a response."

She turned and left.

I just wanted the day to be over with, so I decided to go home. I walked into the bathroom and scooped up my wet suit, hearing the crinkle of paper and putting my hand into my pocket to see the sonography image of my baby. It was crinkled, but dry, and I put it inside my wallet for safe keeping.

I gathered my suit up and put it into the dry-cleaning bag, then pulled my damp shoes on without socks because they were still wet. I checked my cell and saw it had turned off. I couldn't remember if I'd plugged the charger in overnight, so I couldn't even check my messages.

My body ached with tiredness as I walked towards the elevator, but no one was around to see me leaving. It was a little after six p.m., and the freeway was packed, but I made it home in forty-five minutes. Once I was inside, I kicked off my shoes and climbed the stairs slowly.

My only thought was of bed, but I needed a shower first, so I stripped out of my suit and turned the dial before stepping in to the scalding hot shower.

My body began to relax, but I tensed again as the events of the day caught up with me. I was worried about Bailey's reaction to me at her gallery, and I was worried about her health. I was worried about my job and how people would react if they found out that I had knocked up my stepsister, and I was worried I wouldn't be allowed to be involved in my baby's life.

As soon as I was finished with my shower, I dried off quickly and climbed into my bed, sinking gratefully into a deep sleep.

Chapter Twenty Three

MY BODY TENSED UNDER THE COVERS, AND I ROLLED OVER onto my stomach, trying to ignore the sound I was hearing. When I woke up a little more, I recognized the pounding noise as someone battering on my door.

I crawled groggily from my bed and snatched up a pair of sports shorts from the chair by the door in my room. I pulled them on and tied them tightly before making my way down the stairs.

I didn't want to deal with anymore confrontation, and I decided to call the cops if it was Jan, rather than trying to sort out things with her myself.

The person behind the door pounded again, and I couldn't help the sliver of apprehension that tightened around my gut as I put my fingers on the door, unlocking it and opening it to reveal Bailey standing in the doorway.

"Coop, c-can I come i-in?" she asked me, shivering as she stood in the pelting rain. I quickly stepped aside and let her into the house, showing her into the downstairs bathroom and handing her a towel and my fluffy housecoat from my office.

She closed the door and I moved into the kitchen to make us some coffee while she got changed. I was standing at the patio doors when I heard her enter the kitchen and walk over to the island. I didn't look around because I was so scared to see her expression, but I could see her movements reflected in the windows.

She sipped her coffee in silence, and I watched her walking around my kitchen with my bathrobe on. It was like a fantasy come to life, and I had to think of slugs and snakes and jelly to try to keep my erection down because I knew if I turned around with a boner, she'd take it the wrong way.

"Coop," she sighed, and I jumped because her breath touched my skin. I hadn't been paying enough attention to see her cross the kitchen and come close to me.

I turned around as her eyes scanned across my chest and down to my abdomen. My lightly tanned skin and toned stomach made me proud usually, but the fire in her eyes when she licked her lips and brought her eyes up to meet mine made me hornier than I'd ever been in my life.

"I wanted to… erm… well, you know… apologize to you because—" She took a breath and looked away before speaking again. "Can you go put some clothes on?"

"Is my near nakedness distracting you, Bails?" I asked her, laughing as her cheeks colored and she shook her hair down over her face.

"Yes. You know it is. Please, Coop. I need to be serious, and I can't—" She broke off, breathing hard, and ran her fingers through her hair, tugging at it. "Cooper?" she asked with a lilt in her tone, and I grinned at her.

"Two secs," I told her, and I took off into the laundry room at the back of the kitchen, scooping a dry top from the washer/dryer. I pulled it on and returned to the kitchen to see her frowning at her cell.

"Better?" I asked on my return, and she lifted her eyes, smiling broadly at me.

"Much. Thank you." Her words were sincere, but something was off in her eyes.

"You want me to put your clothes in to dry?" I asked her, trying to delay the conversation we were about to have, and she nodded, chewing on her lip.

I left her for a moment and went into the bathroom, gathering all her clothes, but leaving her coat hanging because I was sure you couldn't dry wool. After I'd thrown in her clothes and put the dryer on, I went back out and saw she was standing where I had been, staring out the window. I watched her for a bit before she turned and caught me staring at her.

The gray bathrobe encased her figure in the most appealing way, and she shook her head at me when she saw me watching her.

"Stop looking at me like that," she chastised in a playful whisper as she sat back down at the island.

I laughed and moved towards her, muttering under my breath, "You'd be better telling me to stop breathing."

As soon as I sat down, I leaned forward and faced her across the island. I did it for two reasons. One, she was fiddling with her right wrist and chewing on her lip, which was her nervous tell, and two, I was trying hard to hide my pretty obvious erection.

"Bails, what is it? What's wrong?" I reached out and touched her hand, and she quickly pulled it back. She'd never done that to me before, and I dropped my hand to the table, pulling it back to rest in front of me.

"Coop, I keep making mistakes with you. Every time you touch me, I forget all the reasons we can't be together and I end up hurting you."

I met her eyes and could see the glassines in them as she fought against the tears.

"I'm a big boy. I can cope," I whispered, and she stared at me hard.

"Can you though? Are you still not able to drink alcohol?" Her words cut into me, and I wrapped my arms around my waist, wanting to kill Zane with my bare hands for revealing that to her. "It wasn't Zane," she said, as if she could read my mind. I straightened up to look at her.

"I can handle it. I'm handling it," I stuttered, and she leaned back to look at me.

"I hate what I'm doing to you. I had no right to yell at you earlier, but you took it, and I know you're hurting, Coop. I see it every time I see you. God, when I saw you sobbing, it tore my heart out and I couldn't breathe. I never want you to feel that way again."

I didn't know what to say to her, so I stayed silent, because all the things I wanted to say to her would only have hurt her more.

"Today, I didn't tell Pierre about the appointment. That's why he was mad at you, and I didn't tell my mom you were the father because I didn't want to deal with the fallout from that, but then you did, and my mom called Pierre and your dad." She took a breath and wrapped her hands protectively around her swollen stomach. "I don't want to bring my baby up around all the drama, but I can't cut you out of our lives, and Pierre hates it. He hates you. I mean, he really hates you, and I don't know what to do."

She pursed her lips as she finished, but her eyes watered and a tear broke free and rolled down her cheek.

"He hates me because he's jealous. He doesn't want me involved because he knows our connection is too strong."

"But—" she began, and I held my hand up to stop her.

"No, it is. When we're together, nothing else matters. I see only you, and you see only me." She opened her mouth to speak, but I cut her off. "Don't try to deny it, Bails. It's been this way forever. Since we were kids. That's why my dad put his foot down and made me end things, because I would have moved heaven and earth to be with you. You are it for me and I know I'm not it for you, but—"

"You are," she interrupted, and I stared at her in shock because I didn't expect her to say that.

"You are amazing, Cooper Christie, and you are so special to me."

"Here comes the but..."

"But." She smirked through her tears. "We're going to be parents, and I need to be with someone who doesn't consume all of me. With you, I feel like I'm in a bubble, but I don't feel safe. I feel like I'm home, but never relaxed, and I need to feel that. Can you understand?"

"Yes," I said in a small voice, because I did understand. But, selfishly, I wanted her to want me. I wanted to keep her, even though I knew I couldn't.

"Coop," she pleaded. "Can I stay with you tonight, and tomorrow, can you promise to let me go?"

"Of course you can stay. You can always stay with me, but I can't promise I'll be able to let you go. I will try though."

I knew I'd have to try, or I'd lose her forever, but it would be the hardest thing I'd ever done.

"Take me to bed, please, Cooper?" she asked, and I met her eyes across the table. I reached out to her and she entwined her hand with mine, following me to my bedroom.

When we reached the door, I paused and turned back to face her, seeing uncertainty in her eyes.

"Are you sure you want to do this, Bails?" I asked. Even though I desperately wanted to have her in my bed, I didn't want to pressure her into something she'd later regret.

"Yes. I'm sure. I've never been so sure about anything,

Coop. I just need one more night with you. Just one more night before I let you go forever."

I closed my eyes and asked the question that I needed the answer to, and even though I hated myself for asking, I had to know if she'd really thought this through.

"What about Pierre?"

"What about him?" Her tone was cool, and a shiver rolled down my spine at her words.

"Won't he mind you spending the night with me?"

She laughed and I opened my eyes to look at her. "Yes, he'd mind. But he will never find out about this. As far as Pierre is concerned, I'm spending the night with Lish. This is just between you and me. Promise me, Cooper. Please?"

I stared at her, completely nonplussed, and she stepped forwards, capturing my lips in a soul-shattering, earth-shaking kiss. She pushed me until my back was against the closed door to my bedroom and wrapped her arms around my neck, kissing me harder and more fervently than ever before.

I forgot about everything and picked her up, carrying her over to my bed and placing her gently on top of the covers. My eyes widened as she reached over and opened my bathrobe to reveal her pearly flesh underneath. She was completely naked, and my mouth watered at the sight of her.

Her stomach was rounded, and I dropped to my knees, worshiping her, and wrapped her legs around my head so I could taste her warm pussy again. She writhed and wriggled on the bed, but I made her come furiously after a few minutes. My erection strained against my shorts and I quickly stood, pushing them down and springing free.

Her eyes found mine and I lowered myself, thrusting hard inside her, making her moan my name over and over as I pushed into her hard and fast. I couldn't think of anything outside of us, and I had to slow down so I wouldn't come too quickly.

My eyes roamed over her and my t-shirt flapped against her baby bump. She pulled her hands out of the bathrobe and ran her nails down my spine. My heart rate sped at the sight of her arching her back and I wanted to stay in this moment forever.

"Cooper," she moaned breathlessly, and I leaned down, capturing her lips and pouring everything I felt into the kiss, all the pain, anguish, love, desire, and my devotion to her. My tongue plunged into her mouth, dancing with hers as I slowed down to make love to her.

I licked her lips, tugged on her bottom lip with my teeth and lightly bit her, then caressed her lip with my tongue. She pushed me up and tugged at my t-shirt. I sat up, lifting my arms one at a time to allow her to take my top off.

Her fingers roamed my abs and I groaned as she scraped her nails across them before she rounded my back and ran her nails along my bare skin and her fingers found my ass. She gripped onto my cheeks tightly and tugged me harder into her.

My eyes wandered to her rounded breasts, and I lowered my head, capturing her nipple in my mouth and sucking hard on it while I pushed upwards. She panted harder, so I leaned down onto my elbows and put all my weight on one arm, using my free hand to twist her nipple and give her a little pinch.

I began to feel the telltale tightening at the base of my spine, so I stopped and flipped us over so she was on top of me. Her wide smile, flushed cheeks, and bright eyes made me feel whole in a way I only ever felt with her.

She began moving and I lost all thought. Her tits bounced lightly in front of me and I teased them. Hearing her breathing change and low moans emanating from her made me push up hard as she came down.

Within a few more thrusts, she was coming apart around me, and I detonated like a bomb when her pussy clamped onto me again and again. She collapsed against me, breathing hard, and I just lay there. My dick went limp, but was still partly inside her and I didn't want to move. I didn't want to break the spell because, when the spell broke, I'd remember that she wasn't mine and she'd probably regret this.

I knew I never would. I would cherish this memory, rightly or wrongly. That moment right there was mine.

"Coop," she started, and I glanced down at her. My complete bliss dissipated as I saw the tears in her eyes and the pain on her face. "I—" she began at the same time I spoke.

"Hey, Bails." I paused and nodded for her to continue, praying she wasn't about to crush me again.

"That was incredible," she whispered, surprising me. Her lips pressed against my chest, right above my heart, and I leaned back, swallowing the words I really wanted to say to her.

I wanted to beg her to stay with me. I wanted to tell her how happy I could make her and how amazing we would be together, but all I said was, "Yeah, it was." It always was when we were together. I was about to say something else when a small flutter hit my abdomen and I glanced down. The flutter happened again, and then her stomach moved. I stared at it, completely entranced.

"Will that have hurt the baby?" I asked her without meeting her eyes, and she laughed at me. Her laugh clenched against my dick, which was already beginning to harden again.

"No, Cooper. The baby will be fine."

I looked over at her, needing to make sure she was telling

the truth, and she smiled at me, picking my hand up from the bed and sitting up. My erection, by this time, was back inside her, but she didn't move.

She placed my hand gently on her stomach and my hand was pushed by the smallest of movements. My smile widened and I watched as my hand was kicked again.

"Hi there, baby. I'm your daddy," I said in a low voice, full of love and regret. "I love you and your mommy very, very much."

Bailey didn't say a word, but she began moving against me, and I responded without conscious thought. I sat up, moving my hand to help me up. Once I was upright, my hands went around her and I held her back as she moved against me.

My lips explored the softness of her lips, and she kissed me back fervently. I explored the skin around her neck and nipped gently at her collarbone. Her body moved in complete sync with mine, and I leaned back up, kissing her hard and swallowing her moans as she came apart, harder than the last two times.

I followed after a few more thrusts, and we sat staring into each other's eyes. Her eyes shone with tears again, and I pulled her against my chest, holding tightly to her as my heartbeat slowed.

"Coop, I need to use the bathroom," she said, and I loosened my arms, feeling the loss of her as soon as she was out of my hold. She walked across my room and I watched her naked ass move away from me. It was perfect, rounded, and a sight to behold. She glanced back over her shoulder.

The look she gave me when she saw my heated gaze was one of complete love, and it took my breath away. Maybe there was hope for us after all. Maybe if I could get her to let her guard down, she could let me back in.

I'd prove I was worthy. I'd do anything. I scooted up the bed and climbed into the covers as I waited for her to return. I heard the water running and sat up straighter as the door to my bedroom opened a little wider.

She walked into my room and her smile grew. She twisted her hair back and I devoured the sight because it pushed her breasts out and made her stomach look rounder.

"You really are a goddess, Bails," I muttered, and she turned to smile at me before scooping up my shirt from earlier and pulling it over her, which made my heart tingle. My eyes never left hers as she climbed up the bed and crawled in on my left side, sleeping where she'd always slept on those nights we managed to sleep together when we were younger.

She pressed her lips softly to my cheek and laid her head on my arm, gazing up at me. My eyes roamed all over her face and I breathed her in because I knew this would be a fleeting moment. It would be over way too soon, and if all I was getting was this night, then I was damn sure I'd make the most of it.

"Wanna play a game, Coop?" she whispered, and I sighed, leaning my head onto hers.

"No, Bails. Not tonight. Tonight, I just wanna hold you."

I pressed my lips against her forehead, and she breathed against me. I stayed there for a few moments and then she pulled her head away, lifting her lips and brushing them against mine.

My lips responded, and the kiss was the softest kiss we'd ever had. My body began to respond, and even though I'd just wanted to hold her, I would take whatever she was willing to offer me.

"Cooper," she breathed against my lips, and I slipped my tongue into her mouth and ran my hands up and down her back. One of my hands twisted in her hair and I tugged her neck back gently, exploring again with my lips, teeth, and tongue.

When I brought my lips back up to hers, she mumbled against them, "Make love to me, Cooper."

Her words caused my heart to stutter, and I crawled around the bed, spreading her legs and running my fingers along her glistening pussy.

"So ready for me, Bails," I moaned, slipping first one and then two fingers inside her. She mewled, and I pushed a little more firmly and then withdrew my fingers, sucking the juices from them. Her eyes widened, and I moved my body, so I was hovering over her before I thrust gently inside her.

"I…" I pulled out. "Love…" I thrust in and pulled out again swiftly. "You…" Again, I thrust in, but slowly and precisely. "So damn much." I pulled out and rubbed my dick along her seam before pushing back inside her.

I lowered my body to hers and continued to drive my cock slowly out and in, all the while telling her how much I loved her and how much I wanted her. She didn't speak. She groaned loudly and then bit my shoulder as she detonated around me, clenching and unclenching her pussy.

I went a little harder and she moaned my name. Hearing my name cross her lips had me coming like a firework on the Fourth of July.

"FUCK! I love you," I said as I shot my load inside her. I pressed my lips to hers, feeling her responding to my kiss, and then rolled over onto my back, breathing hard and bathed in sweat. Bailey nudged against my arm, and I turned onto my side and watched as she laid her head on my arm.

She stared up at me through hooded lids. I relaxed against my pillows because, for one night, she was where she belonged, safe and in my arms. There was nowhere on earth I would rather have been in that moment.

I gently kissed her lips as she relaxed into sleep. My lids grew heavy, but I didn't want to drift off because I knew that when I woke, the moment would end and she'd leave me again.

Once I was sure she was asleep, I pressed a gentle kiss to her head and whispered, "I wish I could keep you here forever."

I then closed my eyes and let my body soften until I fell asleep.

I only woke once because Bailey's lips pressed to my forehead and her hair tickled my cheeks. "I love you too, Cooper. I just hope you can forgive me for leaving."

She stepped away from me and I rolled over, sure I was dreaming as I drifted back to sleep.

Chapter Twenty-Four

THE PAIN AFTER THE PLEASURE

I WOKE UP THE NEXT MORNING, SURE I'D DREAMED THE previous night, but when it all came back to me and I glanced towards her side of the bed, my heart shattered. I hoped I was wrong, and I got up, pulling my sports shorts on, and walked downstairs. I went into every room, but she wasn't in any of them, not that I really expected her to be. I'd known as soon as I saw she wasn't there that she was gone again.

She'd really fucking left me after giving me hope again. I went back to bed, despondent and dejected, and just lay there with my eyes open, staring at the ceiling tiles. I didn't make any move to get up, and the day passed with me slipping in and out of sleep.

I didn't want to shower because my body still smelled like her. I didn't want to wash the scent of her away because then I'd be able to convince myself it was a dream, so I didn't.

As night fell, I knew I had to move, so I got up and shoved a shirt on, noting that the one I'd had on the previous night was gone. I went into the laundry room and saw her clothes were gone, but she'd left me a note propped up against the washer.

Coop,

I'm so sorry. I wanted to stay with you. I really did, but I can't. I just needed one more night with you and I'm sorry for leaving before you woke up. I couldn't face you in case you wanted more which, let's face it, you would have, because I know I do too. I've taken your shirt as a memento, and I've left you a little something in your office. I'm leaving my heart with you because that's where it's always been and I will never, ever love anyone like I love you.

Last night was so special to me, and I felt every word you said as we made love. I'll be back stateside in four weeks and I hope you'll be able to come to my appointments from now on.

I love you so much, but we can only be friends and former lovers, and Pierre can never find out about last night. I know this will probably hurt you and, selfishly, I partly hope it does because I know it will always hurt me. I'm so sorry again, and I need you to know I never intended to sleep with you last night, but when I'm with you my intentions never seem to go to plan. I will always be thinking of you.

You have my heart, now and always,
Your Bails

I CLENCHED THE NOTE IN MY FIST AND READ IT A DOZEN times before tossing it and storming away. I bolted up to my room and snatched up some socks and my sneakers and shoved my feet into them. I needed to hit something. I needed to get the pain of her words, her excuses, and her leaving out of my head because it was all over. I knew it when she'd gone. I just wished I hadn't held on to the tiny sliver of hope that I could somehow change her mind. She'd left me and she wasn't coming back. Not now. Not ever.

I moved down to my gym on autopilot and pushed my

body harder and harder until I collapsed on the ground in a pool of sweat. My hands were cut and bloody from hitting the punching bag over and over again, so much that I'd ended up splitting it, and my head swam with my rapid breaths.

Never again. Never again will I let myself have hope for our future. We had no future. She'd made that perfectly clear. I pushed myself up from the ground and walked upstairs on unsteady legs, heading into the kitchen for a drink.

My alcohol stash had been emptied, but I usually kept a bottle in my desk drawer. I turned and moved swiftly to my office. My only thought was getting something to numb the pain. I opened the drawer and saw the bottle, but my eyes scanned the room and I saw a gift on top of my laptop, along with a note.

Coop,

I know you've probably struggled today and I know you won't have reached out to Zane, but let him help you. I know you're hurting right now because I am too, but I have support. You need support and you have to let others help you.

Open up to someone, even if it's not Zane, because you are loved. You are so loved and both me and your baby need you whole and healthy.

Take care of yourself.

Always,

Bails

I DROPPED THE LETTER AND PULLED THE SQUARE PACKAGE ON the table towards me. My fingers itched to open it, but I was scared of what was inside. After a few deep breaths, I was ready.

I slid my finger along and opened up the wrapping, ripping it, and flipping the box inside open.

Inside was a teddy bear frame, and inside the frame was a sonogram picture. The words My Daddy were engraved on the frame, and I sat staring at it with tears in my eyes. The bear was holding a heart, and it reminded me of the one I gave Bailey before I left for college.

I'd wondered if she'd ever found my mom's ring, but then I realized it didn't matter. She'd never be mine to wear it. I picked up the bottle from the drawer with shaking hands and cracked it open.

My eyes stayed on the frame of my baby, and I threw the bottle across the room. He or she needed me to be sober and together and not a fucking mess, so I had to stop drinking when I was overwhelmed.

The bottle smashed open and the liquid inside spilled down the wall and along the floor, but I didn't care. I'd clean it up later. I knew I needed help, and I knew who to call to make sure I stayed sober, so I left the room and searched for my cell, finding it in my briefcase.

My hands shook as I connected it to the charger and I sat in my office, waiting on it to turn on. After a few minutes, the smell of the alcohol was beginning to get to me, so I went into the kitchen for the broom, dustpan, and some cleaning products.

I sat on the floor of my office and cleaned up the walls, the floor, and swept up the glass. Some pieces were pretty large, so I picked them up last, slicing my palm on one and cursing under my breath.

I stood up and watched as blood dripped down my hands and onto the dark gray flooring. It splashed in a circle and was followed by another drop and then another. I clenched my fist and began to move towards the kitchen when there was a knock at my door.

"Fuck," I hissed as I turned back towards the door. I couldn't see who was standing there, but I had to decide whether to answer the door or go clean up my hand. I decided to answer the door quickly, and then I'd deal with my hand. It was alcohol anyway, so it was already sterile.

As I walked towards the door, it was knocked again, and I opened it. My feet carried me back in surprise when I saw Pierre standing in my doorway.

"May I come in?" he asked, his accent curling around the words. His eyes narrowed on my hands.

"Yeah, I guess so." I turned and left the door open, walking into the kitchen and running my hand under the faucet. It stung and burned, but I cleaned it and then wrapped a cloth around it.

Pierre stood at the kitchen door, watching me, and I wondered why he'd visited me.

"Sit?" I asked him as I moved to the island and sat down, but he shook his head and stared at me hard.

"I don't like you."

I gave him a quizzical look because I didn't care how he felt about me. Not really. "And?" I asked after a pause, because he didn't continue.

"And I don't think you're good enough for Bailey. You are hotheaded, selfish, and inconsiderate, and I'm here…" He paused as I pushed up onto my feet and leaned towards him. "I'm here," he continued with narrowed eyes and a sneer across his lips, "to tell you to stay away from her and her baby."

"Our baby. The baby she's carrying is ours. Hers and

mine, and it's not for you or anyone else to tell me to stay away from the mother of my child, or my child."

His gaze darkened and he stepped forwards, separated from me by the island. "Yes, it is. It hurts her every time she sees you, and it stresses her out. You are risking her health and your baby's health, so you need to stop."

I stepped back and glared at him. "If Bailey doesn't want to see me, then she'll tell me that, but until that time, stop trying to push me out of her life. *You* are stressing her out. You're causing her so much pain because she's choosing between us and she shouldn't have to."

He snorted at me and his dark eyes narrowed further. "It is not me who is hurting her or making her cry at night. It is me who is trying to pick up the pieces after her heart is broken by you over and over again."

My heart pounded in my ears and I wanted to punch his lights out, but I knew it wouldn't do any good.

"Get out," I demanded tiredly as the weight of his words hit me and I collapsed onto a seat.

"No. Not until you promise to leave her alone."

I glowered at him and shook my head. "As long as Bailey wants me around, then I'm gonna be there. It's not about you or me. It's about her wants and needs, and if you don't like it, then I really don't give a shit. I love her and I won't let some passing fling come between us."

He laughed and my blood pressure rose. I pushed up to my feet, but his next words took the wind out of my sails.

"We are to be married. Next week. In Paris. So, she'll be my wife and I will hardly be a passing fling."

"What?" I queried in almost disbelief, and he met my eyes with a vicious sneer on his face.

"Yes. She's going to be my wife, and your baby will be

my stepchild, so I'm telling you to back off and leave us alone."

I opened my mouth to speak, but the words didn't come out. With one last glare at me, he turned and left, slamming the door behind him. My legs gave way, and I collapsed onto the cool kitchen tiles, feeling my world crumble at my feet.

I didn't know how long I sat there, but eventually, the pains in my legs made me move and I crawled into my office. I found my cell with a few messages. One from Luke, one from Zoe, two from Bails, and two from Zane.

I ignored all the messages and just sent Zane two words.

COME. PLEASE.

I PUT MY CELL DOWN AND SAT DOWN ON THE FLOOR BEHIND my desk as I waited for Zane to arrive. When he arrived, I crawled along to the door and pulled myself up on the hall table, opening the door to my brother. I stared at him blankly for a moment before my head started to spin, my ears started to ring, and my vision blurred at the edges.

I heard him call my name, and I looked up at him from the floor and saw his face blurring in and out as he stared down at me.

"Cooper, are you okay?" His voice echoed in my ears and I tried to sit up, lying back down when a wave of dizziness overcame me again.

"I… I'm… I'm not sure…" My words were broken as nausea rose in me and I rolled away from him and retched. There was nothing in my stomach to bring up, but I retched again, bringing up vile stomach contents, and then lay with my head resting on the cool floor.

Zane sighed and then helped me to my feet and half dragged, half carried me into the living room. When I was sitting on the sofa, he sat beside me and stared at me until I began speaking.

"Bailey's getting married."

It was all I said, but it was enough, and he stared at me wide-eyed.

"Yeah, I know. You knew that, didn't you? She said she'd told you."

He was rambling. He always rambled when he was nervous. He twisted his lip ring around with his tongue.

"She's getting married next week, Zane."

His eyes shot to mine and he stared at me in disbelief. "Are you serious? How do you know this?"

His face and tone told me he knew nothing about her plans.

"Pierre came over and told me. He told me to stay away from her and the baby." My hands twisted around and around each other, and I finally looked into his eyes. "What am I supposed to do, Zane? How am I supposed to let her go and not be in my kid's life?"

His eyes softened and he sat down beside me, putting his head into his hands. "I don't know, Coop. I'll speak to her and see if I can convince her to postpone the wedding. I think she's making a mistake and she'll regret it."

I leaned back on the sofa as he took out his cell and typed furiously, and then he stood up, walking from the room. I sat staring numbly at the TV. Thinking back to how happy I'd been overnight made me feel nauseated, so I tried to put it out of my mind.

A few minutes passed and Zane came into the living room with a frown on his face and handed me his cell. "Bailey," he mouthed at me, and I lifted his cell to my ear. I could hear her arguing furiously with someone, so I waited a minute and then cleared my throat.

"Hey, Bails," I whispered, trying to sound casual, but failing entirely when my voice broke on her name.

"Hey, are you okay?" The concern in her voice made my stomach roll and I breathed in through my mouth and out through my nose as I fought the urge to vomit.

"No," I said finally. "No. I'm really not. Bailey, please don't do this. Don't marry him. You don't want me, that's fine, but wait at least until after you've had our baby. I'm asking. No, begging you. Please, just wait."

My voice cracked and broke so many times as I spoke. The tears I was fighting rolled down my cheeks. Zane clapped me on the shoulder as I begged her not to go through with the wedding. For a moment, there was silence, and then she spoke so quietly I had to strain to hear her.

"I'm sorry. I really am, but I have to. I have to move on from you. From us. Goodbye, Cooper."

Her whispered goodbye shattered my heart into a million pieces, and Zane's cell slipped from my numb fingers as her apology rang in my ears.

Zane watched as I sat back, numb, hurt, and beyond destroyed. She'd really been saying goodbye to me when she'd been at my place, and like a fool, I'd let her in to stomp all over the shattered pieces of my heart.

My ears buzzed and my head swam when I tried to sit up. Zane took his cell and sent a message. I wasn't sure who he was messaging, and I didn't want to know. After a while of us sitting in silence, he picked up the remote and turned on the TV.

With the sports channel on softly in the background, he turned to look at me and the sorrow on his face was almost too much for me to take.

"Coop, have you eaten today?"

His words were so unexpected that I laughed. "No. I haven't eaten. The girl who owns my soul is marrying someone else and came over last night to fuck me and then leave me, so food was pretty low on the agenda today."

His mouth popped open and he gazed at me in complete disbelief. "She did?"

"She did. She didn't care how much it would hurt me or how hard knowing she was marrying someone else would be. She hates me so much that she used me to scratch an itch and then left me with a note saying she hoped I wouldn't hate her."

His face grew tense.

"Well, she got that part wrong because I do hate her," I went on. "I hate her for using me and for breaking my heart all over again. I hate her for not choosing me when I chose her. I wish I could change what I did to her, but I can't, and it kills me every day."

After a few minutes, Zane stood up and patted his pockets. I watched him and then realized he was looking for his cell, so I picked it up and handed it to him without checking.

He touched the screen, frowned, and stood up, nodding towards the hallway. "I'm just going to text Sam and then I'll order us some pizza. Cheese and pickles okay for you?"

His tone was light and I tried to smile as he grinned at me. The memory of the cheese and pickles fiasco played before my eyes. I remembered how my mom, while she was sick, tried to order Zane and me a pizza for dinner, but she accidentally ordered a pizza with those toppings, which was disgusting, and she ended up making us a frozen pasta instead.

Anytime I saw or ate a frozen pasta, it reminded me of

that, and when I ordered pizza, I was always careful to not choose that because it was vile. I still remembered the taste of it and urgh… it was so gross.

Zane stepped out into the hall and I heard him speaking softly to someone as the door closed. I didn't listen to his words, nor did I care who he was speaking to. It was probably Sam anyway. I leaned back and watched the commercials on TV without really watching them, and when Zane came into the living room after a few minutes to say he was going to the store, I ignored him.

"I'll be back in ten minutes with some sodas and chips, but if the pizzas arrive, I've already paid."

Chapter Twenty Five

GUNS AND NIGHTMARES

THE DOOR TO THE LIVING ROOM OPENED AND A PAIR OF HEELS sounded on the floor. I turned around, hoping to see Bailey, but disappointment crushed me, followed by shock when I saw Jan standing there. Her hands shook as she pointed a 9mm handgun at me.

"Jan, what—" I began, and she shook her head at me.

"You don't get to talk. You get to listen now, Cooper."

I swallowed back my words and stared at her as she moved around to stand in front of me. Her eyes narrowed on my face and I sat up a little straighter, watching as she shifted from foot to foot.

"You are a selfish, arrogant son of a bitch and you are going to pay for what you've done to me. You are going to suffer. I was going to go after Bailey, but then I thought of how much it would kill you to not be there for your baby. You always talked about how you wanted kids, and it gives me some satisfaction to know that you won't ever see your baby in person. Plus, then I get to know that I punished that bitch for stealing you from me. I can't resist that."

I had to interrupt. She was serious. I could see it in her eyes and in the set of her shoulders. If I didn't manage to talk her down, she was going to put a bullet in me.

"Jan, think about this. You aren't a killer. You're hurt and angry with me, and I get it, but you don't want to do this."

"Don't you fucking tell me what I am or am not, you worthless sack of shit. I could have made you happy. We could have been happy, but you left me humiliated, and for what?" Her hand circled the room, encompassing the cream walls, gray sofa, and TV. She moved closer still, hissing at me. "So you could be here all alone, without her?"

She moved closer and pointed the gun right at my chest. I closed my eyes, praying to God, any god, to get me out of this, but I wasn't sure I would be able to.

My life flashed before my eyes as the barrel of the gun touched my chest, and I thought of all the things I'd yet to experience. My baby being born. Bailey as a mom, and fixing things between us. I had to have a chance to put everything right. I needed to fix what I broke by getting on that plane to Hawaii.

"Please, don't do this, Jan."

I met her eyes and she smirked evilly at me. "All you had to do was love me, Cooper. It was all I wanted."

Her eyes narrowed and she glanced away, giving me the split second I needed to push the gun up. Her finger pulled the trigger and I felt the burn of the bullet as it tore through the skin of my shoulder.

I shrieked in agony and shoved her away from me as the gun went off a second time, but it didn't hit me. I didn't know where it hit. I tried to breathe through the pain and dropped to the floor, hearing the front door open and footsteps burst in.

"Zane," I moaned. "GUN!"

I used the last of my stepsy to yell at him, and then everything went black and I was trapped in a world of pain and darkness.

When I finally came around, I was groggy and my shoulder was tied up in bandages. I tried to lift my arm, but it was as though someone had tied lead weights to it and set it on fire. My moan of pain caught Zane's attention and he rushed over to me.

"Cooper, thank God you're alive."

His face appeared above mine, white and pinched, and his eyes were red-rimmed.

"What-what am I doing in the hospital?" I asked, trying to remember what had happened. Flashes of it came back to me, but I couldn't make sense of the pictures in my head.

"Jan." He said her name like an expletive. "She came by and shot you."

"What? Where's Mom?" I asked in a small voice, and I tried to move my head to see if she was still around. She'd been with me when I'd arrived. I remembered seeing her so clearly and I could still smell her perfume.

"Coop, Mom's dead. She's been dead for sixteen years." His eyes widened and he glanced at someone who was standing just out of my line of sight.

"Bailey," I began as I thought about her, and again, Zane's eyes drifted away to look at the corner of the room. "Zane, she's in danger. Jan might go after her. You have to warn her."

My panic came back, and I began to breathe heavily as I struggled to make him understand how serious it was.

"Cooper, relax." The machine by my bed began going crazy, and a nurse came in, admonishing Zane for getting me hyped up.

"Zane, you have to go to her. You have to protect her and my baby…"

My words began to slur as the nurse pushed the green button and I began to float away, my eyes drifting closed, even though I was fighting it.

I woke up a few hours later feeling a little less groggy, but still in copious amounts of pain. Zane stood in the doorway with his back to me. He was speaking to someone in the corridor and I cleared my throat, trying to get his attention.

He turned towards me and closed the door, crossing the room and sitting by my bed.

"Hey, bro. You seem a little more alert today." He smiled at me and took my hand, giving it a gentle squeeze.

"I am, but where's Bailey? Did she go to Paris?"

Zane shook his head and looked at me with wide eyes and narrowed lips, his forehead furrowed. Before I could ask why he looked so worried, he spoke in a quiet, calm voice. "Bailey is fine, Coop. She's just fine. She's with Sam."

My heart rate began to speed up as I thought about Jan coming across them. She'd kill them.

"Did the police get Jan? She'll hurt Bailey because she didn't get to kill me. Please, Zane, you have to protect her. Jan is unhinged."

My voice was high-pitched as the panic set in, and Zane leaned up so he could look me in the eyes. "Coop, calm down. Breathe. Just breathe."

I tried to calm down, but the thought of Jan anywhere near Bailey made me want to leap from the bed and go to her.

Zane watched me struggling to calm down and spoke in a low, measured voice. "Cooper, Jan won't be going after Bailey because she killed herself. The second bullet hit her stomach, and by the time the EMTs arrived, she'd bled out."

She was gone. Jan was gone. I couldn't help the guilt that twisted my stomach. That was partly my fault. She was dead because I'd used her, and I needed to learn to live with the fact that I was too much of a coward to break it off with her sooner. I was partly to blame, but her dad and my dad were the most at fault. If they hadn't tried to bully me into marrying her. God, if my dad hadn't tried to convince me at eighteen that she was the right girl for me, then maybe none of this would have happened. My thoughts were all over the place, but knowing she wouldn't be going after Bailey relieved some of the tightness in my chest.

The rest of the day passed in a blur as the cops arrived to take my statement, and the nurses bustled in and out, checking my wound, changing my dressing, removing my catheter and telling me since I was more alert that I had to go to the bathroom or they'd have to put one back in. When a nurse is at your penis, taking a wire tube out, you listen to them when they tell you you need to take a leak.

The first time I stood, I was unsteady, but my arm was strapped across my chest and I used my IV stand to steady myself as I moved to the bathroom. The small trip exhausted me and I had to sit in there for what felt like hours as I readied myself to go back to bed.

Zane had gone home, but told me he'd come by later. I managed to get into bed, but the pain was too much and I took a push of my green button. They'd lowered the dosage earlier in the day and I hadn't needed to use it too much. Normal pain relief was okay, but I'd exerted myself getting to and from the bathroom.

The nurse, Lindy, came in and smiled at me as she took a look at my wound, assessed my dressing, and read the machines.

"Okay, Mr. Christie, everything looks good. I see you've pushed your button. Are you okay?" Her cool, professional tone made me sit up a little and I nodded.

"Yeah, I'm okay. I just went to the bathroom and I was a bit sore." My voice was groggy and cracked, and she smiled at me.

"And did you manage to pass urine okay?"

"Yeah. It was a little sore, but the nurse earlier told me it would be. There's a cup in there. She told me to pee into it so you can check it out."

Lindy smiled widely and went into the bathroom. She reappeared a few moments later and carried my sample from the room, closing the door softly behind her.

When the door opened again a few moments later, I was sitting with my eyes closed and I didn't open them. I assumed it would be a nurse, but when a gentle hand touched mine, my heart rate sped and I turned my head a little to see Bailey sitting there.

"I thought you were sleeping," she admonished me gently and reached up, moving a lock of hair from my eyes.

"And miss this?" I whispered, wondering if I was dreaming.

Her smile lit up her whole face and her eyes brightened as she looked at me. "That was the scariest thing I've ever gone through. I thought I'd lost you."

The pain in her words made me breathless, and I mumbled, "It was scary for me too. I didn't think I'd be here to see our baby born or—" I broke off because I couldn't tell her how scared I was that I'd lose her and never get to marry her.

"Cooper, this doesn't change anything between us though. I love you so much, but I can't…" Her broken expression and the anguish on her face made me speak up.

"Ssshh." I put my finger over her lips. "Seeing you and knowing you're safe is all that matters to me. I'm here and I'm yours whenever you want me, Bails, but I'm not asking you to choose me. I won't tear you in two. Not anymore."

She pressed her lips to my finger and then stood up and touched her lips to my head.

"Bails, can you stay? Just a little longer."

She met my eyes sadly and shook her head. "I can't. I'm sorry, Coop."

Her eyes filled with tears and one rolled down her cheek as she looked at me before she turned and left the room. As the door closed, I released the breath I was holding and tried to relax.

I wondered if she'd still go through with her wedding. I hoped she wouldn't, but I had to know. Zane had given me my cell earlier in the day, and I'd set it down on the bedside table. I reached over and scooped it up, using my right hand to do everything from opening it to typing the message to Bails.

BAILS, ARE YOU STILL GETTING MARRIED?

I PRESSED SEND BEFORE I LOST MY NERVE, AND WHEN THE vibration went off, I glanced down with my stomach rolling.

No. NOT RIGHT NOW. I POSTPONED IT. WE'RE GETTING married after the baby.

MY HEART WAS A LITTLE LIGHTER, AND I CLOSED MY EYES, letting the morphine carry me off to sleep.

I woke up the next day and was told the discharge plan. I was to be discharged the next day, if all was still okay. The bullet was a through and through, but it had damaged some nerves and torn a muscle, which was why I was in so much pain.

The morphine was stopped, but they would give me oral

morphine if the pain was too much, and I could still take regular pain medication. By the time Zane arrived, I was ready to go home, but he wouldn't hear of it.

"One more day, Coop. Then you can come home." He dismissed my plea for him to break me out early with a wave of his hand as he set down a sandwich, coffee, and a glazed donut in front of me.

"What do you mean *come home*?" I asked, and he shrugged nonchalantly.

"You're coming back to stay with Sam and me until we can get your place cleaned. It's still a crime scene, so I've only been allowed in once to get your stuff and I was escorted by a police officer the whole time."

I nodded, accepting his words, unable to say anything else as the physical therapist and occupational therapist came into the room with Leah, the nurse of the day. Leah was prettier than any of the other nurses with her dark brown hair, tanned skin, and bright blue eyes.

She laughed at me and called me a flirt when I pointed that out to her. She smiled at me while the physical therapist went through the exercises and set up an appointment for two weeks at a follow-up clinic. Phil, the OT, also gave me a few things to do and said he'd see me at the same clinic.

I was exhausted, crabby, and sore afterwards, but I still managed to smile at Leah whenever she came into the room. Later, when Zane had left, I tried to do some of the exercises, but it was too painful, so I stopped and tried to go to sleep.

My sleep was broken, and I was grouchy in the morning as I took my pain meds and was given my discharge paperwork. I had a follow-up appointment with the surgeons in a few weeks to check that they'd done a good job, but I didn't care because Bailey came into the room as Leah was giving me my instructions.

"Hey, I'm here to drive you home," she said with narrowed eyes as she saw Leah and me messing around. Her tone was light, but her face said it all, and I wondered what was wrong with her. She couldn't tell me she was marrying someone else and expect me to stay single for the rest of my life. That wasn't fair.

She didn't look at me as she took my bags to the car, and when she came back, she seemed to be in a better mood. She helped me to get into my hoodie and zip it up. Her hands lingered on my shoulders, and I stared at her lips with longing as she stood in front of me.

She stepped forward, almost but not quite meeting my lips, when a loud shout in the corridor broke the moment. She stepped back from me and led the way towards the elevator bank.

As we stood waiting on the elevator to arrive, she slipped her hand into mine, entwining our fingers together and holding on to my hand without a word. I let her go. I couldn't keep doing this with her. She had to stop fucking with my head, and her mixed signals were giving me whiplash.

"Coop, you okay?" she asked, and I turned to face her.

"I'm fine, Bails, but you gotta stop taking my hand and shit. It fucking hurts and it's not fair to keep on messing with my head and my heart."

Her face fell and I felt like such a shit, but it was too much. All this back and forth wasn't doing us any good, and it wasn't going to get any better anytime soon, so I had to end it.

"Sorry, Coop. I just wanted to support you…" she began, and I cut in because her tone caused a ripple of agony to shoot through my chest.

"I know, Bails, but you told me it was over, that you're

marrying someone else, so you gotta stop because it fucking kills me and I can't keep going over and over it."

The drive back to the farmhouse was silent after that, and it was an uneasy silence because I could feel nerves radiating from her. She gripped the steering wheel tightly and stared stiffly ahead. Her knuckles on the steering wheel were white as she held on to it.

Once we reached the farmhouse, she stopped the car and sat without moving for a moment. I needed her help with my seat belt, so I was stuck inside the car with her.

"Bailey?" I asked when the silence got too much, and she turned to look at me.

"Oh, shit. Sorry, Coop. My bad." She quickly unclicked the belt and then fed it back into the holder. Her top teeth chewed on her lip as she moved away from me. I was about to ask her what was wrong when the door opened behind me, and my unasked question was answered when I saw Pierre glowering at me.

Great. Just fucking great.

Her fiancé was there and he hated me. For a brief moment, guilt flashed in Bailey's eyes before she glanced away and opened her door, stepping out of the car and around to help me get out. Pierre's eyes stayed on us as she helped me to steady myself, and he glared at me when I stumbled a little and she wrapped her arm around my waist to keep me upright.

Once I was safely inside, she went out to get my belongings, and I heard them arguing all the way out to the car. I couldn't help overhearing. He was furious that she'd come to get me, but Sam had an urgent appointment that morning, Zane was working, and Pete was on vacation. Jack was out of town at some work conference and no way could they ask my dad or her mom, so it was down to her.

Bailey was angry too, and I heard her voice rise a few times.

Eventually, I had enough, and I stood up, ignoring the burning pains that shot through me as I marched slowly into the kitchen, pushing my way between Pierre and Bailey.

"Listen, I know you don't like me or don't trust me or whatever, but Bailey is pregnant with my kid and she came to get the father of her child from the hospital, so you wanna lay the fuck off her?"

He glared at me, mumbled something in French, and turned around, storming from the house.

"Cooper." Bailey sighed, putting her head in her hands and flopping down at the table.

"Sorry, Bails, but you need to take it easy. I know your relationship is none of my business, but he needs to back off. You don't need the stress right now. Remember, we have to do this together. You and me, okay?"

My words tumbled out in a rush, and she reached over and grabbed my hand. Her bright blue eyes sparkled and she gave my hand a gentle squeeze as she whispered, "Together."

The rest of the day was more peaceful. Pierre came back and apologized to Bailey and me, which surprised me. When Sam came home, she was all smiles and made a pot roast for dinner. Zane was working late, but made it home in time for dessert. He missed Bailey and Pierre who'd left after dinner.

The next few days passed with Sam and Zane looking after me and forcing me to do my exercises. Bailey didn't come by to see me and left for a trip to Paris a few days later. According to Zane, she'd be gone for four weeks while she interviewed for a management position in the gallery, and then she'd be back home. We'd spoken a few times, briefly, by message. When she got back, I was planning to have a serious chat with her about the baby and Pierre.

He hated me and made his disdain of me very clear, but somehow, we needed to find a way to work together or we'd never be able to co-parent. I just hoped she was agreeable to what I was going to suggest, because I wasn't about to let him push me from my child's life or stop me being a part of her pregnancy.

Chapter Twenty Six

IN THE WEEKS BAILEY WAS GONE, I SETTLED INTO MY routine, returning to work and going to my PT appointments. I'd also gone on a few dates with a girl I met in a coffee shop. Her name was Analyn, and she was pretty, sweet, and funny, and I was trying to be excited about her.

She had long brown hair, dark green eyes, and arched cheekbones, but something was missing. I couldn't help the distance I felt as Bailey's return date edged closer, and I was aware I had begun pushing her away.

I was finally let into my townhouse that week since the cleaners had been and all evidence had been collected. I returned to find flowers on my path and against my door. I couldn't believe people were laying flowers for Jan after she'd tried to kill me.

I shoved them all aside as I opened the door and stepped inside, breathing hard and texting Zane. I'd just clicked send on my message when a call popped up and I answered it. The call was from an unknown number with a New York area code.

"Hey, man." Luke's cheery voice echoed down the line.

"Hey, Luke. How you doin'?"

He laughed and I walked into my house with my heart in my throat as memories of the day I was shot played over in a loop in my head.

I went straight into the kitchen and sat down at the island while Luke spoke.

"I'm all right, man. I was calling to see if you're free and to apologize again for leaving you on your last night. I can't believe I didn't get up to see you off," he said, and I rolled my eyes. He'd already apologized a dozen times via messages and on the phone.

"Dude, again?" I asked him, cutting him off, and he laughed again, although something sounded a little off.

"Yeah, again! Coop, I was wondering if I could come visit this weekend. I need to get out of the city and get my shit together."

His words spilled out in a rush, and I knew he was worried I'd say no by the plea in his voice.

"Of course you can. I'm working 'til six on Friday—" My words were slow and cautious because I was worried. I wasn't drinking at all anymore. Not even light beers, but Luke was and I didn't want to get dragged off the wagon.

"There's a flight that gets me in at five, so six is perfect. I'll meet you at the office, yeah?"

"Sure, but, Luke?" I said in a cautious tone, and I could hear the rustle of something on the other end of the call.

"Yeah, dude."

"I'm not drinking anymore. Like at all. I'm off it, so if that's why you're coming here, then I can't help you." My words were sharp and I heard his sigh at the other end of the line as I glanced around my kitchen, distracted by the fact that my laundry room door was open.

"Nah. It's cool, man. I'm coming to get away from the cycle of my weekends, not to drag you out with me."

"Mr. Jones?" someone called in the background, and Luke swore under his breath.

"Coop, I gotta go, man. I'll book my flights and see ya

Friday."

He hung up without waiting on an answer, and I placed my cell down on the table, walking into the laundry room. My eyes darted around and I saw the note from Bails on the floor. I bent down to pick it up and heard a loud noise close by.

My fingers closed over the note, and I stood up, scooping it up and putting it in my shirt pocket, then wandered through the house, checking each room to see if the noise had originated in there. I left the living room until last because I honestly didn't want to face that room.

When I opened the door, a strong chlorinated smell hit me, and I almost closed the door. My hands were shaking and my legs were like Jell-O as I stepped into the room and glanced around. My heart rattled in my ears as my eyes darted around, taking in the pristine walls and the spotless couch and coffee table.

The room was empty, and I heard another loud bang, so I crossed the room and glanced outside. My heart began to race when I saw Jan's father standing outside. I quickly stepped back, but it was too late. He'd already seen me and he howled in rage, banging on the door again.

I didn't know what to do. I didn't want to open the door to him, but I also didn't want any more trouble. I moved around the living room as his bangs continued in earnest, and I froze at the door to the living room, staring hard at the sofa and remembering the agony of the bullet as it tore through my skin.

On shaking legs, I walked to the door, but the bangs stopped just as I reached it, and when I opened it, I saw Finn being folded into a cop car. The guy putting him inside was vaguely familiar to me, and he turned towards me after he closed the door.

As he got closer, I had an odd feeling of jealousy sweep up inside, and when he stood in front of me, it clicked who he was and why I had remembered feeling jealous.

"Mr. Christie, your neighbor called and reported a disturbance. We'll take him downtown if you're agreeable and let him sleep it off in a cell."

His dark eyes twinkled for a moment and then he turned away from me, heading down the path. As he reached the end, he turned back towards me and spoke in a carrying whisper, "She's making a mistake." His words were clear, and I nodded at him.

"I know," I answered with a sigh. Jay lifted his hand and waved before stepping into the car and driving away. I wondered if Bailey had kept in contact with him. I mean they'd been best friends, and I was sure it was his apartment we'd ended up in after my bachelor party, so I couldn't help wondering if he had heard from her.

I remembered being so jealous of him when we were in high school. I shrugged it off and went inside, closing the door and going upstairs to shower. I had to be careful in the shower, but my dressing was due to be replaced the next morning, so I only washed my right side and winced as the movements tugged on my arm.

Most of the skin had healed, but I'd ended up with a small infection and had antibiotics to take and a cream to apply to it when I changed the dressing in the morning. I quickly dried off and dressed in joggers and a t-shirt before going back downstairs and ordering a pizza.

The next few days flew by, and all too soon, it was Friday. I couldn't help my nerves at Luke coming, and I'd messed up a few times that day at work. Thankfully, Brie didn't mind the rumors and caught my mistakes before the emails were sent.

At six twenty, Luke arrived and was buzzed into my

office by Brie. Her fiery red hair, dry humor, and cheerful laugh had helped me get through the week. She was diligent in her work and only left when I did, unless I made her go, which I did frequently because she had three small kids at home and she was already working hard to help me catch up.

"Hey, man. You ready?" Luke asked as he stood in the doorway. His suit was crumpled and he had an overnight bag in his left hand. His dark curls were wet, and he brushed some water from his eyes as he stood dripping in the doorway.

"Yeah, let's go." I stood up and gathered my papers, putting them into the brief and put it onto Brie's desk with a sticky note attached.

For filing at the court - Monday a.m. Thanks. Enjoy your weekend. Coop.

I grabbed my coat and briefcase, checked my cell, and closed my desktop as Luke stood at the window and glanced out over the city.

"This is nice, man."

He turned to face me, and I saw the pain he was trying to ignore cross his features before he shook it off.

"Ready?" I asked him, and he smirked at me.

"Fucker, I was born ready! Are you ready?"

"Asshole, I'm always ready!" I answered. It was our college motto, and we asked each other about it before every exam, essay, and night out.

He smirked at me and we left my office, crossing to the parking lot. Once we were inside my truck, he blasted the heat and put the radio on. We drove along, singing to the music, and when we reached my house, he hopped down and stood on the street.

"Pretty nice digs, man. That trust fund must come in handy."

My laugh turned to a grimace when my shoulder jarred, but I shook it off and let us in. We both went to change, and I showed him to the downstairs guest room across from my office. I ran upstairs and ordered some takeout pizza and some Chinese food because I was starving and I wasn't sure what Luke would want to eat.

When I got back downstairs, he was in the living room, sitting on the sofa and flicking through the TV channels. Two cans of soda were on the table, and he'd opened some chips and dips.

"Sport or chicks?" he asked, and I smirked at him, sitting on the sofa for the first time since the shooting.

"Chicks," I answered, and he flicked to the movie channels and put on a dumb movie about strippers hunting monsters. Within minutes, we were laughing, and I began to relax.

"I ordered some food. Chinese and pizza."

"Whatever, man. I'll eat anything."

He turned his attention back to the movie and we saw the strippers do some pretty amazing things, like pull a pistol from inside their bras and shoot a dagger from behind their backs. Soon, we were laughing all over again and I completely forgot about the food.

The doorbell rang and I stood up to get it, but Luke passed me, laughing at something in the movie. He hadn't returned after a few minutes, and I called over my shoulder to him.

"Did you get lost?"

"He didn't get lost. He's in the kitchen." The voice caused a shiver to run through me and I turned to see Bails watching me. Her face was white and pinched, but I could see color rising in her cheeks.

"Sit, Bails." My words were inviting, but I cautiously

stared at her as she moved into the room. She perched on the armchair and I couldn't help my eyes roaming all over her.

"Coop," she answered, and I glanced up at her eyes, seeing pain there before she closed her eyes and sucked in a breath.

"What's going on?" I asked her and moved to the edge of my seat.

"I'm sorry. I shouldn't have come here." She stood up and I followed her, catching her hand as she moved by me.

"Talk to me, Bails. What is it?"

She tugged her hand away and I let it go, watching as she walked from the room. I wanted to let her go, but something seemed off, so I followed her.

She stood at the door indecisively for a moment and then turned and ran into my arms. Her arms closed around my back and I leaned down, tucking my face into her neck and breathing her in. Her hair tickled my mouth, so I wrapped my hand around it and just held her.

"Coop, I'm sorry. I messed up."

Her words were low and fearful, and I tried to move back to look at her, but she tightened her hold.

"You didn't marry him, did you?" I asked, dreading the answer.

"No. I didn't marry him. I told you, I'm not marrying him until after the baby, but I'm scared. Cooper, I'm so scared and so, so sorry." She broke down in tears and I just held her as she sobbed into my chest. I didn't know what was scaring her or what was affecting her so badly, but I would always offer my arms to comfort her.

"Ssshhh, it's okay, Bails. I got you." My hand stroked her back and she relaxed into me. The doorbell rang, and Luke passed from the kitchen and answered it as I led Bailey back into the living room.

I kept my arm around her and pulled her down to sit on my knee, marveling at the size of her stomach as she curled in to me.

"I'm so sorry. I shouldn't have—" She broke off and breathed deeply, and I couldn't think what she'd done that would be so bad that she'd appear at my door and break down.

"Bails, whatever it is, it's fine. It's okay. You're safe. You'll always be safe with me. Just tell me what it is..." I broke off as so many possibilities threatened to overwhelm me, and my fear worsened with her next words.

She sniffed louder and twisted her face into my neck. "You'll hate me."

Hate her? How could I hate her? She was carrying my child. I wanted to calm her down and get her to tell me. My heart thudded painfully in my chest, reminding me that she wasn't really mine anymore, but it didn't matter. I had to somehow help her to open up to me.

Her apprehension scared me and I squeezed her tightly. "Bails," I whispered into her hair, pressing my lips to her head and speaking against the skin. "I could never hate you. I am so in love with you. You own me, body and soul, so whatever it is, it'll be okay, but you have to tell me what it is. You're scaring me."

Her body trembled and a sob broke free. I just sat and shushed her, consoling her as she cried.

"I don't deserve your hugs or your love."

"Why don't you let me decide what you do or don't deserve?"

"It's my fault. All of it. It's my fault."

Her words took me back to another place, another time, and I remembered how much I'd hurt her when I blamed her for my dad's assault.

"It's my fault you were shot and I-I'm so sorry, Coop. I'm so, so sorry."

My body froze, going hot and then cold, but I tried not to let her see the impact her words had on me.

"What?" I asked. "How?"

She shuddered against me and pressed her lips to my neck. Her tears ran onto my bare skin and down my neck as she breathed deeply before speaking again.

"I met Jan that day. It was after the ultrasound and I was… I was at the grocery store. I turned around and there she was. Her eyes were narrowed at me, but when she saw my baby bump, she came rushing towards me. She screamed at me and I just laughed at her. When she asked me if you're the father, I smirked at her and told her that you absolutely are and we're so excited about having a baby together."

Her words echoed in my head and the room began to spin as the pieces all fit together. Why she'd come to the office, and why she'd come by the next day. She was dead, and all because she was jealous.

"It's not your fault, Bails," I whispered, trying to reassure her. In part, it *was* her fault, but Jan was certain to find out anyway, and it wasn't like Bailey had given her the gun or told her what to do.

"Yes." She sighed, and another tear hit my neck. "Yes, it is."

"No. Listen to me," I said as she opened her mouth to protest. "You didn't give her the gun. If it's anyone's fault, it's mine. I led her on. I promised to be faithful to her and then I slept with you. Those things are all on me." She shook her head and I leaned back a little to look at her. "Bails, look at me."

She shook her head and hid her face behind her hair. I

reached up and brushed her hair from her face, lifting her chin to meet her tear-filled eyes.

"It's not on you. She made her decision."

"But—" she cut in, and I leaned over and pressed my lips to hers to silence her. Her mouth moved against mine for a moment and then she pushed herself out of my arms, breathing hard.

"No, Coop. I can't do this anymore with you. I just thought you should know about what I did. It's been eating me alive and I can't cope with the guilt anymore."

Her flushed, tear-stained cheeks and her chest rising and falling told me I'd affected her, but her hands were outstretched towards me and she moved back a little.

"Bails," I said as she backed away a little more. "I love you, okay. I'm not going to force anything on you. I respect your decision, but just know you will always be safe with me, okay?"

Her eyes widened in surprise and a tear spilled down her cheek as she stared at me. "No, it's not that." She took a deep breath. "It's hard for me to say no to you. I love you too, Cooper."

Her words made me smile, but before I could respond, Luke opened the door and peeked his head in. "Hey, guys. You want something to eat?"

He met my eyes and nodded at Bails. I gave him a simple nod, answering his unasked question, and he smiled at me, giving me a thumbs-up from behind her back. She turned and he stepped aside, letting her lead us into the kitchen where he'd opened the pizza boxes and set the Chinese food on the island.

He sat on one side of the island and Bails and I sat on the other with our legs touching. My fingers brushed hers, and after it happened a few times, she entwined her fingers with mine. I gave her hand a gentle squeeze, but then removed my hand from hers on the pretense of getting a drink of my soda.

Luke raised his eyes at us, but said nothing, and we sat chatting. Bailey asked Luke questions about himself and he answered her with wit and charm, but I wasn't worried. I knew he loved Hailey, so it didn't bother me at all.

"So, this girl, has she seen you? Luke, you're freaking gorgeous," Bailey mused, and Luke chuckled at my obvious discomfort. I gripped onto my soda tightly and took a sip, trying to hide the fact my hand was shaking in annoyance.

"Yeah, she's seen me and she's gorgeous too, but there are obstacles in the way and I can't reach her."

"Just keep faith. If you love her as much as you say you do, she'll find her way back to you."

I glanced sideways at her and she caught my eye before giving me a soft smile and turning away. If only it was that simple. I toyed around with the food on my plate as they continued to talk, but I tuned them out because her words had opened up the wounds I was desperately trying to heal.

After our food was finished and the conversation stopped, I could sense Bails getting distant. She pushed her chair back and stood, brushing her dress down. I wished I had the power or the words to make her stay, but I knew her well enough to know she wanted to leave.

"Coop, I have to go." Her eyes met mine and I only nodded as she turned to Luke. "Luke, it was great to meet you. I hope to see you again and I hope everything works out with the girl you love."

His mouth popped open and I gazed at her in awe as she turned and left the room. She looked back as the door was closing. Our eyes didn't leave each other until there was nothing to see.

Chapter Twenty Seven

CO-PLAN TO CO-PARENT

LUKE SAT BACK AND STARED AT ME IN COMPLETE SILENCE FOR a few minutes and then he sighed.

"So, that's Bailey? Your stepsister?"

I nodded at him, still staring after her. I wanted to go after her and talk to her, but I couldn't face upsetting her. I desperately wanted to talk with her about how we would parent apart. She hadn't come by for that, but I needed to tell her how I was feeling. I didn't want to parent apart. I wanted us together and bringing up our baby.

"Go after her," Luke said, and I glanced around to see him smirking at me. "You clearly want to, so go after her and talk to her about whatever it is that's turned your smile into a grimace. But go easy on her. She looks exhausted."

I rushed to the front door and saw Bails standing next to my truck, looking down the street.

"You need a ride, Bails?" I asked her, and she turned to look at me. She shook her head and then nodded.

"Yeah, Coop. I could use a ride back to the farmhouse."

I glanced down and lifted my hand to bring her back inside. She came towards me slowly and touched my arm with her freezing cold hand.

"Bails, you're freezing," I said, and she laughed. "I need to put some shoes on, and I'll take you where you need to go, unless you want to stay."

Her eyes met mine and I could see fire, but she shook her head and leaned up, kissing my cheek and whispering against it. "No, Cooper. I can't stay, but I will take a ride from you."

My blood heated and I felt a stirring in my pants when she stepped back and stared longingly up at me.

She was gonna be the death of me. She knew exactly what she was doing to me. Her eyes dropped to my joggers and then she looked back up at me with a raised eyebrow.

I shook my head at her and turned, running up the stairs to get my hoodie and put some shoes on. I made my way to the stairs as I pulled my hoodie on and froze when I heard voices.

"You don't know what you're talking about," Bailey said, and I moved to the top of the staircase.

"I do. I know how much he loves you and how much he's hurting. You should give him a chance."

"I can't. I wish I could, but I can't."

I cleared my throat and began walking down the stairs, grateful to Luke for trying, but needed to stop the conversation before I heard all the reasons that she couldn't give me a chance. Luke walked into the living room and closed the door as I moved to stand in front of Bailey.

"Be honest, Coop," she began as she shifted from foot to foot. "How much did you hear?"

"I… well… all of it, I think."

My voice was low and she shook her head, turning from me and leading the way to my truck. I grabbed my keys and followed her, closing the door behind me.

I clicked the lock open and she climbed up slowly. I watched her ass jiggle and bounce as she entered the cab, and I walked around to climb in beside her.

We didn't speak as I started the engine, and when the silence got too much, I twisted the dial on the radio, switching it on. One of my favorite songs played, and I began singing along softly. Bailey sat stiffly at my side and didn't look at me.

Once we got closer to the farmhouse, she began to relax a little and her shoulders softened.

"Bails," I spoke over the radio, and she turned to face me. "Are you okay?"

"Yeah." She nodded. "Yeah, I'm fine."

I went silent again and she turned back to the window. My pulse was racing as I considered how to broach the subject of Pierre, but she brought him up first.

"Coop, can you like… uh… not come inside?"

I glanced over at her and then back to the road.

"Pierre will be so angry." Her voice was low, and I could hear the fear in her words.

"Bails, we need to talk about that," I said, and she sighed, running her fingers through her hair and curling her arm around her waist.

"Yeah, I know."

There was a passing spot ahead, so I signaled and pulled in, turning in the driver seat to face her.

"Can I—"

"Can you—"

We began speaking at the same time and I nodded to her to go ahead.

"Can you not come on Wednesday to the appointment?" Her words hit me in my chest, and she chewed on her lip.

"Why? I'm confused."

I watched her mull over my words and saw her straighten her shoulders. "Because I'm asking you not to. Is that not enough?"

Her words were icy, and I almost reconsidered my next words, but I had to get it out. "No. I will be there on

Wednesday because you are carrying my child, and if Pierre doesn't like it, then that's too damn bad."

She opened her mouth and gave a squeak of protest, but I held my hands up, stopping her. My eyes burned into hers and I spoke in a calm and measured voice.

"I've already told you I won't beg you to be with me, or get in your way of having a future, but we have to find a way to work together. This fear you have of being seen with me is not okay. You are carrying my child and I always feel that I have to walk on eggshells around your fiancé. I'm over it. I want us to find a way to work together because I'm going nowhere. I will be involved in my child's life…"

I hadn't realized my voice had risen to a yell until Bails reached over and put her hand on my chest.

"Coop. You will be involved, but it's hard for Pierre to accept. Can you understand that?"

She spoke to me in earnest and I wrapped my hand around my waist to stop myself reaching for her hand like my heart was telling me to.

"Bails, it isn't about him, or about you or me. It's about our baby, and I can't deal with any more of his disdain."

She nodded slowly at me and leaned over, resting her head on my shoulder. "Why is it always so complicated with us, Coop?"

Her voice was low and I turned my head, pressing a soft kiss to her scalp. "I don't know, sweetheart, but I wish things were easier."

After a moment of silence, her cell began to ring and her eyes widened when she saw Pierre's name. She ended the call and sat upright.

"Take me home, please, Cooper?" she asked, and I started the engine again.

We drove the rest of the way in terse silence, but when we

arrived, she turned to face me and reached over, squeezing my hand.

"I'll talk to him, Coop. Wednesday will be fine. Don't worry."

She opened the door and took off towards the house. The rain somehow got even heavier on the way back, and the car slipped and slid on the road. I made it back in one piece and ran into the house, finding Luke on the couch engrossed in a movie.

"It's just started, dude."

I collapsed beside him and tried to watch the movie, but exhaustion overwhelmed me and I drifted off to sleep, dreaming of Bailey and our baby and the family we should be, instead of the fucked-up mess we were.

The next few days passed quickly with Luke, and we spent our time going for food, and to the movies, and shopping. We didn't go out to bars and I constantly checked my cell, but I hadn't heard from Bails in days.

Work that week kept me distracted, and so did the two dates I'd gone out on, but my heart wasn't really in it and I knew I wasn't really being fair to her, so after our date Tuesday night, I ended it with her. She took it well and told me that if I got over my ex, I should call her. I went home and collapsed onto my bed fully dressed and fell asleep almost instantly.

The next morning, I got up, showered, and got dressed in a sharp suit, because I had a ten a.m. meeting that I couldn't miss. I'd told the office I had a PT appointment in the morning, so they knew I'd be going straight to my meeting.

I left the house and parked at the office before crossing town and picking up a cup of coffee and a croissant in a coffee shop near the hospital. Once inside the hospital, I went straight to Bailey's OB-GYN office to wait, and arrived ten minutes before her and Pierre.

Her posture was tense and she continuously looked around. Pierre smiled smugly as he approached the waiting area, but his smile slipped when he saw me waiting on them, sipping on my coffee.

He turned to her and whispered something in French, and she shrugged as she approached me.

"Coop, what are you doing here?"

Her terse tone caused my temper to rise and I sat up and glared between them. "I told you I'd be here, Bails."

She sighed and left to go speak to the receptionist, leaving me with Pierre. He glared at me and I sat back nonchalantly.

"You are not welcome here, Cooper," he spat at me.

"That is my child she's carrying, so your feelings about me being here are irrelevant. I will be there every step of this journey, and you damn well better find a way to deal with that and stop putting stress on to her."

His glare darkened and Bailey came over and sat down beside me, almost subconsciously. Within seconds, her name was called. Pierre and I both stood up, walking with her towards the doctor when she held her hands up.

"Sorry, only the father is allowed into the appointment."

Pierre hissed under his breath and I smirked at the ground, trying to control my expression as the doctor led Bailey and me into the examination room.

We went through the same things as before, but the doctor frowned when she checked Bailey's blood pressure. She asked Bailey questions and Bailey answered in a low voice that grew more and more tense.

"Bailey," the doctor began, and she glanced between us. "Your blood pressure is still high, and with the headaches you've mentioned and the fact that there is protein in your urine, I'm afraid I suspect you have a pregnancy condition called pregnancy-induced hypertension or, as it's more commonly known, preeclampsia."

"Wait. I'm sorry, can you explain?" I asked as Bailey sat looking thunderstruck. I reached over and took her hand, giving it a gentle squeeze as the doctor began speaking.

"It's a condition that can occur in pregnancy, usually after the twentieth week of pregnancy. It can cause a breakdown of the red blood cells and liver problems, and is usually identified by protein in the urine, swellings of the hands and feet, and high blood pressure. In most cases, it's manageable, but it can result in babies being delivered early and it can also have dangerous consequences for both mom and baby, so it needs careful monitoring."

Bailey turned to me with wide, fearful eyes and I wrapped my free hand around her, giving her a hug as the doctor's words sank in.

"Is there anything I could have done to prevent this?" Bailey asked in a small voice, and her doctor glanced at us.

"No. It's common in around two to eight percent of pregnancies worldwide, and most often occurs in first pregnancies. It can be a very serious condition and you will need to be monitored for the rest of your pregnancy, but I expect we'll need to deliver this little one a tad early."

Bailey nodded and I pressed a brief kiss to her forehead before I dropped my arms and sat back, but when I tried to let go of her hand, she squeezed it so tightly I was worried the blood supply would cut off.

The doctor leaned forward and placed her hand on Bailey's knee, ignoring me entirely as she focused on Bailey, who was almost hyperventilating.

"Bailey, I know this can be scary, and I understand how upsetting this news can be, but with careful monitoring of your symptoms and medication, you should be able to deliver your baby safely and as close to your due date as possible. We'll take care of you both, but you should prepare to be induced in four to five weeks. We may need to deliver a little earlier than that, but we can deal with that only if we have to."

Bailey nodded and the doctor sat back and looked at me for a second before she turned back to Bailey.

"Do you have any more questions?" Her tone was brisk, and when Bailey and I both shook our heads, she nodded towards the examination table. "Okay then. If you'll pop up on the table, I'll have a listen in to baby to make sure that they're coping okay in there

Bailey shrugged her fingers from my grasp and sat up on the table. Within moments, the steady sound of our baby's heartbeat filled the room and Bailey gave me a small smile and met my eye. I was still shocked at what the doctor had said, but Bailey looked a little numb. Her eyes were fearful and her fingers shook in mine as we listened to our baby's heartbeat on the monitor. Once the doctor was satisfied with the baby's heart rate, she led us back to the seats.

"Okay, I'm going to write you a prescription for aspirin, Bailey, and you need to take it every day. If you begin to feel lightheaded, dizzy, or have any form of vision changes then you are to call me and report to the hospital immediately. Here is a leaflet on preeclampsia, and there is an address on there that gives information about the condition."

Bailey sat stiffly, staring at her prescription, and then shuffled to her feet as the doctor stood and clasped her arm.

"I'll be with you every step of the way and I will do my best to deliver your baby safely. You have my number and you can call me anytime."

Bailey nodded and began to walk towards the door

without looking back. As I stood to follow Bailey, I stopped and asked the doctor for a private word. Bailey gave me a worried glance, but left the room, letting the door close after her with a snap.

"How can I help you, Mr...?" the doctor asked, and pointed to a seat as she sat down at her desk to face me.

"Christie. My name is Cooper Christie," I answered before continuing. "Is there anything I can do to help Bailey, so this doesn't hurt her or my baby?"

"Okay, Mr. Christie. I can only tell you steps to alleviate the stress. The rest is up to you." She paused as she scrolled through notes on her computer and then glanced up to meet my worried gaze as I sat down across from her. "Generally, we cannot discuss confidential patient information with anyone other than the patient, but since you were already in the appointment and privy to the information, then I can discuss this with you. I see here on Bailey's notes that she has already stated that we can discuss things with you."

Wow, she had. I didn't know that and it made my heart sing a little because maybe she hadn't written us off completely after all. Before I could dwell too much on it, the doctor spoke again and I leaned forward to listen.

"Bailey and her stress levels need attending to." She paused and gave me a stern glance before continuing, and my heart raced at the thought of hurting Bails more. "I know what your family dynamic is, but my patient is my priority. The more stress she's under, the more likely it is that your child will need to be delivered early, and the more likely it will be that Bailey's life is put in danger. Pregnancy-induced hypertension can cause a stroke or heart attack, so Bailey needs to rest and eliminate as much stress from her life as is possible. That means that you and the other guy need to work out whatever it is between you before it negatively impacts on her. As the father of her baby, you need to make sure that she's free from stress and drama from now on. That is how you can help. Now, I have another patient to see, but I hope you'll take this on board, Mr. Christie, for Bailey's sake and the sake of your unborn baby."

I nodded at her and mumbled my thanks before I stood up. The doctor stood with me, walking me to the door. As soon as I was outside, she closed the door and I stopped for a moment to catch my breath. Pierre and I were putting her blood pressure up and we needed to stop it or Bailey and my baby was going to be in danger.

I walked slowly towards the waiting room, intending to ask Pierre to meet with me, but they were gone. They hadn't even waited on me to get out from the doctor, and I walked towards the elevators. My finger jabbed at the button and I stormed inside, closing the door and descending.

I went to sleep night after night with my cell right beside me in case something happened, and a few days after our meeting, my cell went off in the middle of the night and I answered the call to hear Zane in a complete panic, telling me to get to the hospital because something was wrong with Bailey. He didn't say what. He just told me to get there as soon as possible.

Chapter Twenty Eight

BIRTHING TROUBLE

I RACED TO THE ER, KNOWING BAILEY WAS THERE. I WAS IN such a rush that I broke the law in so many ways. Once there, I abandoned the car and sprinted through the doors, knowing she was only thirty-three weeks pregnant and it was too soon for our baby to arrive.

I thought back as I ran through to the maternity emergency room Zane had directed me to, to how hard it was when she told me she didn't want to be with me. The last few months had been hell on earth for me, and now this.

Zane was pacing around, and he stopped when he saw me running towards him. He gently touched my arm and I stared at him as he broke me from my thoughts.

"She's in there. They won't let me in, but just so you know, he's with her."

I bobbed my head once to show I'd heard and rushed towards the doors.

A nurse stopped me. "Excuse me. Where are you going?"

Her words made me pause and she stepped in front of me. "Bailey. Bailey Walker is in there and I need in to see her."

"And you are?"

"I'm the baby's father!" I almost shouted at her, my voice rising in panic.

"Wait one moment, please," she said in a patient yet firm tone.

She wandered over to a desk I hadn't noticed and made a call, nodding, then frowning as she listened. She moved slowly back towards me and spoke in soothing tones. "I'm sorry, but the baby's father is already in the room."

My fury at hearing this almost made me explode, and I clenched my fists to stop myself punching the wall.

"He's not the baby's father. I am. I. Need. To. See. Bailey."

Zane came over and put his hand on my shoulder. I think he was trying to calm me, but I was bouncing around like a caged animal.

"What's the problem?" he asked.

"That douche is saying he's the baby's father and they won't let me in!"

The nurse stood uncomfortably as I bounced from foot to foot. Pierre chose that moment to walk out, and within seconds, I had him pinned to the wall.

"Oh my goodness!" the nurse exclaimed as I tried to control my temper.

"You are not the father!" I hissed in his face, and he smirked at me.

"Ah, yes, but I am with the mother, and I will be the father!"

I saw red and brought my fist up, but Zane stopped me just as security appeared. The nurse, who had been standing there for the entire exchange, looked between us and shook her head at security.

"Sir, let him go, please, and I'll go through and try to sort this out!"

I dropped my hands and stepped away from him, hating him even more in that moment than ever before.

I watched the nurse walk through the doors as he spoke again.

"Bailey does not want you in there. You shouldn't even be here!"

I spun around but managed to control my temper. I ignored him as I waited for the nurse to come back through.

She appeared a few minutes later and nodded once at me. "You may go in, but no stressing Ms. Walker, and no fighting. She's in room four and it's on the right of the corridor."

I nodded blindly at her as I flew through the doors. Pierre tried to follow, but the nurse stopped him.

"Ms. Walker has asked to speak to him privately." Her firm tone made him stop, and security watched as I bolted through the doors.

The doors closed and I flew down the corridor and found room four. My insides danced a tango as I stood outside the door, and I took a breath, trying to calm my racing pulse as I knocked.

"Come in," a voice called from the other side, and I slowly cracked the door open to see Bailey on the bed with wires in her arm and a wire around her stomach.

"Cooper," she breathed with a smile. I walked slowly towards her. My steps were slow, even though I was desperate to hold her. I just stood at her side when I reached her.

"This is the baby's father," she told the OB-GYN who was in the room, and he nodded once at me before checking something on his watch and nodding to himself. He walked over to a cabinet and was setting something up, but he didn't hold my attention for long. I turned my focus back to Bailey. She was flushed, and her blonde hair was piled on her head, but she'd never looked more beautiful to me.

"What's going on?" I asked her as I glanced around the room.

"I'm in early labor, but it's complicated."

"Your blood pressure?" I asked, and she nodded at me.

Her eyes met mine and I could see the fear in them. I didn't think, I just reached down and pulled her into my arms, breathing her in.

"I'm sorry, Cooper. I should have called you," she whispered against my shoulder, and I held her a little tighter.

"It's okay. I'm here now. I love you, Bails. I know you're with him and that's okay, but I'm here and I'm staying here until our baby arrives."

She seemed to relax in my arms and then a series of beeping noises began. The doctor came over, calling Bailey's name. Another person rushed in and pulled me away from her as they dropped the bed flat. I was numb, frozen, as I watched them quickly unhook things and toss them onto the bed. Within moments, I was alone as they'd rushed her from the room.

I stayed in the room because I didn't know where else to go, and after an hour and a half, the OB-GYN came back to the room.

"Sir, would you like to come with me?" Her words were formal, and my heart dropped right out of my chest at the look in her eyes.

We walked through the hospital and entered another building. She didn't speak to me the whole time, just led me to a room with sofas. She pointed to a bright purple sofa and sat down in a chair opposite.

"Hi," she said with a smile. "I'm Doctor Mackenzie. I've been looking after Ms. Walker since she got here earlier this evening." She paused and looked at me expectantly.

"I'm Cooper Christie, the baby's father. Is Bailey okay? Is my baby okay?" My words rushed out of me in a panic.

She leaned back and clasped her hands on her lap in front of her. "Bailey suffered a massive internal bleed and is now in a medically induced coma in our intensive care department. I'm sorry to report that her chances of survival are slim, but we are doing everything we can, and the next forty-eight hours are critical."

Bailey was in a coma and might not make it. I felt as though the bottom was falling out of my world.

"But your baby is a healthy little boy who's in the neonatal unit. He's coping remarkably well and is a healthy four pounds in weight. He's on a machine to help his breathing. I can take you to see him if you like."

I nodded at her as the words "baby boy" floated around my head and warred with the fact that Bailey was in a coma.

We walked through a few corridors and reached a brightly lit passageway with murals on the wall. It was calming, and the colors were all muted tones. The doctor led me into a bay where there were a number of incubators.

Each one had a person beside it, with the exception of one at the end. The doctor went to the sink and washed her hands.

"Can you wash your hands, please, Mr. Christie?" she asked in a calm voice as I stood numbly, watching everything that was going on.

I moved to the sink and thoroughly scrubbed my hands, drying them with a paper towel.

She handed me an apron, and I put it on before she led me to the incubator.

My whole body shook as I took in this tiny little boy. His face was covered in part by a hat and a machine that covered his nose.

I stood staring at him for the longest moment, and the person looking after him turned to me and said something, but I didn't hear. I was too busy staring at my son.

"Sorry, can you repeat that?" I asked.

"Would you like to hold him?" she repeated with a kind

smile, and I looked at her and then at him. There were so many wires and machines attached to him that the thought of holding him made me nervous, but I couldn't say no, so I nodded slowly.

"Could you sit there?"

The nurse pointed to a seat and I sat down slowly, watching in fascination as she removed the tubing and then reattached it before picking up the baby and holding him to her chest.

She cradled him carefully and then passed him to me, speaking softly to him as she did. "This is your daddy, Baby Walker."

As soon as he was in my arms, he opened his eyes and yawned before settling back to sleep. I held him tightly and sat thinking about Bailey as the nurse washed her hands and wrote something down. She came over and asked me some questions, taking my name, cell phone number, and other contact details. Then she left me with my son. After a while, she came over and checked on the baby.

When she was done, she wrote more things down and looked at me.

"I know it's daunting in here, but you can rest assured we will take good care of this little one."

I glanced down, and for a moment, I could see Bailey's face so clearly in him that I baulked.

"You can speak to him if you like. Does he have a name yet?"

I liked the name Wyatt, and so did Bailey. We'd talked names just a few days ago, and it was a name we both agreed on.

"I think his name will be Wyatt, but I'm waiting for Bailey to give it the okay."

The nurse nodded sadly at me and went away for a moment.

The next hour passed in a blur as I sat speaking to our baby about the weather, and his mommy. When the nurse came back over to do the check, she asked if she could pop him back into the incubator, and I nodded, leaning down and pressing my lips softly to his forehead.

She gently lifted him and placed him back into the incubator, closing the door thing and turned towards me.

"Hold on, Mr. Christie. Here is the contact number for the unit for you and some details about the care your baby will receive while here. You can call at any time, and if you have any questions, then don't hesitate to ask them."

She handed me a few leaflets and gave me a sympathetic smile.

"Can you tell me where Bailey is? Am I allowed to visit her?"

Her eyes widened. "Let me just check and I'll let you know." She walked away and made a call from the desk before coming back to me with a piece of paper.

On the piece of paper were directions to the intensive care unit and a number to call to get entry.

"Can I come back over later?" I asked her, and she smiled at me.

"You can come back at any time."

With that, she turned from me and started attending to my boy. I left the unit and walked through the hospital on autopilot. I didn't think about Zane or Pierre. My only thought was Bailey, and once in the ICU, I was shown to Bailey's room.

She was hooked up to a machine to help her breathe, and there were infusions going into her arms. She looked so pale, but so peaceful, and I was scared to touch her in case I disturbed anything.

"You go right ahead and hold her hand if you want," the nurse told me, and I took Bailey's hand in mine, noticing how cool it was. I wrapped both my hands around it and prayed to God, even though I didn't believe, that she'd be okay.

"You can speak to her, you know?"

I sat back and looked at her, thinking about what to say.

"Bailey. Bails, please come back to me. I'm begging you. I need you. Our son needs you. Please don't leave me. I can't do this alone."

My eyes burned and I closed my eyes, letting my tears fall.

"Bailey," I croaked. "We have a son, and he's so beautiful, but I need you to come back. He needs his mommy. He needs you! I saw him and I held him and I... I just don't want you to miss out on that, so please, I'm doing what I should have done five months ago and I'm begging you, please, please come back to me and to him. I can't let you go. I can't live without you. I don't want to, not ever again. Please, please come back to me. Come back to us."

I put my head down on the bed and just sat silently holding her hand for a while without speaking.

After a while, the nurse came over and asked if I needed anything.

I said no, and she asked if I could leave for a while as they were going to be doing some stuff to Bailey, but if I wanted, she'd come and get me afterwards. I followed her from the room and checked my cell for the first time in hours. Zane had called twenty-seven times. I dialed his number and walked back through the hospital, trying to find him, but losing signal as I walked.

Chapter Twenty Nine
MIRACLES AND MIRACLE WORKERS

I FOUND MY WAY BACK TO ZANE AND RUSHED INTO HIS ARMS. He held me as I broke down and told him about Bailey and our baby, and how scared I was. He let me talk without interruption until I was finished.

Once I'd told him everything, he stared evenly at me. "Pierre was furious he wasn't allowed back through. He stormed out about an hour after you went in and he hasn't come back."

Zane led me to the cafeteria and we sat drinking coffee as he filled me in.

"He's very possessive of Bails and I don't like it. He tries to control where she goes and who she sees, and when he finds out she's been to see you, it's constant arguments."

I grimaced at him, having surmised as much from our interactions.

"I want to go back to the neonatal unit and see Wyatt. Would you like to come with me?"

Zane smiled and we stood, dumping our cups into the trash. As we walked through the corridor, following the signs, I hoped it would be okay for me to bring my brother in with me.

When we got to the room where the baby was, I went over and spoke to the nurse and she smiled and nodded at Zane. We both washed our hands and stood at each side of the incubator. Zane asked the nurse questions and I just stood staring at my son.

"He's doing very well. I expect we'll be able to have him breathing on his own soon."

The doctor came over and they spoke about pressures and how Baby Walker was coping. I wanted to correct them. His name was Christie, not Walker, but I needed to wait.

Shortly after we arrived, Bailey's mom arrived with Pierre. My eyes narrowed as she walked purposefully towards my son.

"I'm the baby's grandma. Could I get an update now?" she asked the nurse rudely, and I glared at her. The nurse turned to me and I shook my head.

"No. I'm sorry. Only parents are allowed to be updated."

She glared at me. Her next words were low and her tone threatening. "Cooper, I am Bailey's next of kin, and I will fight for custody of my grandson."

Zane stepped between us and glowered at her. "Henri, I really don't think now is the time. Bailey isn't fucking dead, and you're acting like she is. Now, can you please leave and let Cooper bond with his son?"

The nurse stepped in and asked everyone but me to leave, and I leaned against the incubator, staring down at my boy. I would fight for him. I would fight them all. No way was Henri, my dad, Pierre, or anyone else going to separate me from my baby.

The doctor came over and introduced himself as Mr. Lennon. Two other ladies followed him in and he introduced them as one from child protection services and the head nurse of the unit. Neither of them spoke the whole time, just observed, which was a little unsettling.

"Hi, I'm the doctor in charge of your baby boy's care. Could you follow me, please?"

I nodded and followed them to a room, much like the one the other doctor had taken me to earlier.

"Sit down." His tone was firm and brokered no argument, so I sat down tensely at the edge of the seat, taking in the calming gray swirls decorating the walls and the pale green sofas.

"I need to talk to you about your baby and the drama that happened in my unit this afternoon. I'm afraid we will need a DNA sample from you and the baby if you are agreeable, because only then can we ensure that you are the baby's father. Angela here has already approved it, and we can go ahead once we have your consent. The lady who came by has made a claim that you are making it all up, and I'm afraid we need to check."

"Fine," I said, taken aback by his professional tone and his directness. "Take a test. I am his father and I'm going nowhere. She's not getting my child. Bailey would never want her to have him and I refuse to let it happen."

He nodded at me and asked if he could take a blood sample from me and I agreed. He informed me he would be collecting a sample from the baby and that this would be sent off to be tested along with mine. Within a few moments, my sample was collected, and he bustled off to collect the baby's sample.

Once they were sent, he informed me that they would have the results within a few hours and would call me with them if I wanted them to.

"Yeah, please. That would be great."

He led me out of the unit and told me I could come back when the results showed I was Baby Walker's father.

My feet carried me almost without conscious thought to the intensive care unit, and the nurse from earlier let me into Bailey's room.

"You can only stay a few minutes, I'm afraid. Bailey's mom is her next of kin and she was quite insistent that you aren't allowed in. However, you are on her notes from her OB-GYN as the baby's father, so I'll give you a few minutes."

I smiled at her, touched by her kindness, and sat down by Bailey's bedside. She bustled away to get some things and left me alone with Bails. I waited a moment and then picked up her hand, careful to avoid the cannula in her hand, and pressed my lips softly to the skin on her wrist.

"Bails, you gotta come back. Please. Your mom is trying to get Wyatt and I need you. She won't let me see you. Please, if you can hear me, come back to me. Come back to us. I know I asked you this earlier, but you are so loved, and you are so needed." I took a fortifying breath as my tears rolled onto her wrist. "Please, Bails. Fight this. You are the strongest person I know and I need you to use that strength to come back."

I pressed another kiss to her wrist and went to stand when her hand squeezed mine. Her eyes were wide and she began to panic.

"Bails, it's okay. You're okay."

The nurse came into the room and calmly walked over, moving me out of the way as she took in Bailey.

"Wait in the corridor, please, sir." She was so calm that I let go of Bailey's hand and stepped out into the corridor, leaning on the wall. A few more people rushed by me and went into the room, and after a few minutes, the nurse came out and tapped me on my shoulder.

"You can go in, but briefly. She needs her rest and she's a little groggy, but she's asked for you."

My legs were like Jell-O as I walked unsteadily into the

room towards Bailey. Her eyes followed me and a ghost of a smile crossed her lips.

"Hey," she said hoarsely, wincing as she spoke.

"Hey," I breathed, smiling widely at her before I leaned over and pressed my lips to her forehead. "You came back," I breathed into her hair, breathing a sigh of relief that her mom didn't have control over us or over her.

"I heard you. You asked me to." Her voice cracked as she spoke.

"I did, Bails. I need you. Wyatt needs you."

"It's a boy?" she asked, and I grinned down at her, pressing my lips to hers gently before pulling back a little

"Yes, he's a boy and he's perfect, Bails. Just like you."

She smiled at me and the nurse caught my eye, nodding towards the door. Her meaning was clear. My time was up.

"Look, I have to go, but why don't I go back over to see Wyatt and I'll take some photos to show you."

She reached out and linked her fingers through mine, but her hand dropped and I stepped forwards, placing it onto the bed.

"Yes," she breathed. "I'd like that."

"Okay. I'll be back. Love you, Bails." I didn't take my eyes off her, and I saw her mouth the words back to me as I reached the corridor where I slid down the wall and put my head in my hands. I didn't move for a bit, and then I leaned back and took out my cell, seeing a message from Zane.

HEY, THE NURSE CLEARED ME OUT AND I HAD TO GO HOME to check on Sam and the kids. Give Bails a kiss from us and let me know when I can come back to visit. Call you later.

. . .

I QUICKLY TYPED OUT A RESPONSE TO HIS MESSAGE AS I began walking towards my son.

HEY, THANKS FOR CALLING ME AND FOR YOUR SUPPORT. Bails is awake and talking. She's still in danger, but hopefully she's gonna be okay. I'm just heading back over to Wyatt now to take some photos for her. I'll call you later.

JUST AS MY MESSAGE SENT, I HAD A CALL FROM AN UNKNOWN number. My fingers shook as I answered and the doctor from earlier spoke.

"The results are back and it's confirmed you are Baby Walker's father. You can come back whenever you like, sir, and I'm very sorry to have put you out."

He sounded distracted, so I thanked him and ended the call as I approached the doors to the neonatal unit. I went through the first set of doors and my body reacted before my mind because I froze in place as I gazed around and saw my father, Henri, and Pierre all arguing with someone about getting entry.

"He's not the father. I'm telling you."

"I don't know what's going on, but I will be making a complaint."

"I just want to see the baby."

My eyes narrowed on them as they continued to harass the poor girl standing there, and I moved around them, turning to face them.

"The DNA results are back and conclusively prove that I am the baby's father, and I am telling you, not one of you will be getting in to see him right now."

My words were sharp, and Henri turned to my dad and

promptly burst into tears. My dad glared at me over his sobbing wife's shoulder and Pierre stepped towards me.

"I am going to see my son, and I don't care what you all say, there is no way you will be getting in if you continue harassing the staff who have saved him and Bailey today."

I walked in through the doors, going straight to my son. After washing my hands, he was passed to me for a while, and the nurse taking care of him took some photos for me. I sat with him for a while and watched her do her checks, but left when he needed changing. The nurse was very kind and she apologized for what had happened earlier.

My stomach growled as I was leaving and I decided to get something to eat before going back to see Bails. I grabbed a sandwich and a soda and ate it while sitting outside for a few moments.

Pierre came out and walked towards me.

"Hey, I don't want to argue with you," I informed him as he reached me, but he surprised me, sitting down beside me.

"Bailey and I are over. She just told me, and I'm sorry for the way I acted with you. I was trying to protect her, but I guess in trying to protect her, I ended up pushing her away."

He leaned forwards and put his head in his hands. I almost felt sorry for him. Almost, but I couldn't quite make myself say anything.

"I'm going back home. I just wanted to wish you well."

He stood and walked away from me. I watched him go, then went back in to see Bails. There was a spring in my step, and I couldn't stop the happiness from spreading through me.

I made it to the ICU department and walked towards Bailey's room. I took a breath before I entered and walked in to see Bailey sitting up in bed. She looked a little better and her smile brightened when she looked at me.

"Cooper," she breathed as I walked towards her.

"Hey, Bails."

My hand reached out to hers and our fingers locked, and I knew that this was it. She was mine, finally, and no matter what happened in the years to come, it would be okay, because we had each other and we had our son.

He'd been the bright light that brought us together, and I couldn't wait to be a family.

"Coop," Bailey whispered, and I turned to her, seeing the same happiness and contentment I was feeling reflected back at me in her eyes.

"Yeah, Bails," I said as I lifted my lips to hers and gave her a gentle kiss.

"I love you."

Her words, breathed against my lips, set my soul on fire, and I kissed her a little more firmly before pulling back a little and murmuring against her warm skin.

"I love you too. I'm yours, Bailey Walker. I've been yours since we met and I'll be yours until I die."

A tear rolled from her eye and dripped onto my cheek. "Thank you for always loving me. I'm sorry for what I put you through, but I'm yours, Cooper. I've always been yours. You were my first kiss, my first time, and my first love. I will always belong, heart, body, and soul, to you." She took a breath and then kissed me again before moving back. "Now show me our son, please?"

I laughed and took out my cell, showing her our perfect little boy. Her eyes lit up and her smile widened. She stroked his face through the camera and I knew my world was complete. I was the happiest man alive, because I was finally, openly, and completely in love with my stepsister.

Epilogue

Bailey

"Coop," I called from the living room as I sat with Wyatt attached to my breast. He was feeding away, and Cooper was supposed to be getting ready to take us to the farmhouse.

Zane and Sam had just had another little girl and we were due to go to their house to meet her. They hadn't told anyone because of the miscarriage they'd had before and only told us once Bailey was out of the ICU.

Wyatt was dressed in a little white shirt with gray shorts and a small pink bow tie. It was the cutest outfit and seemed perfect for him to be meeting his baby cousin in.

"Bails, what's up?" Cooper asked as he appeared in the living room. He was smiling broadly and his skin was glowing with a tan. He'd been working in the garden while on vacation and his muscles were more defined under his light blue shirt and dark slacks.

"Hey, quit perving on me," he chastised, and I laughed. Wyatt popped off and stared up at me, then started rooting about for my nipple. Once he was situated back on my breast,

I glanced up to see Cooper watching me with the same look of devotion and love he'd worn since Paris.

Every time I thought of Paris and what I'd put him through in the months after, a ball of shame tightened my gut, but he kept telling me that it was okay. We'd come out of it stronger, and we knew that we were both completely and irrevocably in love with each other.

"Did you call my mom?" I asked him.

My mom had been trying to build bridges with us for a few weeks, but it was a slow process. There was still a way to go, but we all agreed that it would be good if Wyatt, Ollie, Serena, and now Millie had their grandma in their life.

Shawn had been prosecuted for driving under the influence and assault on one of his associates at a party, so he wasn't allowed to visit us or the kids. We'd all agreed that my mom could visit, but Shawn wasn't coming near any of our children unless he pled guilty, went to rehab, and stuck it out for at least a year. Coop was adamant on that, and even then he wasn't sure he wanted Shawn in Wyatt's life. I wasn't either. I hadn't ever forgiven him for the torture he'd inflicted on us as teenagers, or what he'd almost done to Cooper with Jan. Just thinking of her made my skin crawl, and I hated it that we'd almost lost everything because of his dad.

"Yeah, I called her. She's out of town until next week, but she's asked if you can send her a picture of the babies together."

We still weren't sure whether letting my mom in was a good idea. Cooper was against it, but I wanted her to be part of my life and part of Wyatt's life because I still loved her, and she was in therapy. She'd apologized and spoken with Shawn about Louis, finally admitting his existence, and that helped me. I'd gone to therapy with her and now attended too.

I glanced down at Wyatt and brushed my finger over his curls, smiling down at him, still feeling a little guilty for all the stress I put Coop through when I was with Pierre. Pierre and I got together just before Cooper came to Paris and he became more and more possessive of me as I struggled with how much I was still in love with Cooper. I wanted to move on and he was willing to stay with me even though he knew I was pregnant, but he hated Cooper and a big part of what went wrong with us was how he would react anytime I saw Cooper or spent time with Cooper. Instead of keeping us together, he'd ended up pushing us apart.

After I came around from my coma, Pierre and I talked and he ended things with me. He told me he'd been possessive and jealous and that he hadn't been happy with me because he knew I still loved Cooper, but when he'd tried to talk to me about it, I'd denied it.

We were still friends, but distant friends because he was back in Paris and was running my gallery, so we didn't talk much. He emailed now and again, and Coop still got tense whenever I heard from him, but I was reinforcing every day that I loved him, and that this time we were together forever. It was us against the world and it was always going to stay that way. He was now happily in a relationship with Toni, a girl we hired to help out in the gallery, and we still spoke on occasion, but Coop always left the room when we did.

"Hey, where've you gone?" Coop asked me with a gentle smile, and I glanced up at him and gave him a small grin as Wyatt drifted off to sleep. He was still sucking a little and I searched around for his pacifier on the sofa.

"He sleeping?" Coop asked, and I nodded up at him and quickly switched my nipple for Wyatt's pacifier. I stood up and moved across the room, placing Wyatt into his car seat and strapping him in, while Coop checked the bag to make sure we were ready to leave.

"Bails," Cooper asked, and I turned my head to see him grin at me. He glanced down at Wyatt and raised his eyes at me.

"No!" I whispered. "We don't have time."

He stalked towards me and I laughed lightly, not wanting to wake up the baby as he picked me up and turned me towards the sofa, dropping me down gently on it.

He lowered himself so he towered above me and then leaned down and licked my cheek.

"Cooper," I whined and wiped at my face, but he laughed and then captured my lips in a kiss that stole my breath. His fingers roamed up my dress and he moaned when he reached my panties and found me wet and wanting.

As he thrust his fingers inside me, I curled against the couch and unzipped his pants, freeing his erection. My fingers stroked his length and he quickly removed his fingers, thrusting inside me and making me moan.

Wyatt made a sound in his seat and we both froze and turned towards him, but he was still asleep and Coop began thrusting into me harder and faster. I kissed Cooper furiously to keep from moaning, and within a few minutes, he'd taken me right to the brink. My body spun out of control and I came apart, panting, and bit on his shoulder as he came inside me.

He pulled out and quickly shoved his penis back inside his pants as I lay on the couch, breathing hard. He watched as I sat up, righting myself, and he grinned as I stood on shaky legs and moved towards him.

"Love you, Bails," he breathed into my ear as he pressed a soft kiss to the skin under my earlobe.

"Love you too, Cooper," I answered, and I did. I really, really did.

He took my hand and spun around, staring at me with a nervous expression as he dropped to one knee on the floor at my feet.

"Bails," he said, and his hand holding mine shook at little. "I have loved you since we met. I know I haven't always treated you right and I know I don't deserve your love, but you are my home, my world, and my almost everything. You have given me our son, and I want to ask you if—" He broke off and rubbed at his face with the back of his hand. "Will you please do me the honor of becoming my wife?"

I stared at him and then smiled as he opened the ring box. The ring was simple yet elegant. A rose gold ring with a gorgeous square-cut diamond solitaire nestled in a red velvet cover.

"Yes, of course I'll marry you," I said, and he smiled wider, slipping the ring, which fit perfectly, onto my left hand where it would remain forever. He stood up and kissed me again harder.

"You have no idea how nervous I was about that. I was gonna ask you later, but I wanted it to be just us because I didn't want to share the moment with anyone."

His lips found mine, and when he kissed me, I knew I'd found my soul mate, my true other half, and nothing would ever come between us again. I was marrying my stepbrother, finally.

LEAVING HOME

Bailey

I woke up the morning after dropping Cooper off at the airport and glanced around the room that had been my home for a few years. I was still so thankful to my grandma for leaving it to me, and for leaving me all her cash, but her loss washed over me again, and a tidal wave of grief threatened to pull me under, so I quickly got up and dressed.

My flight to Paris was due to leave in a little over an hour, and I was partly excited and partly nervous. I would miss Zane, Sam, and the kids, but I wouldn't miss the heartache that was attached with my mom and Zane's dad. I was trying hard not to think of Cooper and what he'd be doing.

I'd sworn that my baby and I would be okay and I meant it. We would do it without him. He'd chosen her again over me and I wasn't about to let my heart suffer anymore because of Cooper's choices.

My stomach began to rumble, and I checked my cell. It was a little after five a.m., but I couldn't remember when I'd last eaten, so I popped some Pop Tarts into the toaster and brewed a coffee. No one else was up and the farmhouse was quiet and peaceful.

My eyes wandered to the window, and I stood and watched the outside for a few seconds until my coffee was ready. I couldn't wait to taste the coffee, and I was so ready to eat that my food burned my tongue.

I ate and drank quickly and then began to move my carry-on luggage and my large suitcase to the door. I was used to carrying heavy things because of the gallery, but I did get a little twinge when I pushed my suitcase to sit by the back door. I moved slowly around the kitchen, writing Zane and Sam a note to say goodbye.

I hadn't told them I'd moved my flight up, or that I was leaving earlier than I'd originally planned, but being home when Cooper and his new wife flew back was not part of my plan. I could cope with a lot of things, but masochism wasn't one of them.

My fingers flew over the words as I said goodbye to them and told them I'd be back around Christmas. I didn't want to miss the holidays with Ollie and Serena. It was their first Christmas here, and with Zane starting his new job and Sam starting hers, I wanted to make sure the kids had a holiday that was special and fun.

Dear Sam and Zane,

I'm so sorry to leave like this, but I can't bear to stay here any longer.

I've moved my flight up, and when you guys get this, I'll be gone.

I'll be back for Christmas and I'll miss you all terribly, but I can't stay because I need to move on. Cooper is getting married today and I honestly wish him all the happiness, but staying around to watch him begin married life with her would make me a total masochist, and he's caused me enough pain to last me a lifetime.

I'm so sorry for not saying goodbye, but I'll be in touch once I'm settled in Paris.

My love to you guys and the kids,
Bailey

My bags were packed and my passport was on top of my cream carry-on bag. I gave the room one last sweep and then picked up my cell to dial for a cab when Sam came into the kitchen.

"Hey, Bails," she said and moved towards the coffee pot, pouring herself a cup and adding creamer and sugar as I stood awkwardly by the door. I didn't speak and she glanced towards me and then towards the door and her eyes widened.

"Were you really going to leave us without saying goodbye?" she asked as I glanced guiltily away.

"I'm sorry. I just wanted to go and save you all the hurt of seeing me leave."

"Yeah, that's not going to happen. What time is your flight?" she pressed, and my eyes shot back to her.

"A little after nine."

She gave me a brief nod and then sipped on her coffee, without another word. I wanted to call my cab and had just lifted my cell to call it when she came over and put her hand over mine.

"I'll drive you to the airport. I'm going there myself anyway. My dad's coming to town for a few days and I'm picking him up."

I hadn't told anyone about the baby, and I didn't want to because they'd try and convince me to stay here. If I stayed in Paris, there was no need to tell Cooper about the baby and he'd be free to live his life without the complication of having a baby with his stepsister.

"Sam, you don't need to…" I whispered, and she gave me a warm smile and then hugged me tightly.

"Yes, I do. I'm not letting you leave here like a thief in

the night. God, Bailey, you deserve so much better than Cooper. He doesn't deserve shit from you."

My eyes began to sting with the tears I was holding back. I swallowed roughly and glanced towards the bags. My bear was tucked up in there, because even though Cooper was marrying her, I'd never parted with the bear he'd given me. Seeing his half a heart yesterday told me he still loved me, but he didn't love me enough to leave her and I wasn't going to wait around forever for him to realize that I was the one, because what if I wasn't?

I was twenty-five and I was set for life, thanks to my grandparents. I didn't need him or his dad, and I wasn't about to stay here and have my heart trampled over and over. It was time to make a break, and I took a deep breath and shrugged out of Sam's embrace.

"Coop and I are over. He made a choice. I asked him to stay with me and he said no, so it's done, and there's nothing anyone can say or do now."

I turned towards the bags and stared at them as Sam moved over beside me.

"Okay, Bails, you're right. Now, let's get you to the airport and get your ass on the plane before Zane or anyone else tries to talk you out of it."

Her words were low and I picked up my suitcase and carried it out to the car, popping it into the trunk as I walked with my purse and carry-on over my shoulders. I took one last look back at the farmhouse and shuddered as I thought about leaving, but it was the right thing to do.

I could start over in Paris. I could build us both a life there, away from my mom and her coldness, and their dad and his heartlessness. I knew I'd miss things at home, like Zane and Sam, the kids, my gallery, and Jay. I had so much here, but the one thing I really wanted was in Hawaii, about to marry a girl who terrorized him and bullied him as a teenager, and I couldn't bear to watch it.

I shook my melancholy thoughts from my head and climbed into Sam's car, noticing that she didn't look back at the farmhouse as we drove away.

"Do you think Zane is really going to go after him?" I asked, and Sam sighed and then nodded, without speaking to me. We drove to the airport in silence, and as we reached the parking garage, my heart rate began to speed because I was really doing this. I was really leaving everything behind and flying halfway across the world to start over.

"Bailey." Sam interrupted my almost freak-out and I turned to face her. She was staring at me, and for a moment, I wished I was somewhere else because I could see the cautious expression on her face.

"Are you sure you want to leave? Are you sure this is what you want?"

I turned to face her with tears in my eyes. "Yes, I'm sure. I can't stay here. This life just hurts way too much and there are so many bad memories for me here."

"Don't you think that running will just make it harder in the long run?"

Her soft words were something I'd asked myself, but I wasn't running. Not really. I was taking myself out of the equation, so I shook my head because, one, I wasn't a total masochist. And two, what if I stayed here and ruined his happiness? I'd never forgive myself for ruining his future. And three, he'd already made his choice. I asked him to stay and he said no, so why would I stay when he'd already answered my question?

"No, Sam. I can't stay," I stammered and she gave me a nod.

"I understand. I knew it was a long shot, but you

understand why I had to check. I love you, Bails. You saved us and have given us a new life here. We'll be forever grateful, but I know you deserve so much more than he gave you. You deserve to be happy and whole and not someone's dirty little secret."

She stopped speaking and took the keys from the ignition. After a second, we both left the car without another word. Our paths split inside the airport as her dad's flight was arriving, so we said goodbye quickly and part of me longed to stay, but I had no fight left in me.

Cooper deserved to be happy, and if being with Jan made him happy, then he deserved every bit of happiness he could get with her. I wasn't about to ruin it for him, and I knew I'd find my happiness someday. I'd find someone to make me happy. Someone who loved me for me, and not as a way to get back at my mom for marrying his dad.

My heart still stung over that jibe, and although he'd apologized, it didn't take away the pain of hearing those words come from him. I closed my eyes and shook the thoughts of that day off before wandering through the airport.

I was in the coffee shop, buying a cake and some coffee when my flight was called for boarding, so I purchased my items and made my way through the airport to the check-in desk. As I waited in line, my panic at moving to Paris began to overwhelm me.

Chill out. I needed a fresh start, and Paris was the perfect place to give it to me. I couldn't help the anxiety I was feeling because the last time I'd had a big move, I'd ended up with two stepbrothers and a boatload of issues with their father.

When I'd told my mom I was moving to Paris, she was ambivalent, but told me it would be good for me to start over and offered me some of Shawn's money, which I declined. I still hadn't told her about the cash my grandma had left me, and I wasn't sure I ever would. After how she'd behaved about Louis, I wasn't sure I'd ever forgive her, and then the way she'd behaved when Shawn was beating us made me resent her even more.

The line began to move, and I shook off thoughts of my mom, Shawn, and all I was leaving behind as I handed over my ticket and my passport. As I walked onto the plane, I wished Cooper had made a different choice. I wished he'd chosen me, but he hadn't.

I didn't hate him anymore. I was sad for him, and I was upset that he didn't know I was carrying our baby, but I knew I wouldn't tell him I was pregnant to him. If and when I saw him again, I'd lie and say It was someone else's baby He didn't need to know, and I just hoped he wasn't around at Christmas because I didn't want to have to face him.

I moved along towards the plane and gave myself a mental slap. It was all over. Cooper and I were history, and when I arrived in Paris, the past was where he would stay. I wasn't going to rehash over and over again all of our mistakes. It was done and finished with, and my future was calling.

As I made my way to my seat, I made a vow to myself to move on, to really truly give myself permission to find my future in a city I loved. A city I was excited to call home.

PARIS LANDING

Bailey

My arrival in Paris was calm, and although I was feeling nauseated and tired, I was also excited. I couldn't wait to start viewing the galleries Pierre had lined up. He'd also helped me to find an apartment. His apartment, to share until I found somewhere of my own.

He'd told me he'd come to pick me up from the airport, but I'd told him it wouldn't be necessary, although I wished I'd accepted his kindness as I walked through the terminal and out towards the cabs that lined the street.

I tugged my suitcase tiredly along with me and popped it into the back of a cab without the help of the driver. As I climbed in, I took one last look at the airport. I wouldn't be going home for a while. I couldn't. I had to give my new life a chance to start and I couldn't wait until I could go home without the constant ache of Cooper's absence weighing on my chest.

I gave the cabbie the address and he glowered at me in the mirror.

"That's not a long drive," he told me, and I gave him a nod because I already knew it would be a short trip. Pierre had told me it wouldn't take long to get to his apartment from the airport, and I sent him a message to check he was home.

Maria was also still living in Paris, and we'd arranged to meet up once I was settled. She was engaged to a French businessman and ran her own bar, which was a far cry from her dreams of coming to Paris, but she seemed happy and settled, so I wasn't going to judge her.

As we drove, I found I was glad I'd listened to Pierre and not hired my own car because the people on the roads were driving like maniacs and we'd almost crashed as we drove down a few streets. We arrived outside the apartment after twenty minutes.

I quickly paid the driver and climbed out, getting my carry-on and my suitcase from the trunk as Pierre came out to meet me. I'd forgotten how attractive he was, with his tanned skin, bright smile, and curled hair.

He helped me into the apartment and showed me to a moderate-sized bedroom with beautiful bay windows and a south-facing view.

"This is adequate?" he asked in a gorgeous French accent, and I grinned up at him.

"Perfect, thank you. And thanks again for letting me stay here. Maria told me she'd help me find somewhere to stay but she bailed on me."

He gave me a bright smile and I couldn't help smiling back. I was really here. I was in Paris and I was going to start a new life.

"This is only temporary though, correct?" he asked, and I turned to face him because I was planning to stay in Paris long-term. "My roommate will be back early next year and will need his room back."

His words sent a bucket of ice down my spine, but I simply nodded at him. Maria hadn't mentioned that when she'd convinced Pierre to let me stay with him.

"Yeah, that's fine. I can find my own place soon."

"Parfait, chérie."

He gave me a quick nod and then turned to walk out of the room, leaving me with an unmade bed and my suitcase to unpack. I'd sent most of my things to storage because I didn't want to carry them all the way to Paris, but that didn't bother me.

I was desperate to go shopping, but I knew my body would change soon and I'd need to buy different clothes for myself as my bump grew, so I'd wait a while and go shopping around December to get new clothes.

Over the next few weeks, I'd busied myself with finding the perfect gallery, making an offer on it, and when the offer was accepted, working with Pierre, Jacques, and Coraline to make sure the gallery was up to standard.

Pierre and I began to become closer, and one night, when I was overwhelmed with searching for an apartment, making doctors' appointments, and sourcing artists for the gallery, I broke down and told him all about Cooper and our past. I told him about the baby and about the fact that he'd left me to go marry Jan.

Pierre opened a bottle of wine and drank as he listened and then we kissed. Our kiss was small and I wasn't sure if it meant anything to him, but he told me after the kiss that he'd step up to stop me getting too emotionally involved with Cooper.

Pierre also asked me to stay in the apartment for a while, which wasn't what we'd originally agreed because Franco, his last roommate, whose room I was staying in, was Pierre's best friend. He'd moved away to Nice to live with his fiancée and couldn't afford to pay both the mortgage on the flat in Paris and his home in Nice, but I'd agreed because it saved me from apartment hunting.

I'd called home that night and was surprised when Cooper

answered. I hadn't expected it and the sound of his voice still did something to my insides, but it was his tone that worried me. I knew I shouldn't have been worried and I tried to keep the conversation light, but I couldn't get the sadness of his voice from my mind.

I called Sam back a few hours later after she'd filled me in on what happened to Cooper via text message. It hurt my heart to know he was struggling so much, but I was trying to harden myself to him. I wanted to move on with my life and not keep getting sucked back into to the Cooper Christie drama show.

"Hey, Sam. It's Bailey," I told her cautiously. I was still unable to get over hearing Cooper's voice and I was so relieved that Pierre had called me away to deal with the painters, who'd painted the café in the gallery a horrid mustard yellow color.

"Hey, how are you?" Sam asked in a low voice, and I wondered if Cooper was still there.

"Yeah, I'm good. Are you and the kids okay? How's Zane? Is his new job going well?" I wanted to find out how things were at home and check that Zane and Sam were coping financially because I didn't like that they were struggling.

"Things are good. The kids are great. Missing you though, and Zane's job is going well. I also got a new job and I start next week, so I'm so happy about that. It will really help us out and we can start to get out of this hole."

"That's great. I'm so happy for you guys. I'm here if you need any help though, okay?" I was firm, because I knew that they wouldn't accept my help, but I wouldn't see them go without. Especially since they had kids.

"Thank you, Bailey, but we're fine," she told me, and I could hear the smile in her voice.

"I got your text. Is Cooper okay?"

"He's fine." Her tone was cool.

"Is Cooper still at the farmhouse?"

"Yeah, he's still here. He needs a place to crash for a bit. I hope that's okay?"

"Yeah, it's fine." I was trying to be fine with it. I really was, but it made me a little uncomfortable to have him staying there.

"Does he still want to come here?" I probed, and I hoped she'd say no because I couldn't face him. Not yet. I was still trying to get my shit together, and him coming here, knowing he'd called off his wedding to Jan and flown home for me was too much to bear.

"Uh-huh," she answered, and I knew he was in the room with her. I had to tell her to ask him not to come, but the thought of actually saying it clogged my throat up and made it hard to even get the words out.

"Sam, can you ask him not to come here? I'm trying to start over and I can't do it if he comes. I need time to heal and to get over the heartbreak. I just don't want to see him right now."

"Okay, sure thing." I didn't know if she was being short because she didn't want to say it in front of Cooper, or if she was annoyed with me for putting it all on her. It didn't matter, as long as she stopped him from coming to Paris.

"Thank you. I'm sorry to put all this on you, but I just can't be around him right now. Hearing his voice earlier was so hard, and I can't cope with seeing him in person. I'm not there yet."

"It's okay. Don't stress, okay?"

"Thanks. I gotta go, Sam. Give my love to everyone."

"Okay, will do. Love ya," she said quietly. I assumed Cooper was still in the room with her.

"Love ya too. Bye."

I ended the call and leaned forward on my hands, but I wanted him out of my house. I needed him not to be there. I waited a few days, and then when I couldn't cope with it anymore, I sent a message to Sam, asking if there was any way she could ask Cooper to leave. It made me so uncomfortable having him around my things.

He'd left the same day, but I'd called Sam later and said he could stay because I knew I was being petty and hurting him out of spite, but it was too late. He'd already left, and I spent the next few days feeling guilty, even though Pierre assured me that I wasn't.

Two days after Cooper left, I'd set my cell by the sink and Pierre knocked it into the bubbles by accident. My cell was damaged beyond repair and I was devastated. He apologized over and over and even bought me a new one, but I couldn't contact anyone because I'd lost all of my numbers and hadn't backed them up.

I knew the farmhouse landline number, but the work on the gallery had picked up massively and I was pulling extremely long days, sometimes in the gallery for fourteen to sixteen hours. When I got home, all I wanted to do was curl up in bed and sleep.

I'd tried calling the landline a few times, but it had just rung out, and the answering machine wasn't working, so I couldn't leave a message. I considered downloading the Facebook app because I knew Sam was on there, but I wasn't really up for the people I left behind knowing where I lived. I didn't want Cooper to show up unannounced at my door, now that Pierre and I had started something, so I held off, hoping my contacts could be restored. Pierre's friend Harry was trying something to fix it, and he was a bit of a technological whiz, apparently.

THE END

Thank you to everyone who has bought a copy of this book. Thank you for your support over the years and thank you for being awesome. Please remember to leave a review as we love to hear your thoughts on our books.

Thank you to my amazing, supportive hubs and my three beautiful boys who let me write when inspiration strikes. Thank you for being amazing and for loving me regardless of my eccentricities.

Thank you to my amazing beta and arc teams. You guys are the backbone of writers and we appreciate your feedback more than you know.

Thank you, Eleanor, for the amazing cover, Karen Sanders for the edits and Judy for the proofread. You guys are absolutely amazing.

Also thank you to the amazing Leanne at Irish ink for the formatting. You always make my book babies look so special and I'm so grateful to you.

Thank you to my crazy family and amazing in-laws. You guys really are the best, always there when I need you and always there for my boys. Love you all muchly.

And to my crazy friends. I love you all dearly and I'm so grateful to have such amazing, compassionate, ride or die friends.

Lastly thank you to my ready, steady, sprint group. You girls really are amazing, and I'd be lost without you all. Love ya girls. Let's kick ass and take names.

Stacy

Stepbrother: Step Dilemma Series Book 1

myBook.to/Stepbrother1

Black Mercy (San Francisco Rock Romance Book 1)

myBook.to/BlackMercy

Destroyed by Deception (Amethyst College Saga Book 1)

myBook.to/Deception

Nothing but the Sheets

https://books2read.com/u/bwdg0P

Available for Pre-order

Broken Mercy (San Francisco Rock Romance Book 2)

https://books2read.com/u/31q1en

Sing me Home

https://books2read.com/u/31q1en

About the Author

STACY MCWILLIAMS

Welcome to the rollercoaster world of Stacy McWilliams.

Stacy McWilliams is a Scottish Author who loves romance. All of her books have a romantic element and her books will keep you on the edge of your seat, make you want to throw your kindle around and her characters will make you either love them or loathe them.

Reviews
"...on the edge reading..." Destroyed by Deception
"...hold on tight and hang on for the ride." Black Mercy
"...captivated from the start..." Candlelight
"...kept me intrigued..." Luminosity
"brilliant paranormal story that pulls you into her world of demons and teenage romance." Ignition
"What can I say... I was left wanting more… More Hunter, more Savannah, just more of everything."-Pride

Contact her on Facebook or Instagram and she will message back.

If she's not writing, looking after her three boys or spending time with her hubs, she's reading or watching TV shows such as Lucifer, The 100 and Supernatural.

She's working on new materials and is hoping to release
three-four books in 2020. Also check out her Facebook page
for updates on any signings she's attending.

Social Links

Goodreads

https://www.goodreads.com/author/show/
9796198.Stacy_McWilliams

Facebook

https://www.facebook.com/authorstacymcwilliams

Twitter

http://www.twitter.com/@stacemcw

Instagram

https://www.instagram.com/stacemcwilliams/

Website

http://authorstacemcwilli.wixsite.com/author